Sani

The German Medic

Aubrey Reiss Taylor

Aubrey Taylor Books

To My Momma
1955-2006

Contents

PREFACE TO THE SECOND EDITION

Occasionally, readers take offense when my books do not line up with what they are used to reading about World War II. Yet one wonders if it is right to expect WWII Fiction written from the German perspective to align with what we've come to expect from the genre.

Historical Fiction should be authentic and accurate. Most readers expect authors to have done their research, and therefore, an author of German-perspective WWII fiction must research viewpoints that conflict with the agreed-upon account of the war, not because of modern-day opinions, but to steep themselves in the Zeitgeist.

Yes, there is a postwar consensus and, as I am occasionally reminded, "even the German generals signed off on it." Who did not sign off on this agreement? The vast majority of the German population, whether soldier or civilian. Whether they were convinced National Socialists ("Nazis"), opportunists, young men who were drafted into the war, or civilians trying to live life, many Germans who lived through the Second World War have stories that they believe few people want to hear. Even those who silently resisted Hitler's regime have a different perspective than their Allied counterparts, though it may not provide readers with as much consternation as some of the others.

I have never written a *truly* biographical piece, but countless primary sources, memoirs, war diaries, and histories have influenced my writing for the last five years. *Sani: The German Medic* was my very first book, and I wrote it in two months. That did not give me time to soak in these diverse viewpoints, and therefore, the First Edition is written through a distinctly American lens...Imagine, writing *the German Perspective* though *the American perspective!*

However, this book was the beginning of a fascination with the German side of the story. I hope that five years of research and seven other books have equipped me to provide a more authentic portrayal of Frederick's German counterparts in this Second Edition. The deeper understanding between American and German comrades might be most clearly illustrated in the book's handling of the invasion of Poland in 1939 and in Frederick's interactions with a Polish family late in the war. It is also portrayed in Frederick and Heinrich's discussions, as well as Frederick's many and varied conversations with Chaplain Schmidt.

My books are not intended to be works of apologetics, propaganda, or revisionist history. They are *fiction*, imbued with the historical opinions, facts, experiences, insights, and sentiments I have encountered since the beginning of this fascinating journey in 2021. I am not a historian, and therefore I am not required to validate or invalidate an opposing viewpoint. Rather, as a fiction author, I strive to create relatable, engaging characters and allow *them* to wrestle through questions according to their understanding *at the time in question.* Readers will undoubtedly bump up against opinions that were valid at the time, regardless of whether they are accepted today. It is up to the reader to chafe at these things or to appreciate the insight. If you are interested in browsing some (but not nearly all) of the sources that have influenced my work, be sure to check out the Recommended Books and Films tab on my website.

A Note on the Faith Content of This Book

Sani: The German Medic was first conceived as a Christian Fiction novel, appropriate for church bookstore shelves. Since then, much of my writing has gravitated toward the General Market because I feel compelled to portray the realities of life both within and outside of the Christian faith in a more honest way. I like to say that I don't "pull punches," but for the sake of the heart of this book, it remains faith-based. Frederick is concerned about the eternal security of his comrades. There are Bible passages and other faith references throughout, though readers of the First Edition will find that they are more concise and condensed. This contributed to readability as much as it did to appealing to a broader audience.

Acknowledgements

Brian, you have endured this winding journey with me, and deserve my utmost gratitude. Our children also deserve my thanks, and if it weren't for our wonderful years of homeschool, I may never have started on this path.

The Christian Mommy Writers, Optimistic Writers and Brave Authors have been wonderful sources of support, along with scattered author friends around the world. The nine clubs of the FGAS, and Joy CC are lifelines. Jen W., you are probably my biggest fan. No one listens to me fangirl over my characters the way you do.

Finally, whether you are just picking up an Aubrey Taylor Books publication for the first time, or you've been with me for a while now, I want to say a huge thanks to all my readers. Your support means the world to me.

Ehre sei Gott!

Aubrey

PART I

CHAPTER 1

PROLOGUE

FRIEDRICH

France

1918

Heavy shelling thundered in Friedrich's ears, yet there was something far more terrifying in the silences that often fell over No Man's Land.

It was then that his thoughts could get to him.

His feet were cold, wet, filthy, and covered with open sores. His hole in the ground did little to shield him from the rain, and the squelching mud of the dugout seemed to seep into his pores.

It was dark. Death was everywhere. Was he even alive?

Why had the prospect of war excited the young men of his generation? Even the stray bullet that had grazed his ear as he first approached the front hadn't managed to dampen his enthusiasm.

Endless hours spent in trenches with the constant stench of death had done what no rogue ammunition could. Instead of aching for action, he ached for the warmth of a crackling fire, the nearness of his bride, and the child in her womb.

His child.

He had married Hannah not long after the war began over in Europe—but as an American he, along with most everyone else, had been blissfully unconcerned with what was going on "over there."

Well, perhaps not *everyone* else. Many in his predominantly German-American neighborhood became rattled. They changed their foreign-sounding names and stopped speaking German on the streets. Young men his age volunteered for the US Army to prove their loyalty to their new nation.

Friedrich had longed for that himself—but not as badly as he longed for Hannah.

Eventually, loyalty was no longer an option: it was demanded of him. Now, the days blurred together in a haze of mustard gas.

He leaned back against the damp, earthy wall and consoled himself with the thought of Hannah's telegram:

EXPECTING. NEW YEARS DAY.

That weekend in March had been his last with her. Though he reassured her repeatedly through his letters that he would be home soon, it was Friedrich who truly needed reassuring.

It all felt like a lifetime ago.

Here at the front, one was either facing certain death or endless downtime, in which one had little to do but sit and think. The stench of death, the seepage of mud, and the squeak of rats made those moments with Hannah feel like a lifetime ago.

A wet sock smacked him in the face. The unmistakable sound of Paul's stifled laughter confirmed the identity of the sock's owner. Friedrich picked up the foul thing and whipped it back in Paul's direction. If there was a sure-cure for despair, it was camaraderie. Until he met death head on—or until the *Boche* finally gave up the fight—he'd do whatever he could to keep their spirits up.

His own spirit was another matter entirely.

CHAPTER 2

HANNAH

Upstate New York

Summer 1938

Hannah looked up from her gardening. Before her stood her only child, Frederick. Tall and toned, with dark hair and blue eyes, he was the exact image of his father, the man she had loved since childhood.

"Hello, dear one." Hannah rose to her feet to embrace her boy, wiping the dirt from her hands on her apron and reaching up to his neck.

Sometimes, he reminded her too much of the man she had loved and lost too early in life. They had only been married for a year when he was called to fight a war that was not his own. No use thinking about that now. She had Frederick, coming of age in a time with its own unique pain and suffering. Work shortages, hunger, lack of opportunity...*At least he is home, and not on the other side of the ocean.* The odd jobs he worked helped supplement the meager income she made selling eggs and taking in occasional boarders.

"Mom," he said, knowing she wasn't quite present with him.

"Yes, my love, I'm sorry."

He laughed, a response borne out of love and their unique relationship—mother and son, constant companions. It had always been the two
of them. "It's all right, Ma. I finished up my work at Mr. Strauss's early.
Can we talk?"

"Of course, dear. Let me get you something to drink. Are you hungry
too? I boiled some eggs this morning, and there's some bread in the
pantry."

Again he chuckled. "No thanks, ma, just a glass of water."

He never asked for much.

Hannah collected a pitcher of water and two glasses and set them on
the small metal table in the backyard. What news would he bring from
Paul Strauss today? The man kept himself well apprised and always gave
Frederick a full report.

She only ever wanted the *good* news.

Frederick stretched his legs out to the side of the table and took a big
swig of water. The late spring breeze tousled his hair. Then he faced her.
"Mr. Strauss was talking about his time in France again today."

"Mmm."

Frederick reached into his pocket and pulled out an old photograph.
"He gave me this today. Him and dad."

Hannah's heart nearly stopped. As if summoned by her recollections,
there he was: Friedrich Schmidt. Twenty years old, in uniform, determination written on his face. Beside him stood Paul Strauss. Short and
stocky. Not as sure of himself.

It had been tough for both of them, going up against their cousins on
the other side of the ocean.

"Mr. Strauss admired the fire in Dad's eyes."

Hannah smiled. "Your grandfather hated it."

"That's what Mr. Strauss said. He told me that when Dad saw the first bands of doughboys marching through the streets, he was ready to join up instantly." Frederick winked and continued, "It was only you that held him back."

Her heart tingled with remembrance. "Yes...the fervor of the American Spirit was not lost on him. But we were newly married." Warmth still burgeoned within her when she thought of him, and she hoped someday Frederick would understand what would keep a man home when the men around him were marching off to war.

Friedrich had not been as self-assured as he seemed in the photograph. His family was rent down the middle between the Old World and the New. It seemed, at the time, that the war had bound those who supported the Kaiser together in one camp, and those who wanted to be known as loyal, full-blooded Americans in another.

As the boys marched off to war, they were no longer Polish, Italian, Irish, or Jewish. They were *American*. All of them, except the German boys. Even in American uniforms, the German boys were looked on with suspicion.

That same feeling of being *suspect* had led Hannah to change her last name from Schmidt to Smith, severing her connection to her husband before he even arrived at the front.

Frederick shifted uncomfortably. The table and chairs were built for ladies to sit at while they sipped tea, not for a six-foot young man with a boy still pent up inside.

You grew up too fast, Hannah thought to herself. *You had to*. Hannah and Frederick had played caregiver to her parents. Instead of skipping stones with his friends at the creek, he had been called upon to run errands for his mother. Instead of playing war games in the woods, he'd measured medicine for his grandparents and bandaged wounds when they'd tried to function too independently.

His knee bounced. Too often, it seemed as though he was waiting for something to happen.

"Mr. Strauss says you can keep that," he stated as if remembering suddenly.

"He's so kind."

"He sure is." His leg continued its nervous jitter as he tossed back a sip of water. He'd been extra preoccupied for days, but she need not ask why. She knew he was getting the itch to move on and begin a life of his own.

"Have you been getting a lot of work done for Paul?"

"Nah," he chuckled. "Spend most of the time chatting. You know how lonely he is."

"I do." She sighed. "It's good you're a friend to him."

He took another sip of water. "I don't think I'm a friend so much as a connection to my father."

She had to laugh. "You could be both."

The truth was, Frederick *was* a connection to his father. Almost everything about them was identical—save that Friedrich had been marriage-minded from the beginning and had always wanted to be a preacher. The things that had anchored her husband were the very things her son wanted nothing to do with. She'd stopped telling Frederick long ago how badly his father had longed to serve God. Her late husband's dream was lost on their son.

FREDERICK

Paul Strauss was around forty, the age his father would have been if he were still alive, though the two could not have been more different. From what he'd heard, Father had been tall, broad shouldered, with dark hair and blue eyes. Mr. Strauss was short, solid, and stocky, with sandy blond hair that was turning gray.

His father's hair would probably have been turning gray too, if he'd returned from the war.

Mr. Strauss had been wounded, which had probably saved his life. Shell shock, exposure to gas, and the lasting injury to his leg had given the Great War veteran a host of health problems. He walked with a limp and had a hard time getting things done around the house.

In theory, that was why Frederick went to visit him. The work was easy enough, but what he'd found was a fascination with his heritage, something he'd lacked growing up. Paul Strauss gave him fresh perspective—though for the older man, that perspective had come years earlier when he was in Europe. Old views and beliefs had been refined through fifteen years of hindsight. Likewise, Mr. Strauss seemed to understand the times they were *now* facing.

The clock struck eleven. Frederick turned off his desk lamp, lay down in his bed, pulled up the covers, and closed his eyes. Every time he and Paul Strauss talked of Germany, Frederick felt a stirring in his heart, as if he were homesick for a place he'd never been. Life at home was boring, and he was restless.

In spite of Mr. Strauss's concerns about the political leadership, it sounded like life in Germany was more interesting and exciting than any of his prospects here. It was time for a change. He was willing to take a risk.

CHAPTER 3

HANNAH

She pulled a yellowed letter from her dresser drawer and unfolded it gently. It was dated June 1918.

Dearest,

I hope you received the letters I wrote while on the ship. I mailed them as soon as I was able. This letter is my first since we arrived in France. We have been marching and drilling but have seen no real action. I think that will change soon.

This country must have been beautiful before it was torn apart by war. I can feel it, Hannah—I belong in Europe as my forefathers did. Perhaps when the war is over, we can return—you, me, and the baby. We can help the French with rebuilding. Perhaps we will stay on, find a small cottage, and sit in the doorway sipping wine as our children run barefoot through the countryside.

I know, I know. I am a dreamer, but you love every moment of my fantasies.

I keep the small Bible you gave me tucked in my uniform at all times. Tonight, I read this verse: "The Lord watch over us while we are absent one from another." He has done so, and will continue to do so. Perhaps by Christmas, I will be in your arms once again.

Love, Friedrich

She laughed to herself. *Yes, Friedrich, you were a dreamer.* In his eyes, no endeavor had been out of reach as long as God led them to it. His parents had struggled to keep his feet on the ground, but she loved the way his passion had made her want to follow him anywhere. If she hadn't been pregnant, she almost certainly would have gone to France herself as a nurse. As it was, she was destined to remain a nurse much closer to home, her years of training would lie in caring for her ailing parents.

"Mom."

Frederick stood in the doorway, looking as though he hadn't gotten a wink of sleep. "Hello, my darling." She placed the letter on the dresser and approached him. "You look like you didn't sleep well. I don't have any coffee, but I can brew some nice strong tea."

"I'd like that, Ma."

Along with tea, Hannah served him some eggs. They sat down to breakfast together, a rare treat now that he was often out of the house before she arose in the morning. His odd jobs usually had him up before dawn.

Something was weighing on him. She knew it. Biting back her questions, she took one of his hands and prayed for the meal. "Dear Father, thank You for Your continued provision for us, for Your great love, and for Your peace which surpasses all understanding. Bless this food, and give Frederick comfort and wisdom." She paused, wondering when his hands had grown into those of a man. Then she closed the prayer and opened her eyes. Did his silence have to do with a young woman? *No. Not yet.* If he left her, it would be for adventure, not love.

After a brief and silent breakfast, Frederick returned to Paul Strauss's. Hannah resumed her housework. In Frederick's room, she saw evidence of his restlessness. The sheets were tangled, and a few books were strewn about his bed and his desk. A German language manual, a history book, and his Bible.

It was comforting to know he'd attempted to seek wisdom from this book, rather than innumerable other sources.

FREDERICK

"Ah, Frederick, *Guten Morgen.*" Paul Strauss opened the door and motioned for him to enter.

"Hallo, *Herr* Strauss. Is there anything I can do for you this morning?" He hadn't planned to work today, but it felt right to offer.

"*Nein, danke.*" He offered Frederick a spot on the sofa and took his place in a large rocking chair. "Something tells me you didn't come here to work."

"No," Frederick said, lightly. "I didn't." He ran his fingers through his hair and looked at his friend. Mr. Strauss was only forty, but sadness and poor health had turned him into a much older man. "I kind of wanted to finish our conversation from yesterday."

The man nodded. "Of course."

"You've never expressed anger or hatred at the men you fought against in the war."

"That's because I had no anger or hatred for them. If anything, we were kindred spirits." He scratched his chin, thick with two days of razor stubble. "We were led to believe we were going to fight a tribe of barbarians, monsters who were set on wiping out neighboring cultures through any means possible. The nation had to sell the war, you know."

Mr. Strauss placed an unlit pipe between his lips and sucked thoughtfully for a moment. "Someone once said that when you begin to think of your enemy as human, you cease to be a good soldier."

"And?"

"The same day the shrapnel tore my leg, I was down in the mud, face to face with a man my own age. He could've been my brother or my cousin. I don't know how we ended up in hand to hand combat. It's different, you know, wrestling in the mud instead of launching bombs at each other. At some point, I accidentally looked into his eyes." The man paused.

"You killed him?"

"No. He was injured—there was no more fight in him. I cried for a *Sani* to come to his aid and ran for my life. That's when the shell exploded between us. My leg was hit"—he touched the place on his leg that still carried the scar—"but he could not have survived."

Frederick let out a deep breath.

"I'm not a religious man like your father was," Mr. Strauss continued, "but I know I was divinely taken out of the battle that day because I could not fight anymore."

"You saw his humanity."

The older man shook his head, filled his pipe with precious little tobacco, and lit it. "It was more than that, Frederick. I realized, for the first time, what it meant to kill your own brothers."

The two sat quietly, Frederick mulling over the fresh perspective. "It's strange to think of them as brothers."

"It was strange to me too, once."

"I feel like I've lost something. You're the first person who has ever talked to me about *Germany*. Most of my family wanted to be *Americans*."

"It was not always that way."

"That's what my mother says." He shifted in his chair. "I've been thinking about reconnecting."

"Have you now?"

"*Ja*...I think I'd like to go back."

Mr. Strauss huffed. "That's a marvelous thought, son. Under other circumstances, I would say it was a fine idea. But now?" He shook his head. "You want no part of what's going on over there."

"The country is thriving."

"Compared to ours, yes...but at what cost?"

Frederick chafed at his words. "They must be doing *something* right."

"We only see what they want us to see. Who knows where it will lead?"

"You've said before that we only see what *our* press wants us to see as well."

Mr. Strauss waved his comment away. "Yes, that is true. Still. Germany is in the throes of a fascist dictatorship. Much of Europe is. You don't want any part of that."

Frederick shrugged.

"All right, then, what about your mother?"

Again, Frederick lifted and dropped his shoulders. "I don't know. Maybe she can finally get out and meet someone instead of feeling like she has to care for me all the time. I'm nineteen, for goodness sake. If not, she can come live with me once I'm settled over there."

The older man laughed out loud. "Yes, yes. I remember. Your father had the same ideas. Conquer Europe and then bring his family over." With a pull on his pipe, he added, "My friend, *Friedrich Schmidt.* You've left quite a legacy."

CHAPTER 4

HANNAH

Her mind wandered back to the day her husband had been called up by the United States Army. It was the day after New Year's, 1918. Friedrich had burst through the door, seeking to pull her into his arms as he always did, but she remained at the table, an envelope in her hand. Without further greeting, he'd taken it from her, aware of what it was.

She'd watched his stony-blue eyes scan it, his lips tracing the words. When he set it back on the table, his response wasn't the one she'd anticipated. Rather than the excited peaking of his eyebrows, he'd simply said, "I've been called to report to basic training."

Frederick's entrance broke her reverie. "Hi, Ma." He stood in the doorway, smelling of Paul Strauss's pipe.

"Did you get any work done?"

"Nah." He pulled out a kitchen chair and sat down, stretching his legs out alongside the table and tilting his head back, rolling his neck and shoulders. His eyes still evidenced a lack of sleep. "I needed to talk to Mr. Strauss."

"Of course you did." She smiled knowingly. "He's been a good friend to you, Frederick."

"I know."

Again she noticed how much he looked like his father now that he was a man himself. Even the alternating tones of excitement and nerves in Frederick's voice paid homage to Friedrich.

It was wrong to avoid talking about what was *really* going on simply because she couldn't bear the thought of him leaving. The Lord hadn't provided them with a carefree life together, and she regretted not being able to allow him the kind of childhood she and his father had enjoyed together as playmates. After years of asking him to rush home from school to help her, was it right to deny him the opportunity to spread his wings now?

She took his hands in her own. "Honey, what's bothering you?"

FREDERICK

Frederick looked his mother in the eyes. A rush of courage came over him but disappeared instantly. His father had been standing in this very spot when he announced he was going off to war.

"Mom, can we go sit under the tree like we did yesterday?"

She looked confused, laughed a little, and said, "All right. Would you like me to make some sandwiches first? It won't take me but a minute to spread some jam on this bread."

He was honestly grateful for the extra time to rehearse what he might say. When she'd finished, they made their way to the backyard and took the same places at the table as the day before. It had become their spot in the warmer months, when they had a moment to share together.

Hannah blessed the food, and they each took a few bites. Then Frederick looked at his mother. She had a youthful complexion, and it surprised him that she'd stayed unmarried all these years. Perhaps it was the wedding band his father had given her, which she still wore on her left hand. Everyone in their community knew Friedrich had died in the war, and they'd never seen her with a man other than her father, Frederick, or occasionally Paul Strauss. But the message was clear: *I am not available. I am not interested.*

His father was the love of her life, and that didn't make this any easier.

"Mom." He sighed. "I don't know how to tell you this, so I'm just going to shoot straight. I know this won't be easy for you, but—" He breathed deeply. Even Mr. Strauss had tried to discourage him. "I've been thinking about going to Germany." He twisted his mouth. That wasn't quite right. "What I mean is, I'm *going* to go to Germany."

"For a visit?"

He hesitated. "No...I'm going to move back there."

Hannah dropped the piece of sandwich she was holding and the two stared at each other. So much for the extra time spent planning what to say. Frederick shook his head. "I know it's out of the blue."

She nodded in disbelief. "Um...When did you decide this?"

He couldn't discern the tone behind her question, but it didn't matter. "I've been talking to Mr. Strauss for years. I've fallen in love with my homeland, and I want to be there. I've been trying to learn the language and—"

"Honey, you know nothing about it. I've never even been there myself. Wouldn't you like to visit first? Where would you live? What would you do for work? What about this Hitler fellow?"

He had anticipated most of her rapid-fire questions. He didn't have a lot of answers, but his mind was made up. "I just feel like it's the thing I must do. I'm young, I'll figure it out as I go along. Surely we have family there."

"Not close enough for you to descend upon them without notice."

He shrugged. "I've been trying to pray about it, like you always say. I don't get any answers, but I just don't feel like I belong here anymore."

"And you assume, therefore, that you belong in Germany."

"No. I feel like I belong in Germany, and therefore, I feel like I no longer belong here. Maybe I'm being called there."

"By God?"

"Maybe. I don't know. I'm still not sure I believe all that stuff. I'm not like you are. Not like my father was." He scraped at the peeling paint on the chair and avoided her gaze.

Still, he felt the penetrating disappointment in her words as she sighed. "I know, Frederick, I know. I can't force you."

HANNAH

She understood. A parent could only guide their child, not force him. Hadn't she learned that when she was Frederick's age? Although they shared a common creed, her faith was nothing like her parents' had been. They loved the liturgy and the prayer books. She loved the freedom to sing, read the Bible for herself, and speak to Him with her own words.

She put her hands on Frederick's. "When I went to make your bed and fetch your laundry this morning, I saw that you'd been reading your Bible."

He chortled. "Trying to."

It was good enough—the words he'd underlined revealed his heart: *Teach me to do Your will, For You are my God: Your Spirit is good. Lead me in the land of uprightness.* "Help me understand, Frederick. What specifically makes you want to go to Germany?"

He tossed his head slowly, stretching his neck from side to side.

He must be so tense.

"It's just a longing. The picture postcards, the old books—even the language feels like it could become natural to me, if I just had someone to talk to."

"Doesn't Paul Strauss speak some German?"

"Not nearly enough."

Hannah tried to wipe a tear from her eye with her shoulder. "Where would you go?"

Frederick's hands moved to envelop hers. "Do you think *Opa* and *Oma* Schmidt might know someone who could take me in for a while? Just until I get situated. I'd be willing to do work in exchange for room and board. Unless you have any relatives left over there?"

That was a long shot. Hannah's family had been in the United States far longer than Friedrich's, giving the ties generations to loosen.

She rose from her chair, reluctantly removing her hands from his grip. "I have to be alone." She didn't want to though. She wanted to throw her arms around him and never let go. He was her only child, her companion, and her only connection to the man she had loved from a tender, early age. So young, in fact, that she could not remember a time in her childhood when Friedrich hadn't been there, until the day he'd left for the army.

Still, it's not right to keep him here.

It was dinnertime before she saw Frederick again. He'd worked outside all afternoon, and she'd let him. Meanwhile, she'd worked inside, trying to name the feelings surfacing from deep within. Anger? Numbness? Fear? There was no way she could argue with her son, no way she could force him to stay, but this feeling of loss was all too familiar.

When he entered the kitchen, his hands and clothes covered with dirt and sweat, she handed him a glass of water and smiled sadly. "Go get cleaned up. I'll have dinner ready shortly."

He drained the glass and went upstairs. *He must be exhausted.* Not only had he slept little the night before, but he'd worked all afternoon in the warm summer sun without stopping for a break. He was a hard worker, but he usually took better care of himself than that. Would he remember to take care of himself once he was on his own?

When Frederick had returned for dinner, he'd bathed, shaved, combed his hair, and put on clean clothes. He sat at his place and eyed her cautiously. Nothing like this had ever come between them before.

She grasped his hand and whispered softly, "Dear Frederick. Kind, wise, passionate Frederick. Your adventurous streak runs a mile wide, and yet all these years you have sacrificed it for your grandparents and me. This decision of yours wasn't made in a day. I can see it in the wear and tear you've made on that German language manual. I know in my heart that I can't persuade you against it, though I wish to God you'd stay." She placed an envelope before him. "I've placed a call to your father's Aunt Maria. She is Opa Schmidt's younger sister and lives in Sternberg in Northern Germany with her husband Werner Bergmann. Her address is on a paper inside the envelope along with something else." She breathed deep and pushed the words out, "Promise me you will take one more week to think about this before you do anything."

He nodded his agreement and opened the envelope, revealing a thick pile of bills. "Mom, where on earth did you get this?"

She sighed. "It's yours. Grandpa Hauser gave it to me before he died, telling me it was for you to use when you came of age. I believe he intended for you to put it toward buying a home or perhaps getting an education. I don't know what he would think of your plans, but if you're going to go, you'll need money for passage. There is enough to cover that. You'll have to exchange the rest when you arrive, but it should be enough to get you there and get you started."

Frederick tucked the bills back in the envelope, folding and pocketing it. "Thanks, Ma."

She nodded, swallowing back tears. He stared at her silently for a moment. When she could stand it no more, she moved to throw her arms around him. As she touched the linen of his shirt, the tears came. He wrapped his arms around her. There were no words for a long time.

CHAPTER 5

Frederick often booked odd jobs for Sunday mornings. Even if he was working for a family that had gone to church, they happily welcomed him into their backyard to trim branches or paint shutters. Once in a while someone asked *why aren't you at church, young man?* But most people didn't bat an eye when they came home from Sunday service and saw the work had been done, and done well. It gave him a few more profitable hours in his week, along with a convenient excuse to avoid going to church with his mother. Hannah's church was small, and remaining anonymous was impossible.

Today, however, he owed it to her.

"Oh, Hannah, you brought your son," an older woman greeted them as they entered the house. "Frederick, it's so good to see you. I don't know if you remember me. I'm Susannah Jones."

He nodded shyly, and Susannah motioned to her husband, who was standing across the room speaking to a young couple who had a baby and a little boy. "Mark, come here. Hannah has brought Frederick."

He didn't relish the immediate attention being drawn to him, but he extended his hand anyway.

"Mark Jones." The man's green eyes smiled up at Frederick. "It's good to see you, son."

He didn't blame Mark and Susannah for wondering if he remembered them. His attendance was scarce at best. "Thanks, sir."

With that, Mark raised his voice and called for everyone to find a seat. Susannah slipped onto the piano bench and began playing lightly as Mark prayed. Then, as seamlessly as could be, she began to sing. None of the songs were familiar, until she hit upon the familiar chords of "Be Thou My Vision." Those who had been singing moderately raised their voices higher, and even Frederick sang along. As they reached the third verse, his mother squeezed his hand. "This is my favorite part."

"I know, Mom."

A verse that had been left out of many hymnals entirely was cherished in their home:

Be Thou my Battle Shield, sword for the fight
Be Thou my dignity, Thou my delight
Thou my soul's shelter, be Thou my high tower
Raise Thou me heavenward, O Power of my Power

The song had always captivated him, but by the end of the fifth verse, he prayed Susannah would lead them to the final cadence. Blessedly, she did. Mark prayed again, and opened his Bible. Frederick sank back into the couch and mentally prepared himself for what promised to be a lengthy sermon.

"In ancient times, the watchman was obligated to sound the alarm for his people when war came to their shores. If not, their blood would be on his head."

The words were chilling, but Mark's voice was too gentle to keep Frederick engaged. His mind began to wander. His plans were out in the open now, and there was no turning back. The only thing left to do was to make good on his promise to wait a week. Then, he was bound for Germany.

The service was followed by a humble meal at Susannah and Mark's table. Then, as the other families departed, Hannah followed Susannah into the kitchen, leaving Frederick alone in the parlor with Mark.

The older man gestured to a set of chairs, and the two seated themselves.

"Well, my son, it has been a while. I understand you've been working on Sunday mornings."

Everything about this man was gently disarming. Instead of feeling trapped, Frederick relaxed in his presence, stretched out his legs and crossed his ankles. "I work whenever people need me."

Mark nodded. "Your mother is very proud of you. She knows you've sacrificed a lot to see that she's cared for."

Frederick gave Mark a simple nod of his head and a nervous smile.

"Your mother is like a daughter to us, and Susannah and I pray for the two of you often. The other night, I realized you've reached an age where you might consider striking out on your own. Many young men have left their homes, their cities, and even gone to other states to find work. In my heart I began to feel how difficult a choice that would be for you."

Frederick nodded again.

Mark leaned forward and put his hand on Frederick's shoulder. "Frederick, the same God who has provided for you and your mother all these years will continue to provide for her when the time comes for you to leave."

He'd regret it if he didn't take this opportunity to share what was on his mind with this fellow who cared so deeply for his mother. "Sir—"

"Call me Mark."

"Mark, sir—" Frederick uncrossed his legs and leaned forward in his chair, resting his palms on his knees. "Thank you. I am worried about her. I talked to her about this exact thing yesterday. I am headed for Germany next week."

"A family connection?"

"Somewhat, yes."

"I know your father's family was German."

"Yes."

Mark pursed his lips in thought. "An interesting time to be going there, to be sure."

The man's tone evidenced less shock than Paul's or his mother's, though Frederick still felt the need to explain himself. "In spite of whatever's going on there, I feel like I need to be there. I don't want to find a job and settle down here."

"Do you feel the Lord has work for you to do there?"

Frederick gave a short laugh. "I don't know. I—I tried to do what Mom always does, pray and read the Bible for answers, but I'm just not sure I believe in all that yet, honestly."

Mark smiled knowingly. "Fair enough. Perhaps there is a reason you have yet to discover. Let's pray.

"The LORD bless you, and keep you;
The LORD make His face shine upon you,
And be gracious to you;
The LORD lift up His countenance upon you,

And give you peace.

Amen."

Frederick started as Mark's eyes lit on him. *That's it?* The women returned from the kitchen at that moment, and Hannah looked at Frederick. "I guess we should be going. Unless we're interrupting something?"

"No, no. We were just finishing up. This young man has much to do, I'm sure." Mark smiled broadly as he rose and extended a hand to Frederick.

The afternoon was pleasant, and Frederick led his mother the long way home. It was hard to shake the feeling that he was buttering her up, striving to make as many happy memories for her as possible before he abandoned her. Not that she'd given him any reason to feel guilty.

He didn't need her help with that.

CHAPTER 6

HANNAH

July 1938

Saturday morning dawned, already sultry in the summer heat. Frederick's bags sat packed in the corner. Hannah rose early to prepare eggs and real coffee, with a side of bacon she'd purchased especially for the occasion. She preferred tea, but poured them each a cup of "bean broth" just as she heard Frederick's footsteps on the stairs.

He entered the kitchen, buttoning his shirt. Another night he had barely slept. Surely anxiety and anticipation had kept him awake for most of the night. Placing the cups on the table, she moved to embrace him.

He pulled her in close. "Good morning, Ma."

This was it. Their last morning. He held her for a moment, resting his chin on top of her head. "Thank you for the coffee."

She released him and nodded. "Of course. You have a long journey ahead." She gestured for him to sit.

"There's only one plate."

"I'll eat later. I guess I'm as nervous as you are."

He chuckled. "Yeah. My stomach's been bothering me."

She could feel a look of concern spread across her face as they took their seats.

"It's nothing, Ma. Just nerves."

She nodded and pushed a wrapped package toward him. He opened it carefully and looked up at her. "A German Bible?"

"It was your grandfather's. I know you struggle to believe what's written in here, but I don't want you to be without it."

"How'd you know I didn't pack my Bible?"

She shrugged. "I didn't."

He thanked her again, set the Bible aside, and dug into his eggs.

When he returned upstairs to brush his teeth, Hannah shook her head. The Bible still lay on the table. With a sigh, she tucked it into his rucksack and turned to see Paul Strauss appear at the door.

"Good morning, Paul." She breathed, holding the door open for him.

"My dear." He doffed his hat and kissed her on the cheek.

"Thank you so much for offering to take us to the station." She frowned slightly. "I don't think I could've done this myself."

"I know. That's why I suggested it."

Frederick reappeared and grasped Paul's hand heartily. "Herr Strauss."

"Well, young man. This is really happening."

Frederick grinned wide.

"Are you sure you're ready?"

"Ready or not, I'm on my way."

More awake than he'd been at breakfast, his thrill was evident.

The three climbed into Paul's old Ford and made their way to the station in relative silence, save for the hum of the engine and Paul's occasional whistling. When they arrived, they made their way through the station to the platform. The train was already approaching in the distance.

Hannah's stomach lurched. Every memory of Friedrich's departure fell back upon her, fresh, new, and heavy with unfulfilled longing.

She threw her arms around her son and cried Biblical words she wished she'd prayed over her husband. "Dear God, please protect Frederick. Be his shield and buckler. Bless him and make your face shine upon him. And please, *please*, make a way for me to see him again."

She continued to cry softly as he kissed the top of her head and promised, "I'm going to be all right, Mom."

The train came to a stop, and Hannah released her son. Frederick grasped Paul's hand. "Thank you, Herr Strauss. Please take care of her for me."

"*Ja, mein Sohn.*" He smiled and nodded toward the train. "You be safe now. Be smart, and do good."

Frederick took up his things and boarded the train without hesitation. Hannah watched as he struggled through the aisle and chose a seat close to where they stood, sliding in and immediately meeting her eyes through the glass.

Paul wrapped an arm around her shoulder. She reached into her pocket and pulled out a handkerchief, dabbing her eyes and smearing her makeup. The final whistle sounded. She lifted a hand and waved at the young man in the train who was waving vigorously back at her.

When the train was out of sight, Paul led her to a bench and pulled her close, allowing her to rest her forehead on his shoulder as bitter sobs tore through her.

"I know, Hannah," he whispered. His gentle hand patted her back, somewhat awkwardly at first. "I was thinking about that day too."

"The day you and Freddy left."

"Indeed."

They sat until she'd released enough grief to stand. Wiping her eyes, she looked at Paul. "I think I'm ready."

He nodded, and guided her back to the beat up old Ford.

Once home, he stayed with her long into the evening until she assured him for the fourth time that she would be all right.

CHAPTER 7

FREDERICK

Two long, agitating days in New York had convinced him he was *not* cut out for big city life. Their small city upstate was as much as he cared to see, and he hungered after the wide open spaces he'd seen on the way to the Big Apple.

On the ship, he shared a cabin with Otto, an older gentleman who was returning to Germany after visiting his daughter in the United States. Frederick was grateful for the opportunity to practice *real* conversational German. It helped that Otto spoke some English.

After exhausting the topic of Otto's visit with his daughter and first grandbaby, they began to talk about Frederick's plans.

"So, young man, where are you going in Germany?"

"Sternberg...I have family there."

"*Achso!* You are going my way."

"*Wirklich?*"

"Ja..." the older man gestured in the air, as if Frederick had some mental map of Germany he could just pull up at any moment. "Sternberg is here. I will be going on to Güstrow."

"Achso."

"You are welcome to travel with me."

"Thank you."

Five days later they docked in Hamburg. The sun had risen on a beautiful summer morning. As their feet touched the ground, a sensation crept up Frederick's spine, both terrifying and invigorating. Would life here in Germany *really* be all that different? And would different mean *bad*? That's how his mother and Paul made it sound, but how could they know? Perhaps this would be the best thing for him. Back home, his mother complained of loose women and conniving politicians. Paul didn't trust anyone who leaned too far left.

Otto moved quickly, and Frederick had to hurry to keep up. The man was no novice traveler, even if this had been his first time in America. To Frederick, the chaos was dizzying. He continued to observe as he made his way through the station and out onto the street.

Otto stopped abruptly. "We must eat."

"Ja."

"I know a nice little place. We can stop there before we catch the train."

Frederick nodded.

Ten minutes later, coffee and pastries in hand, Frederick and Otto settled down at a table at a small outdoor café. Finally, Frederick had time to think over everything he'd seen in his first hour in Germany.

"What's on your mind son?"

He took a sip of coffee and contemplated. "Beautiful...Lotta uniforms though."

"*Jup*."

"I had no idea what to expect."

"No reason you should." Otto leaned in. "You must be careful, that is all. You are wise. You will figure it out."

"What?" Frederick was confused.

Otto leaned back and examined him. "Do you remember our conversation about freedom?"

Frederick nodded. The older man had explained that many Germans saw themselves every bit as free as they'd ever been, and many were grateful for the way the new regime had shut the floodgates on the excesses of the past. Yet not everyone felt free, and some felt threatened. They were free to go, Otto had explained.

When Frederick had asked the man for his personal opinion, his traveling companion had simply said, "Admittedly, things are better. That does not mean I support the regime."

Otto tapped him on the hand. Frederick's eyes had been wandering as he processed it all. "If you feel differently, *Junge*, best to keep it to yourself."

Frederick nodded.

"I prefer to spend my time away from the cities anyway," Otto continued. "Life out there doesn't change with the wind." He popped a piece of pastry in his mouth. "Does your uncle have a telephone? You should probably let him know you've arrived."

"Yes."

Otto nodded approvingly. "Finish that up. We must get to the *Bahnhof*. I am sorry that I do not have time to show you around. I must get home to my Margaretta."

"Of course." Frederick finished his pastry and tossed back the last of his coffee.

"Perhaps you would like the window," Otto offered, extending a hand into the compartment.

"Sure." Frederick ducked in ahead of him, stowed his things, and slipped into the seat against the window. Otto took a seat beside him. His eyes drank in the scenery as they pulled out of the station and passed through town, but the rhythm of the train was too much. Frederick's eyes grew heavy, and soon his head followed. He leaned against the windowpane, closed his eyes, and fell asleep.

Something banged against the compartment, ripping him back to reality. Two men in uniform were escorting a man and woman through the corridor. Frederick turned his head to Otto and opened his mouth to speak, but the expression on Otto's face told him to keep quiet. He rested his head against back the glass in an attempt to reclaim the sleep which had been far too brief.

All he really wanted was to be done traveling.

The train arrived in Sternberg a few hours later under a warm evening sun. Frederick peered out the window. "This is my stop."

Otto rose and stepped out so Frederick could pass.

"Thank you for everything." He extended a hand to the older gentleman.

"It was my pleasure, son." Otto leaned toward Frederick and added, "Try to stay out of trouble."

After disembarking and passing through the station, Frederick took a seat outside, hoping he would recognize Uncle Werner when he arrived or that Uncle Werner would recognize him. He ran his fingers over his hair and looked around.

"Frederick?"

He turned to see a diminutive man with white hair and a mustache. "Uncle Werner?"

"Ja." He paused and narrowed his eyes. "*Sprichst du Deutsch?*"

"Ja...*bisschen.*"

Uncle Werner patted his cheek. "We will work on that, ja?"

After a short drive, they arrived at a small cottage on the outskirts of town. The surrounding area was picturesque, wooded and set along the Warnow River. "You will have to work hard," Uncle Werner said, "but when you are finished you will be able to explore."

Aunt Maria was short, just like her husband, and quite plump, with her graying blonde hair tied back in a bun. "Ah, Friedrich!"

"The boy prefers to be called by his *American* name, Mother," Werner chided.

Maria tsked and pulled him into an embrace. "You'd be better off getting used to being called *Friedrich*, young man."

He nodded and patted the older woman's back. It was both thrilling and unsettling to be called by his German name—his father's name. "Danke, *Tante* Maria. It is kind of you to allow me to stay."

"Our children have all grown and moved away, and we never see our grandchildren." With a step back, she looked him up and down and added, "You may not be a child anymore, but you are still bringing some energy to this house." As if to prove her point, she nodded toward her husband, who had already reclined into a chair with his pipe.

"I am resting for a moment, Mother," Werner teased. "The boy will learn soon enough that farm work never ceases."

Maria gestured to an old wooden table, on which she'd set some sausage, rolls, and jam. "You must be hungry."

"Ja." He sat down to the table and filled his plate.

LATE THAT EVENING, HE lay awake, staring out the window at the starlit sky. It was good to be away from crowds of the city and the inability to find any solitude on the ship and the train. Otto had been an excellent traveling companion, but he longed for autonomy. Here, he would have it. Work, yes, but with it, freedom, space, and fresh air.

The time he needed to figure out his next move.

CHAPTER 8

FREDERICK
Sternberg, Germany
August 1938

Uncle Werner had no trouble putting Frederick to work right away on the small farm. There were machines to be fixed, tools to be sharpened, animal pens to be mucked, vines to be trimmed, and weeds to be pulled. Dirty and smelling of animals, Frederick ended every afternoon with a dive into the small pond before making his way to the house. After the first two times he entered her kitchen dripping from head to toe, Aunt Maria began leaving a towel for him on the porch.

"You must have a friend," Maria announced one morning. "Herr Müller is sending his son Fritz over to show you around town today."

Frederick smiled, grateful that it appeared he was being given the day off from work. A knock came at the door less than five minutes later. Aunt Maria went to open it, returning with a tall, muscular young man with blond hair and blue eyes. "Frederick, this is Fritz Müller. His family owns a farm not far from here."

Frederick extended his hand to Fritz, who grasped it and shook firmly.

"Would you like something to eat, Fritz?" Maria asked.

"No thank you, *Frau* Bergmann. I just ate."

"Well, then, if Frederick is done, you boys must go. Two boys in my kitchen will be twice the mess." She turned to Frederick with a twinkle in her eye. "And Frederick is not shy about making a mess."

Fritz cackled in a friendly way. "My *Mutti* says the same thing."

"I'm sure." Maria waved a hand. "Now off. Both of you."

With a bow, Fritz turned and extended a hand towards the door. Frederick followed to the sound of Maria collecting his dishes from the table. Once outside, Fritz turned to Frederick. "Do you like to hike?"

"Ja, it's great."

"Good. We'll hike first and then I'll show you around town." Fritz turned and walked briskly toward the woods, and Frederick followed eagerly. Perhaps this really was going to be a new beginning.

"So, Frederick from America. What do you think of the Fatherland?" Fritz stepped onto a bridge that crossed a stream.

Fatherland. Germany. "It's beautiful."

"And it is becoming more beautiful all the time."

As they continued to hike under a canopy of leaves, Fritz told about his years in Hitler Youth, his parents' involvement in the National Socialist Party, and his future plans. "It's the army for now, but after my two years is up, I'm going to join the SS."

Frederick listened with intent. As they returned to the house, Fritz paused and looked at Frederick. "I am guessing you have never had to salute your leaders in America, *oder?*"

"Ha...nope. Just wave."

"*Na ja*, it is like a wave, oder?" He thrust his right arm stiffly in the air. "Now you try."

It was funny, the thought of actually doing the infamous salute he'd seen in the pictures, but he thrust his arm in the air.

"Try it again."

He thrust his arm in the air again.

"Now. *Heil* Hitler."

Frederick repeated the motion and croaked out the words.

Fritz shook his head. "One more time."

Frederick summoned his enthusiasm and saluted an imaginary *Führer*.

"Much better." Fritz punched his shoulder playfully. "You will fit right in. Now let's eat."

Fritz popped open the door of his father's car and slid into the driver's seat. Frederick followed suit, and soon they were headed into town.

Entering a small café, they were greeted by other young men, some of whom wore their black and brown *Hitlerjugend* uniforms.

"This is Frederick," Fritz announced with pride. "He is a *Volksdeutscher* from America."

Frederick was staggered by the interest of the other young men. Everyone had questions which were only interrupted by the appearance of a young woman with blonde braids and traditional clothing. "I see you brought a new friend today." She eyed Frederick in a friendly way. "And you are?"

"Frederick," he said simply.

"I'm Gertrud, nice to meet you." She turned to the rest of the boys. "*Also*, what will you gentlemen have? Potato pancakes? Sausages? Schnitzel? Fried fish?"

It had been years since he'd enjoyed authentic German food, and it all sounded good.

When she had taken their orders and returned to the kitchen, one of the young men piped up about *Böhmen und Mähren*. Soon, the conversation took on a liveliness with which Frederick could not keep up.

Fritz leaned in. "Czechoslovakia."

"Achso."

"The Führer wants to unite them with the Fatherland, but their leaders resist."

Frederick had heard of the annexation of Austria earlier that year, a month or so before he'd begun his journey. Now Germany was looking to expand its territory into Czechoslovakia as well? "Why?"

Fritz laughed. "You do not know your history, *Frederick from America*. It is German territory. The Germans living there are suffering at the hands of the Czechs and want to unite with Germany." He chuckled again. "I can see I'm going to be explaining things to you all summer long."

A lot to chew on. Thankfully, their food arrived and the conversation slowed, though occasionally someone would ask him a question between bites.

It all made for some uncomfortable reevaluation of his entire thought process. *What am I doing here?* Suddenly, his answers seemed flat. He felt out of touch and idealistic, but then again, these boys were full of idealism themselves.

Perhaps they understood more than he thought.

"Are you going to work on the farm forever?" Fritz asked as they returned home that afternoon.

Frederick shrugged. "Well, I'm sure I won't be there forever." He really hadn't thought much beyond his initial plan of staying with his aunt and uncle, but he figured something else would present itself...eventually. Aunt Maria made no secret of her desire to see him married, although that was the furthest thing from his mind.

"I will be joining the *Heer* in a few months," Fritz said. "You should come with me."

"The army?" He hadn't considered that, although how could he not? It was the next logical step for every young man he'd met that afternoon. The idea had its merits. It would be an opportunity to see more of the country, perhaps even other parts of Europe. It could provide the adventure he'd always craved. He also enjoyed Fritz's companionship. "I'll think about it," he finally said.

Fritz came to visit regularly over the following weeks and even helped Frederick on the farm. Frederick found himself opening up about things he couldn't have back home. Frustration with being unable to play ball with the other boys, and how his family had lost touch with their German roots. He expressed his lack of interest in his mother's faith, but was careful to qualify that he admired her for it.

Fritz continued to share stories of his childhood adventures, especially his experiences in the Hitlerjugend and Labor Service. Hearing these things only made Frederick's hunger grow deeper, and at last he decided he too would enlist in the army.

He wasn't sure what kind of reaction he expected from his aunt and uncle as he made his announcement, but he chose dinnertime over Aunt Maria's pork schnitzel to share his plans with them. Placing his fork next to his plate, he looked across the table at his aunt and uncle. "I want to thank you both for taking me in."

When he had their attention he continued, "As planned, I'll be moving on soon."

Werner raised his bushy eyebrows. Maria startled a little. "So soon?"

Frederick nodded. "I'll be joining the army."

Werner nodded knowingly and returned to his food. Maria stared at Frederick. "Na ja. You will be very handsome in your uniform."

"WELL, AT LEAST HE didn't say he was going to join the SS."

"He would be an easy choice for them. He has the height, *oder*?"

Frederick chuckled. Werner and Maria's voices were traveling farther than they intended them to—either that or they believed Frederick to be asleep. *The SS.* They were both revered and feared—he wasn't sure *what* to think.

Unable to sleep, he switched on the small light in his room and opened the desk drawer. There beside a small stack of paper was the Bible his mother had given him. *No.* He shut the drawer quickly, preempting the urge to pick it up. He had shared his plans with Aunt Maria and Uncle Werner. The harder thing would be telling his mother.

Hello Mom,

I'm sorry I haven't written before now. Uncle Werner is keeping me very busy on the farm, and it's hard to believe it's already the end of September. I've made a friend, Fritz, and he also keeps me busy. Just when I think I have a few minutes of free time, Aunt Maria seems to find things for me to do as well, but she feeds me, so I have no complaints.

Fritz will be joining the army soon, and I have decided to accompany him. I am sure this news is a surprise to you, and although I'm nervous,

I'm excited at the idea of doing something new. I hope to see much more of this beautiful land and maybe even other parts of Europe.

I will try to keep in touch.

Much love,

Frederick

CHAPTER 9

FREDERICK

As a foreigner, Frederick was required to travel to Berlin for enlistment. Thankfully, Fritz was thrilled by the idea of accompanying him to the German capital.

While there were still few passengers on the train, Fritz leaned in and whispered to Frederick. "We are friends, Freddie, oder?"

"*Sicher.*"

Fritz stared at him hard. "You came here because you wanted to get in touch with your roots, ja?"

"*Natürlich.*"

The blond shook his head. "You act so funny about our worldview. The things we hold dear."

"I wasn't aware."

Fritz continued to stare. "It is no surprise that you don't understand, being from *Amerika*. I know there are people who view the Führer with suspicion, and there have been years of propaganda against us." He pursed his lips and shook his head again. "Do not believe everything you've read. You do not have to agree with us, but you must find a way to keep that to yourself."

"I am proud to be a German."

"You do not truly understand what it means to be a German."

"No…I guess I don't." Perhaps it was more accurate to say that, what Frederick thought it meant to be a German was not the same as what Fritz thought it meant to be a German.

"You Americans do not hide your feelings very well. You must change that." He nodded to the front of the train. "Especially now that you will be in the *Hauptstadt*."

Was he being corrected? Warned? "It's not that I don't agree…I just don't know what I think."

Fritz patted his shoulder. "You will, soon."

<hr>

HAMBURG HAD BEEN FULL of men in uniform, but Berlin was the epicenter of National Socialist pride. Swastika flags hung from every building. Uniformed officials were all around. Frederick's curiosity warred with the part of him that had been warned Germany was up to no good.

"It's too bad I told my aunt and uncle we'd be returning this evening," he commented.

"Send them a telegram. They will understand."

"No, no, no…" Frederick glanced around at the shiny cars, the smiling people, the colorful floral sprays, and the blood-red flags. It was absolutely mesmerizing. He wanted to run—but more than that, he wanted to stay and explore.

His enlistment was taken with great pride and assurance of the Führer's gratitude. More young men, he was told, should return from abroad to serve their Fatherland.

He stepped out of the office with a new sense of confidence. Had it really been necessary to tell his aunt and uncle he'd be returning that evening?

Fritz was glancing around, bouncing on the balls of his feet. "We should at least grab a bite to eat. There is so much good food here. Anything you want."

Frederick pursed his lips. "I can imagine."

"I know a café a few blocks away where there is often dancing."

"Midday?"

Fritz shrugged. "At the very least, there will be food, beer, and pretty girls."

He shuddered. But then his stomach growled.

Fritz pulled at his wrist. "Come on, Freddie. We're in Berlin." The blond tugged harder, so Frederick's feet were forced to follow.

It was still warm enough that people had gathered outside. Music played and indeed, a few couples were dancing. It was a light-hearted scene—beer was flowing and the air smelled of schnitzel and bratwurst.

"Two?"

"Ja." Fritz flashed a flirty grin at the waitress.

She led them to a table not far from the dance floor. Fritz took a brief glance at the menu and then ordered *Pommes* and two beers. "Anything else, Freddie? It's on me. We're celebrating your new career!"

"Oh." The waitress gasped. She was young and pretty, and obviously quite entertained by the two young customers. "What are we celebrating?"

"My young friend here just joined the army!"

She bowed politely. "How wonderful."

"He came all the way from America just to serve the Führer."

Frederick rolled his eyes, but the young woman was clearly keen to play along with Fritz's sales pitch.

"Amerika, oder? I have *always* wanted to go there." She gathered the menus but continued her questions. "What part of Amerika are you from?"

"New York."

"The big city? Wow..."

He shook his head. "Na. Upstate..." he glanced at Fritz. "*Nordlich*?"

Fritz shrugged.

"My big brother loves stories about the Old West. Cowboys and Indians. Karl May...you know?"

Frederick nodded. "Ja. Not much of a reader myself..."

She giggled. "You should. It's a great escape."

A woman hailed the server from a nearby table.

"I'd better go. I'll get that order right in."

"Oh—" Frederick raised a hand to stop her. "I don't care for beer. Do you have Coca Cola?"

The girl grinned amusedly as she made a note of his request. Then she darted off to the next table.

Fritz leaned in. "That is no way to win a girl's heart, *Kamerad*."

"I'm sorry, I didn't realize we were here to flirt."

The blond chuckled. "We weren't. But since the life lesson presented itself, next time, make yourself sound interesting. Instead of telling her all the stuff you *don't* do."

"I'm just being honest."

"You save honesty for the girl you want to marry."

Frederick rolled his eyes.

A moment later the waitress arrived back at their table with a beer and a Coke. "My favorite thing from America," she said with a wink. "I prefer it to beer myself."

He nodded his thanks and wrapped his hands around the glass.

"When she comes back with those Pommes, you should tell her something else about America."

"Like what?"

"Like you know Jesse Owens."

"Who?"

Fritz rolled his eyes. "American track star. Won big here in 1936."

"Oh yeah." Frederick rolled his eyes. "I'm not gonna lie, Fritzi."

"Have it your way. I'm just telling you, girls love that stuff." He threw back a sip of beer.

When the girl returned with the Pommes, Fritz announced, "You'll never guess who this fella's neighbor is."

The waitress turned to Frederick. "Who?"

Frederick shook his head as Fritz chirped, "Jesse Owens."

"Really?"

Frederick shook his head. "Na, my Kamerad here is making a joke. What he means is"—Frederick thought quick—"compared to, you know, living in Berlin, it's *like* we're neighbors."

"Oh...all right." The girl seemed genuinely disappointed. "Well, let me know if there is anything else you need."

"Yes ma'am." Fritz watched her walk away and jerked his knee hard against Frederick's. "Come on, *Bruder*."

Frederick held up a hand in the hopes Fritz would just move on.

"All right, all right." Fritz raised his beer. "To Freddie. Who prefers Coca Cola to just about everything, including women. *Prost*."

Frederick shook his head. "Prost."

CHAPTER 10

FREDERICK

October 1938

A horn sounded in the driveway, announcing the arrival of Fritz and his father. Frederick embraced his aunt and uncle then gathered his belongings, which weren't many. Glancing around the small cottage, his eyes landed on the older couple one last time. Maria wiped a tear from her eyes. "I only wish you were leaving us to marry some lovely *Fräulein*."

Werner chuckled. "Do you want more children standing dripping wet on your kitchen floor?"

Frederick was grateful for his uncle's solidarity. "I'll be back before you know it. Thank you for everything."

The two nodded.

With one more glance around the quaint interior, Frederick bid them *auf Wiedersehen* and ducked out the door.

———

THE COACH WAS BURSTING with the energy and hubris of dozens of young recruits as they made their way toward the camp that would finish the work the Hitler Youth and Work Service had begun: changing them from rough-mannered boys to disciplined soldiers. Fritz was a knucklehead, but he was disciplined and worked hard.

The Sudetenland had been added to the Reich only days earlier in a bloodless, jubilant annexation for the ethnic Germans living under the thumb of Czech leadership. A few of the boys had relatives living there, and they declared their family's relief. Frederick sat, leaning against the window, listening quietly. He did not want to appear too far removed from the excitement, but he did not understand. How could he?

Occasionally someone broke out in a song of victory. He moved his lips along with the words, but again he felt his exclusion keenly—he didn't know many German songs, save for the few Fritz had taught him as they wandered in the woods around Sternberg.

So many songs.

"What's wrong with you, man," Fritz said, playfully punching his arm.

"Nothing, I just didn't sleep last night." Keeping up a front might be harder than he thought. "I wrote my mom," he continued, in an effort to change the subject. He was ready for what was happening, wasn't he? "I told her I was going to be a soldier. My dad was a soldier—" he stopped. *Yes, my father was a soldier. He fought against Germany in the Great War.* Was that the kind of thing a person could say?

"You better send her a picture of you in your uniform," Fritz cawed giving him another elbow. "She'll see how handsome her boy is now that he's embraced his roots."

"Ja," Frederick sighed. Did he really look any different, save for the muscles he'd developed working on the farm and hiking in the forest?

"Maybe you will finally meet a nice girl," Fritz continued, leaning back against Frederick's shoulder and gesturing in the air as if painting a picture of the future. "Someone as boring as you. You will raise a brood of children together. Then your Mutti will come. I promise."

Frederick chuckled. "What?"

"Grandchildren. They are sure to bring your Mutti to Germany."

He wasn't sure his mother was going to be as proud as Fritz imagined.

"Hey," a voice called from across the aisle, "Where did you say you are from?"

"America," Frederick said.

"This man is a Volksdeutscher," Fritz said proudly. "He heard the call of the Fatherland!" Another punch to the arm. "I'm lucky to have him as a best friend."

Frederick smiled. That was one thing he was absolutely sure of: after years of having no one his age to associate with, it was good to have a friend. Although Fritz was more energetic and outgoing, they were alike in many ways. How different would their stories have been if they'd grown up down the street from one another like his father and Paul had?

Fritz was still conversing with the tall, slim blond-haired boy across the aisle. "Freddie," Fritz was saying, "This is Heinrich Schuyler...Freddie?"

"Ja, sorry," Frederick shook himself back to reality. "Name's Frederick."

"I know. Frederick the American Volksdeutscher," Heinrich said with a laugh. He was friendly, and the conversation came easily. Although he'd been told American culture was eschewed in Germany, the boys were obviously hungry to hear his stories. Once in a while, Fritz motioned to him to tone it down, saying, "Ja, we don't have that here."

He never got out to movies anyway, and he wasn't much of a reader. But jazz? How could one *live* without jazz?

Fritz's father was a Party member. Apparently, he had some influence in their small town, but even Fritz evidenced fascination with the world outside of the borders of Germany. America, he said, was like a fantasy kingdom, although Frederick wasn't sure he meant that as a positive.

"Just wait," Fritz said finally, "a few more months here, you will not miss a thing. We have beautiful music, beautiful scenery, excellent movies—and girls love a man in uniform, oder?"

The boys around them laughed, a few quipped and nudged one another. Frederick grinned.

FREDERICK, FRITZ, AND HEINRICH made their way up the last flight of stairs to their assigned rooms.

"We're bunk mates, Kamerad," Heinrich indicated.

"All right." Frederick was pleased.

Rüdiger Johannsen plopped his things down on the bunk next to theirs.

"You're in here too?"

"Jup."

Heinrich winked. "Super."

Fritz smacked the door frame. "I'm down the hall. Two doors."

Disappointing, but it wasn't any big deal. He was here to make all the friends he never had growing up, right?

A surge of adrenaline ran through him as he changed out of his street clothes into the training uniform provided for him. Turning toward the mirror, he stared hard at the young man staring back at him. Just one more in a series of unexpected moves. He'd never really thought much about joining the military, probably because his father had been killed doing so, and truly, there was no need.

But now? He was told he was becoming part of the long and proud military tradition of his Fatherland.

He straightened his shoulders and tightened his core. *Brust raus, Bauch rein.*

You're a soldier now, Freddie.

CHAPTER 11

HANNAH

Upstate New York

November 1938

The quick knock at the door no longer served as a request—it had become a welcome announcement of Paul's arrival. She looked up to see him enter the kitchen, holding the mail he'd picked up on the way in. Beneath the mail was a small box of chocolates.

Since Frederick's departure, an awkward romance had begun to blossom between them, sparking a fresh flame in Hannah's heart and, it seemed, a fresh wind in Paul's sails. After years of eking out a living repairing clocks and watches from the spare bedroom of his house, Paul had begun to seek more gainful, regular employment. No easy task, but the prospect alone seemed to get him out of bed in the morning.

As the two began to take walks in the evening, she saw visible improvement in Paul's health. He was young again, and so was she.

"Oh, Paul." She smiled. His charm was vastly different than that of the man she'd married. Friedrich had been tall and handsome with dark brown hair and clear blue eyes. Paul was stocky and his hair was already gray, but there was something charming about him as well—something that emerged the day he sat comforting her at the train station. Was it his genuine concern? His eagerness to assume the role of *protector* in her son's absence? His awkward arm around her shoulder had quickly gone from hesitant and stiff to tender and relaxed, then finally, confident and sure.

"There is a letter here from Frederick." He took a seat at the kitchen table.

She dropped the lump of dough she'd been kneading, wiped her hands on her apron, and took the envelope from his hand. Sitting beside him, she opened and read it, then dropped it on the table and put her face in her hands.

"May I?" Paul asked, reaching for the letter.

She nodded but said nothing. His expression turned grim as he read her son's barely legible scrawl. "Oh, Hannah." Paul scooted his chair closer to hers and embraced her. "He will be all right."

She shook her head, trembling as the emotions of losing Friedrich came over her like a flood. She'd been proud of her husband as he stood before her in uniform, but she hadn't realized it would be the *last* time he stood before her. When Frederick had left her at the train station that evening in July, she'd tried to push away those memories and the inkling that she might be seeing him for the last time as well. There hadn't been any real reason for her to suspect that, anyway. She'd never dreamed he'd join the army—*over there.*

Had he been seduced by propaganda?

Paul placed a hand on her forearm, seeming to sense her thoughts. "Many men join the army purely out of a hunger for adventure. Wasn't that what caused him to go to Germany in the first place?"

She nodded, but didn't truly find his words comforting. "But how will he stand up against all the propaganda?"

"You can't worry about that. Besides, our press has always had its share of propaganda as well." He chuckled and reached for Hannah's Bible, which lay at the far end of the table, and placed it in her trembling hands. "If you have taught me one thing in the last five months, it is that God is in control of all of our circumstances. He will watch over Frederick."

She chuffed, unable to deny her doubts. "It doesn't mean he won't get into trouble. It doesn't mean he won't suffer. It doesn't mean he won't become a Nazi. It doesn't mean—"

"Hannah," Paul said gently, "you have been a good influence on this old non-practicing Lutheran. Just this morning, I read, 'The steps of a good man are ordered by the LORD.' How about what Mark said on Sunday?"

Hannah nodded. "For such a time as this."

"Yes." Paul stroked her hair and took her hand. "Don't you think these things apply to Frederick?"

She laid her head on his shoulder. Paul's words were comforting, but she feared it would be a long time before she could place her son's life in God's hands. She had placed Friedrich in God's hands, and he'd never returned.

CHAPTER 12

FREDERICK
Germany
February 1939

Three months had flown by. The pace was dizzying, rising at 5:00 AM and drilling for two hours before breakfast. When breakfast was served, it was meager. Afterwards, more drills, hiking, weapons training...the officers *loved* training during winter. It forced a higher level of discipline, and if he had known what he was getting into—no. There was no point in thinking like that now.

There was a classroom component too—where Frederick always struggled to stay attentive. He needed to move, or his mind wandered. Ideological lessons were the worst, but he was pleased to find plenty of the other boys were bored by them too. Not that they would admit it openly, but he could tell.

In their limited downtime, there was the inevitable: *so much talk about girls.* He thought he'd gotten used to it with Fritz, but this was a whole new level.

Aside from being called a prude a few times, the guys actually seemed to like him. They knew he had their backs—even if they did call his masculinity into question. Eventually they let him go out for a walk without anything more than friendly, feigned harassment. He'd pop into Fritz's room and invite him to come along—which Fritz always did. At least Fritz knew to let the subject rest.

Fritz's true passion was politics anyway. Frederick let the blond babble on while he nodded, smiled, and swallowed his own misgivings. *If you don't agree, just keep your mouth shut.*

Maybe he was over thinking it. He'd formed his *own* opinions based on what others had told him, after all. Still, the whole thing gave him a knot in his stomach. Was the New Germany right? Was it wrong? Was it just different?

Whatever the truth, that knot was beginning to take up permanent residence. Some nights, sleep was nearly impossible.

<hr>

A HEAVY BARRAGE OF snow beat against the windows of the barracks. The fierce howling of wind ripped Frederick from a restless sleep. In his stupor, he groped for his boots, pulled them on, and wrapped his blanket around his shoulders. Could he make it past the guards?

Even they had taken shelter on this freezing, blustery night. He pulled his blanket tighter and walked on. The piercing cold felt blissful, like tiny daggers of ice pelting his skin. It was just him in the world, no demanding superiors, no Fritz yammering on about the Thousand Year Reich, no high-ranking officials appearing to review the troops.

Some of the young men had seen the Führer with their own eyes—their emotions were stirred even as they spoke. They recounted stories of girls fainting and women crying. It all seemed like an awful lot...but then, he'd led a pretty sheltered life. Was that what people did when a ruler came to town?

We don't have rulers in America...

He had to admit he'd gotten caught up in the fervor himself once or twice. His father had been stirred by the sight of AEF soldiers marching to war back in 1918.

Emotions were funny things.

He tightened his blanket again and steeled himself against the cold swirling around him. His body trembled, his throat tightened, and his stomach complained. Emotions were funny things, yes, but it felt good to give himself to them. He refused to regret his choices. *I'm here now. I've made my decision. It will get easier. It has to.*

Germany is where I belong.

Slowly, he turned his back to the wind and retreated into the barracks. The stark contrast between idealistic young men like Fritz, and men like Otto and Uncle Werner—what was he to make of it all? Weren't Otto and Werner grateful to have someone who brought their nation from miserable to thriving? From despair to hope? Hitler had come along at just the right time. Was he a gift from God? Or a false messiah? Or just...*the right man for the job?*

Freddie returned to his bunk and curled beneath his blanket in an effort to warm himself from his recent, possibly foolish escapade. He was still lost in thought. It wasn't all bad, but some of the National Socialist notions were just stupid. He chuckled softly. *One can't even listen to jazz...*but he understood. Too much had infiltrated German society, and the bad had come with the good. God knew, his mother complained about smut in America.

So far as he could tell, Germany had been responsible for some of the worst of it, and it had needed to be rooted out. *Sometimes, you have to pull up plants along with the weeds...*But really, folks, *jazz?*

"Go to bed, Freddie," Heinrich grumbled.

"Sorry..." Had his body been tossing and turning along with his mind? He rolled onto his side and clutched his pillow. He couldn't figure this out on his own anyway. If only he had someone like Otto or Uncle Werner to talk to.

There was no one around willing to risk their necks to be honest about how they felt—or maybe they really just bought into it all.

Unteroffizier Sauer forced them ever so gleefully another five kilometers in spite of the ice. The frozen structure they'd hoisted themselves up to so many times before was threatening in its sleet-slick surface.

"Up you go," Sauer crowed. With a boost from Rüdiger, Heinrich slipped up and onto the top with no effort, his slim, lanky body like that of a primate. Freddie pulled himself up behind Heinrich, dusted the snow from his trousers, and laughed as Fritz followed, hoisting himself up with his thick arm muscles.

Then, a slip and a scream.

"Jürgen!" Rudi gasped. Sauer cursed. Below, their comrade lay, helmet on the ground three feet away, blood soaking his head.

Freddie dashed for the quickest way down, and with a hand from Rudi leapt the last few feet to the ground.

Sauer shook his head and cursed Jürgen again. "Helmet, Seitsmann." He dipped and grabbed the *Stalhelm*, dusted it off, and tossed it at the recruit.

Freddie shook his head and knelt at his comrade's side. "Jürgen needs treatment, Unteroffizier." He forced respect into his voice—Sauer lived up to his name.

"Ja, ja, well, he should've thought of that before he neglected to strap on his helmet, oder?"

Freddie swallowed a growl and returned his attention to Jürgen. "Where is the first aid kit?"

"Seitsmann was supposed to have it," Sauer growled.

He shook his head. Yes, Jürgen Seitsmann was a *Dummkopf.* But he was also someone in need of help. "Let me carry him back to the nursing station."

Sauer harrumphed.

"*Bitte*, Unteroffizier."

"All right. Go. Take Schuyler with you. But hurry back."

"*Jawohl.*"

Heinrich hopped down and came to Frederick's side. They hoisted Jürgen between them and began to make their way off.

"Don't dawdle!" Sauer yelled.

"Jawohl."

Frederick grinned at Heinrich. "Thank you, Kamerad."

"*In Ordnung...*" The tall, slim blond looked nervously around. "Bet Sauer's got his eye on his watch already."

"Ja."

They picked up the pace. Even in a reasonable amount of time, Sauer would find fault with *something*.

CHAPTER 13

FREDERICK

Rather than being disciplined for returning five minutes beyond Sauer's *reasonable amount of time*, Frederick found himself receiving a commendation the next day and being recommended for training as a medic.

He was sure the recommendation hadn't come from Sauer, but it also hadn't been the first time his rudimentary medical knowledge had come in handy on the march. Relief washed over him at the thought of exchanging his rifle for a medical kit.

He returned to Sternberg with Fritz, anticipating the fresh country air and hikes in the woods without Sauer's barking.

Maria threw open the door, took a long look at Frederick in his brand new, freshly pressed uniform, and pulled him into her arms. "*Liebling.* Welcome back."

Uncle Werner rose from his chair and strode over to shake Frederick's hand. "You are just in time. One of the goats is due to have her baby any day."

Frederick thought it was a joke, but as they walked out to the barn later, there was no doubt Ingrid was with child. She was awkward, with her tiny frame and bulbous belly. Frederick laughed and patted her head. "Wouldn't you figure my first official act as a *Sanitäter* would be to deliver a baby goat?"

"You're a *Sani*, are you?"

"Ja." Frederick continued to pet the goat and feed her a carrot.

"You have always been a caring young man. I guess even Prussian discipline couldn't drive that out of you." Werner turned serious. "Have you talked to your mother?"

"Nein."

"*Na dann.* Not caring enough."

Frederick rose and wiped his hands on his pants. Placing a call to his mother wasn't going to be easy—but if he didn't do it now, it wouldn't be any easier the longer he waited.

HANNAH

Interrupted by the ring of the telephone, Hannah closed her Bible and rose to answer it. "Hello? Yes? Yes, I will take a call from Germany!" Her heart raced as she heard the voice of her son for the first time in months, an answer to the silent prayers she'd just sent to heaven.

"Hi, Mom," he said gently. His nerves were obvious even through the wires.

"Hello, my love." How she longed to throw her arms around him. Tears streamed down her face, and she leaned her forehead against the wall.

"How are you doing?"

"Oh, Frederick, I'm surviving. How are you?"

"I'm fine mom," he said with a light chuckle.

Although she'd thought of a thousand questions over the last eight months, she stood speechless, afraid to hear what he might have to say. During sleepless nights, her mind had conjured up all sorts of images—from the young boy who was always at her side to the marching Nazi columns in the newsreels.

She pushed the image from her mind and tried to think of something more pleasant.

"Mom?"

"Yes, Frederick, I'm sorry. I have so many questions, yet here I am wasting time."

"It's all right, Mom."

Hesitantly, she said, "Tell me—tell me about the army."

Another light chuckle came from the other end of the line. "It's great. I mean, it was tough, but I survived. I'm going to be a medic."

Her spirit lightened a little. Her son, a medic? "That's wonderful, Frederick."

"The German word is Sanitäter. Sani for short." As he began to share a few anecdotal stories with her, his voice became more animated, and her heart lightened as well. He was happy in the role the army had chosen for him, and his passionate spirit had not been crushed by the fabled Prussian discipline. He said nothing about the Nazis, good or bad.

Her stomach loosened.

After a few minutes of nonstop talking, Frederick paused. "You haven't told me how you are, Ma."

She smiled, knowing the news she had to share would be shocking indeed—but in a good way, she hoped. "Honey, Paul Strauss and I have—well, we've fallen in love."

The sound of amused disbelief came from the other end of the line. "What?"

"Frederick, Paul and I are beginning to talk about getting married."

"Mom"—he gasped—"that's wonderful!"

She gave a sigh of relief. He approved...though she had not truly imagined him disapproving. "Yes, it is, sweetheart. He has changed so much. He used to be so sad, and his health was failing, as you know. His whole life changed the day you charged him to look after me. He began taking better care of himself, got a job, and he's over here every evening and sometimes even checks in on me in the morning before he goes to work. You gave him purpose, Frederick." She smiled at the thought of the charming, well-groomed Paul Strauss. "He's been coming to church with me as well. Mark even asked him to begin teaching a midweek Bible study on Wednesday evening."

"I'm happy for you, Mom. I really am."

She could hear the smile on his face.

"Look, Ma. I have to go." Again Frederick's light chortle came across the line.

"Of course, sweetheart."

"Bye, Ma."

"Goodbye, Frederick dear."

Hannah replaced the receiver, her eyes filling with tears once again. His words had soothed her misgivings and allayed her fears. For now. *A medic in the army.* They had not stolen the gentleness of her sweet boy...but still. The nations were rattling sabers. Paul had been speaking of the next European war for years, seeds sown in the last war.

Would her son be caught up in it?

CHAPTER 14

FREDERICK

"Frederick! Frederick, it's Ingrid. The baby. It's coming."

He lost no time, rolling up his sleeves and rushing to the barn. Uncle Werner was already on the ground beside Ingrid, who was on her side, panting. "She's having some trouble," he gasped, straining almost as heavily as the animal. "She's so small..."

"The army didn't train me to deliver baby goats, but I'll help however I can." Frederick knelt on the other side of Ingrid and began stroking the animal's head and whispering to her soothingly. Then he looked at Werner. "Did you call the veterinarian?"

"Nein. We can do this—I'm glad you're here, though, son. I'm getting too old for this."

Frederick wrapped his arms lightly around the animal, resting his cheek against the top of her head. His gentle touch seemed to impart a sense of relaxed determination into her little body. Werner moved into position to receive the baby, and within a few minutes, a tiny goat was in Werner's big hands. Frederick released Ingrid gently and reached for a cutting tool, severing the umbilical cord. He took some rags and dried the baby a little as his uncle helped Ingrid deliver the afterbirth. By that time, Aunt Maria had come to the barn and was watching from the doorway. "You have a way with people and animals, Frederick." She clicked her tongue and shook her head. "I was very concerned for her."

Frederick placed the baby beside its mother and wiped his hands on his pants. "Why don't you two go in? I'll clean up here and put down some fresh straw."

He'd missed farm work in the quiet outdoors or in the barn with animals who only spoke their simple languages. They made no demands on him, no coarse jokes, and no foolish ideas. They were happily oblivious to the world they were born into, and in some ways, he envied them. He'd come from America, where people were entitled to their world view. As long as you didn't force it on anyone else, you could go your way in peace.

In Germany, there was only one world view. Even after eight months, it made his stomach ache with discomfort, fearing he'd say something that got him in trouble, or that somehow, things would go awry.

Did anyone else feel like they were squeezing themselves into a mold in which they didn't belong?

Having washed and changed, Frederick sat down beneath the ancient oak in the backyard. Aunt Maria set out tea and cake while Werner sucked on his pipe. "So, Frederick, what is it like to be an American in the German Army?"

He breathed deeply, emptying his lungs of months of pressure. He was grateful for the training, honored to serve Germany and ready to fight if the Fatherland called.

Fritz would've added that he was ready to die for the Führer and reclaim Germany's ancestral lands. He chuckled. Yes, Fritz would've gone on and on.

Instead, Frederick closed his eyes and inhaled deeply. The blue sky, warm air, and singing birds all ushered in the long, pleasant days of summer. "I'm not sure it suits me," he finally said.

"No?"

"It's difficult to have someone try to cram your head with all kinds of new ideas, especially after you've been told all your life that those ideas are wrong."

"You didn't have anyone back in America cramming ideas into your head?"

He shrugged. Sure, he'd questioned things from time to time. He tossed his napkin on the table and continued, "We aren't perfect over in the States. At least people are allowed to share their opinions."

"I gather you don't believe the Party has a corner on the truth."

"Nope. Some of it I agree with, but some of it"—he leaned in, as if someone were still around to hear what he might say to his uncle—"I was taught never to mess with the Jews. That they are God's chosen people."

"So I've heard."

"Some of the best businesses back home are run by Jewish families. Others are just common workers like the rest of us. They seem to be an upright, honest, and hard working group of people."

"There are scoundrels in every race," Werner observed, "and the distrust of Jews is not unique to Germany. I'm sure you heard whispers of it in America too." Werner shrugged. "The belief that the German—or European—race is superior is nothing new either. Every race thinks they are the cream of the crop, though they may not vocalize it. This fellow

Hitler came along at a time when we Germans needed to reclaim our place of honor among the nations."

Frederick nodded. Uncle Werner was beginning to sound like Paul Strauss.

The older man's eyes grew sad. "You Americans love the idea of the patriot. Is it possible to be a patriot without being overzealous?"

Frederick considered his uncle's words. "I moved here because I love being German, and I want Germany to be a part of my life, but since I've been here, I've come to appreciate growing up in America." He chuckled and emphasized, "I mean *really* appreciate growing up in America. My father was the same. He grew up with his German heritage, but when the time came to serve America in the war, he served proudly."

"So, young man, if you don't like what Herr Hitler preaches, do you suppose you can serve Germany without serving Hitler?"

"I am determined to find a way."

Uncle Werner looked Frederick directly in the eyes. "I hope you do. I know Hitler and his men say they have good intentions, and I agree that things are better here in Germany than they have ever been. The problem with humanity is, we edge ever more toward one extreme or the other. Those who don't are either buried by their own problems or *choose* complacency...Nooses have a way of tightening, and I am afraid one day, you will find yourself unable to resist."

The thought stung. Frederick pushed himself away from the table and stood. "Excuse me, Uncle Werner. I think I'm going to go for a walk. It's been a while."

"They didn't march you enough at camp?"

Frederick laughed. "It wasn't the same. Too many boots tramping. I want to be alone."

"Well, I can understand that. Enjoy yourself, son."

The sky was blue and the leaves on the trees were beginning to fill the ceiling of the forest as Frederick walked under its canopy. He breathed in deeply, letting the clean air permeate his lungs. Nothing could match the peace of this moment.

<hr>

FREDERICK OPENED THE SMALL drawer in his bedside table and laid eyes on his grandfather's Bible—the one he'd intentionally neglected to take along. A twinge of guilt tickled his spine. *I'm sorry, Mom.*

He'd tried her way, and it hadn't suited him. Still, he lifted it out and flipped through the pages of the Book of Isaiah.

When I called, no one answered,
When I spoke they did not hear;
But they did evil before my eyes,
And chose that in which I do not delight.

He'd been determined to come, not realizing the challenges it would present. Everything he believed was now foreign.

Paul had warned him, yet here he was.

A quote that hung on the wall back home flashed through his mind: *You have made us for yourself, O Lord, and our hearts are restless until they rest in You.*

A man could stick his head in the sand or risk drifting to one or the other extremes.

Wasn't there another way?

He placed the Bible back in the drawer, turned off the light, and settled back into his pillow, trying to draw comfort from the blue skies and green hills he'd wandered through that afternoon. Plenty of the other young men he'd met in the army were religious. They had no problem working both National Socialism and God into their lives.

He kind of wanted neither.

PART II

CHAPTER 15

FREDERICK

Pomerania, Germany-Poland Frontier

August 1939

After ten days at the farm, Frederick returned to his battalion to begin what he believed would be two years of service in the army. He'd read the news and heard radio broadcasts all summer long, listening as Fritz and the other *Landsers* discussed the situation at length, offering input only when pressed. There had been the issue of Danzig, but once again, Fritz's concern was for the Germans living within Polish borders—an increase in reports of Pole-on-German violence, and the suggestion that Poland might even be mobilizing for war. *All of the Führer's attempts at reconciliation have been rejected, Frederick. He vows to speak to them in the same language they have been speaking to us.*

Together with the reserves, they made their way to the German-Polish frontier, and awaited orders. If the other boys felt anxiety, they didn't show it. Most of them just snored silently. His stomach ached. Foreboding gnawed at his spirit.

At 0430 on September 1, the Stukas hummed overhead.

"Can you walk?" Frederick yelled over the noise of battle.

The soldier made an uncertain gesture. Frederick steadied the man's arm around his shoulder and prepared to rise. "You lean on me as much as you need." He bore the man's weight on his shoulders and stood to his feet. Together they made their way to a small dugout guarded by a semicircle of trees. He lay his comrade down and began to look him over. The left side of the young man's gray-green *Feldbluse* was soaked with blood. Frederick forced the shirt open, revealing a deep bullet wound to the man's side.

Applying pressure to the wound, he called for the stretcher bearers. The boys were at his side speedily. One replaced Frederick's hand on the wound with his own, allowing Frederick to clean away the excess blood and control the bleeding until he could be taken to the larger nursing station behind the front line.

"He's losing a lot of blood," Frederick warned. "Hold him at an angle so the wound is above his heart." He looked at the injured soldier and said, "Are you able to keep your hand here on the bandage until you get to the station?"

The young man nodded and placed his hand over the bandages on his side. The stretcher bearers lifted the stretcher and marched off quickly. Frederick turned to find another injured comrade stumbling before him, clutching an arm which had been sliced clean through. "Johann," Frederick gasped. He lowered Johann to the ground and began to bandage his wounds. Tears streamed down the young man's cheeks but his stare was blank. Johann was one of the youngest soldiers in the platoon—the only son of his mother. "You're going to be all right," Frederick whispered, securing the limb. "Can you walk?"

Johann shuddered and shook his head through tears. Frederick glanced over the trembling body—his legs were fine, but the boy was in shock and losing a lot of blood. "Up you get," Frederick ordered. He swung Johann's good arm around his shoulder and supported him to the bandaging station himself.

Frederick settled down onto the sidewalk alongside his comrades and leaned his back against a wall. They'd been alternating marching and fighting for days as the army continued its push into Poland. The men received news that Britain and France had declared war on Germany, but it had little effect on their campaign. It would be some time before any Brits or Frenchmen showed up—if they showed up at all.

Besides the skirmishes, there were long marches across the flat Polish countryside. When they paused to rest, the men would lie on the ground and be asleep in minutes—except Frederick. Rest periods meant checking blistered feet, treating sunburn, and giving medicine for headaches or digestive woes. They preferred it to visiting the hospital staff. He wasn't a caregiver—he was a comrade.

The Vistula River, to which they were headed, was in distant view. The village was under German control, allowing them a short break. Frederick reached for his mess tin while Rüdiger reclined on his elbow next to him. "Not a bad spot. Maybe I'll settle down here someday."

Frederick huffed.

"This land used to be German, Freddie. Apparently they didn't teach you that in America." Fritz took a swig from his canteen, wiped his mouth, and looked at Rudi. "Maybe a little closer to the river for me though."

Their chatter was broken by a barrage of fire from a house a dozen meters away, where another group of soldiers had taken their rest. The bodies of two Landsers slumped against the wall while others dove for cover.

"Partisans," Fritz hissed as the three of them flew behind a wagon. Heinrich, Pieter, and Klaus dove behind the wall of a nearby house.

Fritz grappled for his gun. Behind Frederick, *Feldwebel* Baumann appeared out of nowhere. "Smith, I don't want you to get killed. The partisans are in the house opposite them, and we don't know how many there are." He pointed to the house in question. "Stay here until we clear it out."

Fritz motioned to Pieter and Klaus, who raced to his side as Heinrich and Rüdiger slung their Mausers into their hands and prepared to follow Baumann.

More shots from the house. Fritz mounted his machine gun on the side of the wagon and took aim as Pieter strung the cartridges through. Baumann led Rüdiger and Heinrich along the sidewalk, tight against the walls of the houses that lay between them and the partisans.

Picking up a fist-sized stone, Baumann threw it hard, breaking the glass window. Then he primed a grenade and, with the same force, threw it into the open window.

Frederick didn't wait another second. As smoke burst from the house, he ran to the soldiers. There was nothing he could do for the first two, but a third comrade lay shored up against a plant pot, grasping a bloodied thigh.

"Hey," Frederick said, ripping open the young man's pant leg. The bullet was easily visible, and he searched his medical kit for forceps. They were on the move, and there was no field hospital nearby, so he bandaged the wound and stood cautiously to find someone to help the man to a truck.

Fire was beginning to pour from the houses. Women and children were running to and fro, many of them in tears, while his comrades tried to herd them into a corner. "What the—" Frederick threw himself back on the ground and ripped off his *Stahlhelm*, running his fingers through his sweaty hair. He couldn't believe what he was seeing.

"The orders are to burn any villages that are housing partisans." The wounded Landser gasped.

Frederick nodded. He knew the order, though he had imagined a major resistance, house to house fighting with Polish soldiers, not women and children. "The shots only came from one place," he said.

"Ja. Those are the orders, Sanitäter."

Frederick rose to find transport for the injured man and a burial team for the bodies of their fallen comrades.

As he fell in line and began the march, the stench of smoke coupled with the searing pain in his gut and forced him to double over. He swallowed the bile that came up his throat and dug through his medical bag, only to find his supplies had been completely exhausted—nothing to calm the nausea.

He'd have to endure until he could resupply.

CHAPTER 16

FREDERICK

He'd walked off his nausea by the time they reached the Vistula River, but he hadn't quite worked the image of the burning village and crying, helpless villagers out of his brain. They'd been in Poland for a week, and it wasn't the first time he'd seen crying women and children, but it was the first time he'd witnessed something so senseless.

"This is what I'm talking about." Fritz came up from behind and clapped Frederick on the back. He extended his arm and drew it across the skyline. "One day, Freddie, you and I are going to settle down here with a couple of blonde beauties, work the land, and have lots of children."

Fritz's enthusiasm never ceased to amaze Frederick. If only he could share it. Just then a number of soldiers ran past, having exchanged gear and uniforms for black swimming trunks, and splashed into the river. Heinrich was among them. He turned and splashed in Frederick's direction. "Freddie! Fritzi! Come on!"

Fritz looked at Frederick, his blue eyes twinkling. "Ha!" He was in the water like a shot, clumsily pulling off his boots and the outer layers of his uniform as he ran. Frederick shook his head, laughed, and followed suit. It was the end of summer and the water was warm. As he fell into the river he could almost feel the dirt and grime of days of dusty marches and fierce battles melting off of his skin. The moment he righted himself, Fritz and Heinrich jumped on him and held him under playfully. He wrestled out of their grasp and lunged at Heinrich, bringing the tall, slim blond down with him.

"*Achtung*!"

Fifty wet Landsers stopped splashing and snapped to attention, facing the Leutnant who had appeared on the bank. "When you are done bathing," he said, in a tone that told them he knew full well there was no actual bathing going on, "we will take shelter in the homes here for the night."

There was a collective shout of "Jawohl" followed by a salute, and the Leutnant marched off. "He'll be down here himself as soon as we clear out," someone whispered. Laughter broke out and a few of the young men resumed their play.

Frederick gave one last splash in the direction of his friends and headed for the shore, stopping to pull his uniform back on as he climbed up the bank. A few young Polish women stood a short distance off, giggling. He met their eyes and smiled but continued walking. The medical unit had rolled in and he desperately needed to resupply.

"Sanitäter."

He was greeted by the chaplain as he neared the supply truck. The man carried himself like an officer, though his uniform bore no rank and he wore the *Pfarrer's* cross on a chain that fell to the center of his chest. He appeared to be in his early forties, tall and fit, with blue eyes, glasses, and graying hair.

"Herr Pfarrer Schmidt." Frederick hurried past, giving the impression that he was in too much of a rush to engage in conversation. After receiving his things, he returned to the center of town and found Fritz, Heinrich, and Rüdiger standing outside of one of the homes, waving to get his attention.

"They've got room for one more." Fritz grinned.

They entered the house and were greeted cordially by an older Polish woman and less hesitantly by her two teenage daughters. Frederick recognized one of them from the waterfront and acknowledged her with a brief nod.

The woman chided her daughters in Polish, and the girls disappeared into the kitchen, giggling and stealing glances at the four handsome Landsers. The homeowner gestured toward a spare room as if to say, "Well, you might as well make yourselves comfortable," before disappearing into the kitchen herself.

One of the girls returned with a pot of coffee and mugs.

Real coffee, Frederick thought as the girl poured the dark, aromatic beverage into a cup and handed it to him. "Danke."

She nodded and curtsied a little, then served his three companions before retreating into the kitchen.

"Well, I guess we can tell which one of us is her favorite," Heinrich whispered to Rüdiger.

"Ja," Rüdiger chortled, looking at Frederick. "She easily gave you twice as much coffee as the rest of us."

"And curtsied." Fritz attempted to repeat her graceful movement which only resulted in spilling his coffee.

Frederick rolled his eyes and shook his head, but ultimately found it hard not to laugh at Fritz's lack of grace.

It was a small house, but colorfully decorated, and there were enough chairs for them all to sit in, as well as space for them to quarter for the night. The woman cooked a dinner of sausages and potatoes, then stood in the doorway, watching as they ate. Her daughters would occasionally try to peek out from behind her, but she'd shoo them away briskly.

After supper, Frederick and his comrades took time to brush their uniforms, polish their boots, and resew their buttons. Frederick also took time to shave, which the other boys had done when he'd gone to the medical supplier. Heinrich and Rüdiger thumbed through the few meager books on the shelves, but abandoned the prospect when they realized they were all in Polish.

FREDERICK VOLUNTEERED TO TAKE first watch, knowing it would give him the best opportunity for an uninterrupted night's sleep. The next morning, however, he awoke before the sun came up, threw on his boots and tunic, and stumbled past the other three toward the front door. He gave Rüdiger, who had fallen asleep on fourth watch, a swift kick as he slipped out the door.

In the dewy morning, he breathed deeply and walked around to the back of the house. The garden reminded him of home, though there was no oak tree or table with chairs, and his mother wasn't there. An ache of homesickness passed over him, quickly driven away by the sound of the bugle.

He returned to the house and was greeted by the smell of coffee. He paused and inhaled. Back home, coffee was a luxury—his mother had always preferred tea anyway.

Fritz and Heinrich appeared in the main room of the house, looking the part of exhausted soldiers who'd recently been awakened out of an overdue night's sleep. Rüdiger had also dozed off again after being kicked.

Lazy bums. He moved to where his bedroll and pack were on the floor and knelt to grab his canteen. Behind him, the kitchen door swing open, and when he stood to his feet, the daughter who'd taken such a lavish interest in him the previous day stood in the doorway.

She held out her hand and gestured toward his canteen. He gave it to her, his cheeks reddening as she stared at him silently, a broad smile lighting her face. Behind him, the boys whispered and stifled their laughter. She turned and disappeared into the kitchen, returning moments later with Frederick's canteen, full of hot coffee with cream and sugar. He thanked her as she gestured to the other three, offering to fill theirs as well.

"You wait," Fritz said, a hint of laughter still in his voice. "He gets coffee, we'll get water."

Frederick strode past him, intentionally knocking his shoulder into Fritz's.

After filling their canteens, she placed rolls on the table, which Frederick and his comrades gobbled down.. Minutes later, they were assembled in the field adjacent to town, with the rest of the unit which had arrived the day before. Everyone stood at attention, and *Hauptmann* Becker stepped forward. "We have secured the northern bank of the river. This unit will remain posted here until we receive further orders." More instructions were given, along with a glowing report of the progress of the Eighth, Tenth, and Fourteenth armies, which were making rapid progress through southern Poland.

After dismissal, Feldwebel Baumann approached Frederick and the other soldiers under his direct supervision. "You heard the Captain. We are stationed here to maintain order and protect German interests from partisans or unexpected attacks from the Polish Army. Remain alert. Be ready to provide assistance to your comrades at all times. Maintain professional conduct with the locals." Baumann chuckled and leaned in. "You know what that means, ja?"

The men saluted. Fritz made a subtle elbow jab into Frederick's side.

Shouts erupted behind them. Frederick spun to see a detachment of SS men herding a group of men and women toward the fields.

Shovels. The peasants have shovels.

The *Untersturmführer* shouted for the peasants to dig. His soldiers aimed their rifles as the men and women began their laborious task.

Frederick's stomach tightened.

"Come on, fella." Fritz smacked a hand on Frederick's shoulder. "Our orders are to sit around and wait for something to happen." He chuckled. "Let's take a walk around."

He tried not to think about the trenches as they explored a bit and returned to the house for the midday meal.

Heinrich and Rüdiger had begun to refer to the matron of the house as Frau *Schelte* because of the way she always seemed to be scolding her daughters. She was cordial to the soldiers, neither warm nor unkind, but simply resigned to having four uniformed Germans living in her home.

Fritz wrinkled his nose and dipped his spoon in his soup. "Dill pickle soup, oder?"

"Really?" Frederick dove right in.

Rudi shook his head. "I'm with Fritzi on this one."

Lunch was interrupted by commotion outside. They shot to their feet and grabbed their weapons. Frederick reached for his medical belt, and they piled outside.

The home's backyard bordered the field where the soldiers had assembled that morning, and where the trench was being dug at the far end. Though the work detail was hidden by trees, Frederick hadn't forgotten.

The trench was complete. The SS Lieutenant barked orders, insisting that the men stand at the edge of the trench while his soldiers took aim.

"You three," he snapped, jerking a finger at Frederick's comrades. "Assist my men."

Fritz, Heinrich, and Rüdiger joined the line of SS men who stood with their Mausers raised. Helpless, Frederick longed to turn away, but he couldn't. His eyes remained fixed on the scene before him. *Keep it together,* he commanded himself as nausea welled in his stomach.

When they returned to the cottage, Frederick spotted Frau Schelte's daughter in the kitchen. Although he had no romantic interest in her, he enjoyed her interest in him, and he'd hoped that seeing her smile might lift his spirits. Instead, when her eyes fell on him, her expression became icy, and she turned away.

Coffee was left on the table for them. It was tepid and black. Frederick sat down to drink it anyway. His comrades sampled it, complained about the temperature, and then picked at the dirt and blood on their uniforms. He felt no desire to talk, nor was he really even listening. After finishing his coffee, he rose from the chair and walked out of the house, hoping there was a way he could be alone in a town occupied by hundreds of his comrades.

Grim brokenness had descended upon the village. When the Germans had arrived, the inhabitants had been obliged to quarter and feed them.

Some, like Frau Schelte, had offered a marginal level of hospitality. Now, however, the roles were clearly defined.

Who were the people shot in this village? There'd been no report of partisans...Were they Communists? Jews? Intelligentsia?

Frederick's shoulders slumped as he walked the streets. When he thought of it, he fixed his posture, but his heavy soul dragged his features back down. *How many more will there be?*

CHAPTER 17

FREDERICK

Days passed with little action. Although they drilled and marched daily, there were also hours of time to bide. Their boots were polished, their uniforms brushed, guns cleaned, buttons checked and rechecked. Frederick was sure they would never come off.

He regretted their stay in a house so close to the open field. Fritz, Rüdiger, and Heinrich were once again tapped for a firing squad by the tall, muscled SS Lieutenant.

Frau Schelte laid out supper as always, though she and her daughters now kept their distance. She'd also begun to allow the meals time to cool—perhaps a passive way of expressing her indignation toward the occupiers.

This evening was no different. Rüdiger cursed and threw his fork down hard on the table. "When that woman served tepid coffee the first time, I let it go. The second time, I let it go. Then dinner was cold, and it has been cold every night since."

"*Keep* letting it go, Kamerad," Frederick said with a laugh. "Who cares? It's better than we'd get on the road."

The woman appeared in the doorway. Rüdiger threw his napkin on the table and stormed over to her. "I need a *hot* cup of coffee! *Now.*"

She fled into the kitchen, returning a few minutes later with a tray of coffee and mugs in her hands. Without glancing at Rüdiger, she set the tray before him and began to pour. Her hands shook. She looked up as one of her daughters entered the room.

It took only an instant. Her hands shifted. The coffee missed the cup, falling instead onto Rüdiger's lap. He shot to his feet with a curse, grabbed her in both hands, and shook violently. Frederick dove between them, but Rüdiger forced him away, grasped the woman again, and shoved her into a cabinet. Porcelain crashed. She slid to the floor.

Rüdiger stormed out of the house. Frederick flew to her side, kneeling and holding up his hands in innocence. "I just want to make sure you are all right," he tried to explain.

Receiving a barely recognizable nod, he began to examine her, and though she was shaken and scared, she was uninjured.

Grabbing a clean napkin from the table, he ordered Heinrich, "Go wet this with cold water."

Heinrich nodded and obeyed, returning shortly.

"Danke," Frederick whispered. He wiped the woman's tear-stained face with the cloth and then turned back to Heinrich. "Help me get her up."

Together they lifted her and walked her slowly to her bedroom. Easing her down, Frederick swung her still-shaking legs onto the bed. "I am sorry," he whispered. Although he too had been irritated by the cold meals and tepid coffee, he felt they deserved what they were getting. No, they didn't even deserve that. Something in him whispered, *You deserve to be in that trench, Frederick.*

He hadn't participated in the firing squads, but he also hadn't done anything to prevent them…as if he could have.

The woman motioned to her neck, grimacing as if she were in pain.

He nodded softly. Retrieving his medical bag, he gave her some medicine, and encouraged her, "Call me if you need me, ja? Sani. *Tzah-nee.*"

She nodded, and he left the room, returning to the chair he had occupied at dinner. Leaning forward, he rested his elbows on the table and buried his face in his hands. He thought about Rüdiger and his other comrades standing in line with the rest of the firing squad, and wondered what happened to men's hearts when they were forced to commit senseless and repeated acts of violence.

Fritz was still seated at the table. He put a hand on Frederick's shoulder, but what he said wasn't comforting. "The Poles have been doing it to us for years. We're speaking to them in the only language they know."

"The only language they know?" Frederick lifted his head. "What about *two wrongs don't make a right?* What about *turn the other cheek?*"

"This is not time for proverbs and old wives tales, *Kamerad.* This is a time for action. You know, *a time for peace and a time for war…*or however it goes." Fritz chuckled, unimpressed by Frederick but obviously amused with himself.

Frederick said nothing. What was there to say? Was Fritz *right?* If he remembered correctly, there was plenty of killing in the Bible—even in the New Testament, people dropped dead.

He talked little the rest of the evening, spent a restless night of sleep, and rose early again to wander around town.

When he reached the area where the medical unit had set up camp, a voice called out behind him, just loud enough to be heard. "*Guten Morgen*, Sanitäter."

Chastising himself for winding up where he could be waylaid by the chaplain, he turned, snapped his boots and saluted. "Guten Morgen, Herr Pfarrer Schmidt."

"As you were, Sanitäter. Would you like some company?"

Nein. He gave the chaplain a nod anyway, and the two strode off to the outskirts of the town.

"You seem lost," the older man said gently. His expression bore the stoic appearance of the other officers, but Frederick heard a gentleness in his voice that those in command lacked.

"We've been here almost a week. I'm beginning to learn my way around."

"*Achso.* That isn't really what I meant."

Uncomfortable with the judgment, Frederick huffed. What was a chaplain doing here anyway? Did his presence give legitimacy to the crimes being committed? Burning villages. Shooting civilians. *Speak to the Poles in the only language they know.*

He searched his mind for anything Paul Strauss might have said over the years that would have hinted at what was going on between the Poles and the Germans. *I wish I'd paid more attention early on.*

But then again, maybe Paul didn't know.

They were only about twenty yards from the trenches now. He turned his back to them and looked up at the sky.

"Sanitäter." The older gentleman paused, adjusted his glasses, and continued, "You are restless. Anyone can see it. I am afraid that will only make your job more difficult."

"Thank you, Herr Pfarrer." *Now please, mind your own business.*

Rather than the sound of the trumpet, it was the sound of alarm that broke the early-dawn silence. Both men quickened their pace in the direction of battalion headquarters.

The Hauptmann and his assistant stepped out of the door just as they arrived. Frederick saluted, barely acknowledged by the captain as the older man turned and saluted Chaplain Schmidt. "Herr Major."

Beneath the formalities, he sensed a familiarity between the two men he hadn't expected. And the chaplain...*Herr Major?*

"They are in need of immediate reinforcement to the south. We will leave a skeleton crew here to keep the river bank secure until replacements arrive. The rest of the men are to advance toward the Bzura."

The chaplain nodded to Frederick, indicating his dismissal. Frederick saluted again and strode quickly to the house where he was billeted. His comrades were already pulling on boots and strapping on belts. "Reinforcements are needed at the Bzura," he announced.

They shouldered their packs, secured their helmets, and headed for the door. Last in line, Frederick turned back as he heard the kitchen door swing open. The woman's daughter stood there, smiling at him once again. He smiled back.

"Danke," she whispered.

His smile widened. He nodded and turned to go, confident his kindness to her mother, and the fact that he did not carry a Mauser, had not gone unnoticed.

CHAPTER 18

By the time Frederick's unit arrived, the Poles had been driven back by the tanks and artillery, aided from above by the Luftwaffe. Now it was the infantry's job to engage the enemy face to face.

Frederick knelt in a roadside ditch behind Heinrich, Rüdiger, and the other men from the rifle platoon to which he was attached. Farther down, Fritz and Pieter manned their MG-34. Klaus was poised beside them, rifle in hand. Tension hung in the air as they waited for the signal. In spite of the power of the German artillery, return fire from the Poles still exploded nearby.

Finally, the call came. Frederick watched as his comrades poured out of the trench and into the fray. His heart raced, and he moved closer to the edge, peering over the side.

Suddenly, a cry came from down the trench, and an explosion knocked Frederick onto his backside. Regaining his posture, he heard Pieter cry from the MG-position. "Sani! *Hilfe*! Freddie, where are you?"

Frederick pulled himself to his feet as shells exploded on either side, pelting him with dirt and debris. He ran, bent double, toward the sound of Pieter's voice, falling to his knees beside his comrades.

Fritz lay crumpled on his side, trembling and clutching a gaping hole in his chest. Blood soaked through his uniform. Pieter moved away and let Frederick come to Fritz's side.

"Freddie…" Fritz gasped. Frederick pulled Fritz's body into his lap. With one arm around Fritz's shoulders, he placed his free hand over the wound in Fritz's chest. Shrapnel had embedded itself close to his heart.

"Freddie," Pieter pleaded, "do something!"

Klaus echoed the sentiment. "Come on, man."

He couldn't move. Couldn't think. He pressed a hand into Fritz's chest as if to stop the flow of blood, but his mind and body were in shock, and his fingertips were numb. Fritz's blood soaked into his own uniform as they stared into each other's eyes.

"Sieg Heil," Fritz whispered as the life drained from his body. His sweat-drenched, blond head dropped back against the wall of the trench. Frederick's chest seized. "No, God, no!" He wrapped his arms more tightly around Fritz's body and let the tears come. Curse-laced laments and angry accusations streamed from his lips, making even Pieter and Klaus blush.

Baumann stuck his head over the side of the trench and put a firm hand on Frederick's shoulder. "Pull yourself together, Sanitäter. There are men who need you." He turned to Pieter and Klaus and ordered Pieter to retake Fritz's position.

Frederick looked up. In the time he'd been sitting with Fritz, the bodies of four other German boys had been brought into the ditch. Two more Sanis were busy at the other end of the trench.

Trembling, he slid his arm out from under Fritz's body and rested his fallen comrade in the dirt.

"Get his identification tag," Klaus barked.

Of course. Frederick mechanically tore Fritz's shirt open wider to reveal the oval disc, broke it in two, and shoved the bottom half into his pocket. With a last look, he rose to his feet and stumbled down the trench toward injured, but still living, comrades.

FREDERICK SAT ON HIS bedroll, resting his back against the wall of the blown-out church that served as their billet for the night. His comrades were exhausted from days of pressing the Polish army back toward Warsaw, and he longed for the heavy silence of sleep that fell upon them, but it wouldn't come. Deep pain coursed through his abdomen, and his heart felt like it had been freshly ripped asunder.

He'd helped bury Fritz days ago, and personally placed Fritz's *Stahlhelm* on the wooden cross marking the grave. There would be no jubilant homecoming for Fritz. No future in the SS. No hope of farming ancient German lands. No beautiful wife or barefoot, happy children.

Was this what Fritz had wanted? To die for Germany? No. He'd wanted to live—though he had been willing to risk death so other people might enjoy the things he'd dreamed of.

Frederick's stomach was gripped by the need to weep. He couldn't shake the image of Fritz lying helpless, his uniform ripped and saturated with blood. Fritz had been his first real friend, and Frederick should've been able to force himself out of his stupor long enough to save him—but he'd only sat there, staring blankly as Fritz's eyes had gone dim.

Guilt began to supplant sorrow as he considered how ugly the war had become—traditional warfare, accompanied by the senseless slaughter of civilians—as if he knew what war was supposed to look like. Did his opinion even matter, if he didn't do anything to stop what was happening?

How foolish he'd been. And what was his excuse? A longing to return to Germany? His mother had asked if *God* had told him to go to Germany.

Would God have wanted any of *this*?

He sat up, slipped his arms through the sleeves of his uniform, and pulled on his boots. Silently, he crept to the door and opened it just enough to step out into the cool, cloudless night. He couldn't go far if he wanted to avoid attracting the attention of the guards, so he fell to his knees.

Where was Fritz now?

Frederick had never asked himself this before, but his heart begged it of him. He *cared* where Fritz was.

If Fritz didn't make it to heaven, it wasn't because he was a Nazi. It wasn't even because he had innocent blood on his hands. It wasn't even because Fritz never spoke about God—though all of those things were true.

Fritz didn't *care* about God. He didn't care about Jesus, and he certainly didn't care about eternity.

Frederick bowed his head. Fiery tears burned his eyes. *I don't want to be the kind of man who doesn't care.*

From his kneeling position, he leaned farther down. His forehead sank into the damp earth. He had eschewed Fritz's fanaticism and fancied himself a better man than a lot of the boys around him. He didn't smoke, didn't drink, didn't chase girls—even the religious boys did that stuff. He secretly laughed at them as they rose for Eucharist on Sundays. *Really, fellas?* Yet when it came to trying to save his best friend's life, he'd frozen and let his best friend go to hell. People would go on dying, and he was powerless to save them.

"God forgive me," he whispered between noiseless sobs. "I don't want to be a man who doesn't care. I'll do whatever you want. Just don't let me be useless."

It was a small thing, but he felt comforted. He rose and crept back to his bedroll, lay down, and fell into a deep, peaceful sleep.

CHAPTER 19

FREDERICK

The battalion marched Northwest through a flat countryside which still bore the scars of battle. They would be garrisoned in Western Poland before being allowed to return to Germany.

He mouthed the words in sync with the rest of his comrades, but his mind wandered back to the home of Mark Jones, where he'd sat uncomfortably on a sofa listening to a boring sermon about the watchman. It was ironic, considering he'd just helped invade another country in a war that wasn't even his to fight.

Fritz had told him as much. *You don't understand, Freddie.*

What am I doing here?

He glanced down at the Asclepius patch on his sleeve. He had some vague understanding of the story. Probably, he'd heard it from his mother. The Asclepius, a serpent on a pole, was an ancient symbol used by pagan cultures before being given to Moses as a sign of healing for the tribes of Israel.

So he was to dress battlefield wounds and—and what? Was he being called to be some kind of preacher?

He shuddered. *Yeah, right.*

But as the march continued, the thought wouldn't go away. He tried to raise his voice, but the words got muddled.

Fritz was right, he *didn't* understand, and it was a lot to unpack. The American newspapers would have one believe Hitler was a madman, yet he'd gotten a few things right. *More than a few.*

Maybe it wasn't about Hitler at all. Even the churches couldn't agree. The ones that supported him were vilified by the ones that didn't—and vice versa.

Did it matter?

He glanced at the living souls around him. Each one was a young man whose life was at stake every time he set foot on the battlefield—and sometimes off the battlefield.

So he'd gone from being an agnostic to being a preacher overnight? An evangelical? A missionary? He touched the Asclepius on his sleeve. *This is* not *what I wanted.*

They needed to pass three abreast through a narrow curve in the road between a higher embankment to their right and a lower one to their left. Frederick's platoon was in the strait when the sound of marching and singing was broken by machine gun fire. Men dove to the ground as Feldwebel Baumann flew behind a rock and lifted his binoculars, scanning to find the source of the hail of bullets.

A few comrades crawled to the embankment to return fire. From behind, someone screamed for Frederick.

Instantly, he was in motion, crawling along the ground in the direction of the voice. "Sani," the cries continued, through bursts of machine gun fire and rifle shots. Baumann and another NCO were barking orders, but Frederick tuned out their voices, listening for the voice of the injured comrade.

"Sani!" The call came from a tangle of tall weeds. He rose only slightly and made a dive next to his comrade's body, narrowly avoiding a spray of machine gun fire. "I'm here, Viktor." He gasped, catching his breath. The young man lay curled on his side, clutching his left leg where a bullet had ripped through his flesh. He hurriedly bandaged the wound to the sound of others crying out for a Sani. "We'll be back for you," he whispered. "Take cover here for now."

He dove back toward the road, striving to locate another comrade's voice in the fray of battle. Finally he spotted Josef, waving an arm wildly and pointing in the direction of a large clump of weeds where Rüdiger and Heinrich lay, bloody and trembling, grasping each other tightly.

Pain gripped his heart. How could this happen so soon after losing Fritz?

He prayed silently and drew nearer, reaching forward to force them apart. But they fought his hands away, each struggling to shield his wounds with his comrade's body.

Frederick called his stretcher bearers, and they arrived to join the fight to separate their wounded comrades.

"Mutti." Rüdiger sobbed as his body was torn from Heinrich's.

Heinrich lay back, shuddering but unable to speak. Their blood mingled in the dirt, staining their hands, their uniforms, the reeds, the ground. Their breaths were labored. Neither was going to make it. He shook his head and motioned to his stretcher bearers to return to Viktor. Reluctantly, the two retreated. Frederick turned his attention back to Rudi and Heinrich, drew in a deep breath, and thought about his new-found responsibility. "I am going to try to make you more comfortable. You must relax."

Heinrich was unresponsive but Rüdiger still fought for a grip on his comrade. Slowly, Frederick eased him back against the embankment and removed his helmet, tossing it aside.

*All right...*He folded his lips into a line. What did it *mean* to be here as a minister as much as a battlefield medic? Didn't they already have a chaplain for that?

Frederick took a quick glance around. Chaplain Schmidt was nowhere in sight. *He can't be everywhere.* "Um, Rudi..."—he gasped awkwardly—"I am going to pray for you." He'd never heard Rudi talk about church or faith or God. Heinrich seemed to have grown up in church, and they both attended field services from time to time, but this? This was different. He almost felt *wrong*. With one hand he grasped Heinrich's hand and with the other he grasped Rüdiger's. "Lord, Rüdiger and Heinrich have been my friends. Please give them comfort, please ease their suffering."

Was that it?

Heinrich's breathing had slowed a little, though he remained unconscious. There was enough breath left in Rüdiger's lungs that he choked out a few words. "God doesn't want anything to do with me."

If I was God, I might not either. Along with the firing squads, Rudi had taken his rage out on an old woman who'd tried to serve him tepid coffee. There were other things Frederick didn't want to acknowledge, but was Rüdiger a bad fellow? It wasn't his fault he'd been ordered to shoot civilians.

Rüdiger's hair was matted and sweaty. His brown eyes were barely perceptible through the thin slits of his eyelids. His breathing was shallow, but his hand clung tightly to Frederick's.

Frederick came to himself and shook his head. "*Doch.* The very reasons we think he should hate us are the reasons we need him most."

Rüdiger attempted a laugh. A thin smile spread across his pale lips. "Pray for me again, Freddie."

Frederick nodded. "God, forgive us for all those things we think will keep us from You. Receive my friends Rüdiger and Heinrich into heaven, to be with you forever. Amen."

A soft breath left Rüdiger's mouth. He was gone. Frederick felt Heinrich's pulse. Faint, but there.

"Sani!"

The machine gun fire had died down, though a few volleys of rifle shots echoed over the moans of the injured. Frederick leaned forward and whispered to Heinrich, "Hold on, man. We'll be back for you."

CHAPTER 20

A chill descended from the cloudy October sky, worsened by the winds blowing in from the plains. Frederick donned his greatcoat as he walked through the streets, his collar turned up and the flaps of his field cap flipped down. It made precious little difference against the biting wind.

"Sanitäter!"

Frederick turned, snapped his boots together, and saluted. In the whistling of the wind, he hadn't recognized the voice of Chaplain Schmidt.

"As you were, Frederick," said the older man. "Walk with me." The chaplain turned and began to walk, and Frederick fell into step with him.

"I hear many things as I'm ministering to the wounded in the hospital." The chaplain clasped his hands behind his back as they continued. "*You* have a particular reputation for having gone above and beyond the call of duty."

Frederick felt his cheeks redden. "Danke, Herr Pfarrer Schmidt."

"What made you want to be a Sani?"

He shrugged. "The army noticed I had some skill and offered me further training."

"And so it is."

They arrived at a parklike area with a few clusters of pine trees. No one else seemed to want to be outside unless ordered to be, so they found themselves alone. "We are not that different, you and I," the chaplain mused. "I was a young soldier back in 1918, injured in the final days of the war, and after my recovery I became a pastor." He smiled nostalgically. "I couldn't get the military spirit out of my bones though. Joined the *Reichswehr* as soon as they would take me."

Frederick nodded. *Not surprising.*

"I attended officer training and rose through the ranks, but at some point, I realized my heart was no longer in it. I cared deeply about the young men under my command, but I myself was no longer a warrior. That is why I resigned my command and applied for a chaplaincy."

"Yes, sir."

At a distance, one could not *really* tell Chaplain Schmidt from the other officers. Up close, however, warmth emanated from the man.

Perhaps he's not so bad.

"Are you a Christian, Sanitäter?"

Frederick shrugged. "I was baptized as a Lutheran...my mother moved to a little church that met in somebody's house. I don't know what we are anymore."

"I did not ask what sort of Christianity you practice. I asked whether you were a *Christian.*"

"Aren't most of us?"

"Mmm. To one degree or another...if such a thing is possible."

Frederick huffed.

"I saw you one night, your face to the ground. You seemed to be in deep distress."

"I guess I was." *Might as well be honest.*

"I only saw you because I too was wandering around, deeply disturbed and unable to sleep."

The words struck. "Permission to speak freely?"

"Of course, Sanitäter. I am your chaplain."

"I—I did not expect to see so much bloodshed, sir."

The man huffed sadly. "Well, Frederick, it is war...though I think I understand what you are referring to."

"There has to be another way."

The chaplain sighed. "I too was...*unprepared* for what I saw. There was a temptation to ask myself if I had been wrong all this time."

"Wrong about what, sir?"

"I have always supported Herr Hitler. Not unquestioningly, but in good faith that God tears down one ruler and raises up another."

The cold October breeze blew against the pines surrounding them. The chaplain grasped his cap and pulled it farther down over his graying hair. "Frederick, I believe you and I are both here for a reason. You must follow the path to which God has called you, and so must I."

"Jawohl."

The chaplain chuckled. "I am not your commander, Frederick. I am here to be your pastor, if you wish. Though you never answered my question."

"Which question was that?

"Whether you are a Christian."

"Oh, right..." Frederick sighed. "Yes, I am a Christian."

"It is something you take seriously, oder?"

He twisted his mouth in thought. "Trying to."

"Achso." The older man stood back a bit and stared, as if making an estimation of Frederick. "Please do not hesitate to seek me out, Sanitäter. I am here for you, as I am for all the men."

"Thank you, sir."

As Frederick turned to go, the chaplain added, "There is one more thing, young man."

"Ja, Herr Pfarrer?"

"Your friend Heinrich Schuyler was brought to the hospital here in town after the ambush on your platoon. He is asking for you."

Frederick's heart began to race. *Heinrich is alive?* "Danke, Herr Pfarrer Schmidt."

He tried to walk with an air of soldierly composure, but it was difficult. When he arrived at the hospital, he saluted the guard and entered, breaking into a run when he saw the stairs were clear of people.

He found Heinrich in the infirmary, a large, stark room with high windows and at least thirty beds in it, most of which were occupied.

"Kamerad?" Heinrich opened his eyes.

"Heinrich? How—"

His entire torso was bandaged, and his skin was pale, but he was alive. Frederick pulled over a chair and sat so his face was only inches from Heinrich's. With a smile, he clasped his friend's hand in both of his. He'd seen the wounds the machine gun had torn through this young man's body. He should *not* have survived, and yet—

"I should be dead, Freddie."

Frederick folded his lips.

"Your prayers..."

Tears formed in Frederick's eyes.

"Thank you."

He nodded and squeezed Heinrich's hand.

"When are we leaving Poland?"

"There should be a train in the next day or two."

"Do you think we'll be sent to France?"

Frederick shrugged. "Probably eventually." France and Britain had declared war on September 3rd but had done nothing since.

"Do you think they'd put me back on the front lines?"

"Don't worry about that now, man. You just need to get better."

"Excuse me," said a female voice. A plump nurse with round cheeks and shiny brown eyes stood at the end of Heinrich's bed. "We need to wash and redress your wounds."

"Let me help," Frederick said, rising from his chair.

"Ilse"—Heinrich labored to move a little on the bed—"this is Frederick. He was the Sani who helped save my life."

"Oh, yes." She smiled. "Well then Sanitäter, yes, you may help."

Frederick helped Heinrich sit up while the nurse began to unwrap the bloodied bandages. Deep scars were just beginning to heal. Frederick was further amazed that his comrade had survived.

Reaching for the cloth and wetting it in the basin Ilse had provided, he began to cleanse the scars on his friend's back. The nurse smiled approvingly. "You'd better be careful, Sanitäter, or the hospital won't let you go home."

He laughed gently and continued his work. "It wouldn't be so bad. Heinrich would keep me company."

After they'd finished, Frederick re-bandaged Heinrich's wounds and spent another few minutes sitting at his bedside until his friend began to doze off. As he reached for his coat, his hand brushed the buckle of his uniform belt, reminding him of the words emblazoned upon it. *Gott mit uns.* Not a formality. Not hypocrisy. Yes, things had gone awry, but that did not mean God was not with them.

Apparently, it was his job to remind them of that.

CHAPTER 21

CHAPLAIN SCHMIDT

He'd considered returning to Berlin, to his sparsely decorated flat where no one was likely to bother him for a few weeks. *A chaplain needs to refresh his spirit after all.*

In the end, he couldn't leave his boys.

The medic stayed too. Strangely, the wall the medic had thrown up upon their first few encounters was beginning to crumble—the young man had actually visited a few times, and they'd begun to talk about life, religion, and of course, the ever-present topic of war.

Though smaller, the chaplain's quarters were about as simple as his apartment back home. A small suite in an old hotel which the army had commandeered, two rooms with a small desk and swiveling desk chair, two comfortable red upholstered chairs for conversation, and a door separating his private sleeping quarters. Private bathing quarters had also been provided to him, although he would've settled for less.

The medic's familiar knock came on the door—it had been happening about this time every day.

"Come in, Sanitäter." As the young man entered, the chaplain laid aside the Bible he'd been reading and motioned for Frederick to have a seat.

The twenty-year-old soldier's passionate spirit reminded him of the man he used to be, before the takeover of militarism and...*heartache.* He sighed. It was still hard for the three facets of his personality to cohabit.

"Heinrich mentioned that you are an American," the chaplain began. "I'm surprised you never told me. I'd noticed your accent and that you still stumble over your words sometimes, but I never thought to ask where you were from."

Frederick chuckled. "My grandparents came to the United States as children. I grew up in a community that used to have strong ties with Germany. Over the years I think we became more and more American, but as I grew older, I became curious about our homeland...*the Fatherland.* When I came of age, I decided to return."

Chaplain Schmidt shifted in his chair and began speaking in English. "I was born in America too. I've been here since the Great War."

Frederick raised his eyebrows. "What? Your German—it's impeccable!"

"Well, I have been here many years."

"You even speak English with a—"

"Slight German accent."

"Yes."

"It's funny what twenty years in your ancestral lands will do to you. I have to think hard to remember English sometimes."

Frederick shook his head and leaned back in his chair. "I never would've taken you for an American."

"I came over here as a Doughboy." With a slight laugh, he added, "But, you don't need to remind my superiors of that."

Frederick chuckled along with him.

"I am joking, of course." A distant longing began to creep into his heart as he thought back to 1918. "Oh, how I loved that uniform. It was nothing compared to the fine *frocks* the Wehrmacht gives us"—he pulled at the front of his uniform for emphasis—"but I felt ten feet tall the first time I put it on."

"I have seen pictures...my father and his best friend Paul."

I had a best friend named Paul too. He allowed the memory to linger for a second, then closed his eyes and released it. "You are never prepared for the reality of the trenches."

The young man nodded in agreement.

"It was a horrible war. Horrible." He removed his glasses and polished them with a blue and white cloth he'd drawn from his pocket. "It is amazing anyone ever made it through No Man's Land." He placed his glasses on the table and looked at Frederick. "Like your friend Heinrich, I should have died. I lay in the mud for hours with shrapnel embedded in my back, my side, and my legs. I faded in and out of consciousness, but I could not die. *God, I wanted to die.* I was yards away from the German trench. I finally called for help, hoping they would appear long enough to end my misery."

He leaned forward a little, engaging Frederick with his eyes. "You know, I was rescued by a Sani. He and another soldier carried my half-dead body back to their trench. He gave me a drink of water and something to ease my suffering. We all believed I was going to die—me and the Germans, who didn't know I knew their language." Mist came into his eyes. He tried to wipe it away casually. "When I awoke, I was in a hospital behind the German line. I was in pain and could not move easily, but I was alive. The war ended not long after."

"You decided to stay in Germany?"

"I was in the hospital for a long time. I fell in love, as young men do. A nurse named Greta helped me learn to walk again. When I was put out of the hospital and had no place to go, she took me in. We fell in love, yes, but it was there that I saw the suffering of her people. I knew they were my people too." Again he fought the mist forming in his eyes. "I couldn't leave. Do you understand?"

Frederick nodded.

"Germany was so broken after the war, and my heart broke with it. Whatever wrongs had been done during the war, innocent lives had been destroyed. Families had been torn apart." He sucked in a breath. "Germany was being blamed for *all of it*."

Again, the young man appeared to understand—or at least he was trying to.

"I—I left a family in America." This was the hardest part of the story by far. The part he rarely told, but somehow he knew—this young man *needed* to know. The words came, almost before he could stop them. "I had married back in the States. My wife was pregnant when I left for Europe. It was wrong, yes, but by the time I could walk again, I'd made up my mind. I reasoned that the war had changed me, that I was *not* the man I'd been when I married Hannah. She was too pure, untainted by the stains of hell like I had been. She would not understand, and I couldn't bring that back to her and the child she bore. Greta understood me. Like me, she'd been exposed to the bombardments and seen countless bodies ripped apart." He shook his head as the tide of words slowed to a trickle. As if to justify himself, he reiterated the phrase, "She understood me."

The medic only sat staring at him, mouth open but speechless.

Chaplain Friedrich Schmidt waited.

"Chaplain," the boy finally said, "with all due respect, what did you say your wife's name was? The woman you left in America."

"Hannah. My first wife."

The young man's eyes turned dark. His brow furrowed, and he leaned forward, clenching the arms of the chair. "It can't be...My mother's married name was Hannah Smith—Hannah *Schmidt*. My father Friedrich Schmidt left for the war when she was pregnant with me." He clenched the arm of the chair with one hand and ran the other over his face. "I am the son you left in America!" With that, the boy stood up and threw the chair at the wall, then collapsed onto his knees.

Friedrich sat stunned, trying to work through how this could be true, that this American could possibly be his own flesh and blood, and that he'd ended up *here*, of all places. He rose from his chair and walked over, kneeling beside the medic who had begun to weep bitterly. *How is this possible?* Cautiously, he reached out and put a hand on the young man's shoulder. Frederick turned a tear-stained face towards him, confirming everything that had just been revealed. Their toned build, their straight stature, the shape of their faces, their blue eyes and dark hair—he was the spitting image of Friedrich at 20 years old.

Friedrich took a deep breath and asked, "How—how is your mother?"

"My mother is married to Paul Strauss." The words had been aimed like daggers, and he felt them. Every single blade.

Friedrich nodded and settled back against the wall. It was too much. *God, only you could have done this...but why?* He stared at his son. The boy's weeping had settled, and he sat motionless, head between his knees, arms hugging his shins. His body rose and fell with his breathing.

I have asked for forgiveness a thousand times. Why do You now confront me with my sins?

Could there be reconciliation?

If the gospel I preach means anything, there must *be. At least, it must be possible.*

A knock at the door broke the silence. "Herr Pfarrer?"

"*Moment,*" Friedrich replied in German. He rose and went into the bathroom to splash water on his face. Replacing his cap, he strode to the entrance of his quarters and opened the door, stepping into the hallway and closing the door behind himself.

The young staffer saluted. "Herr Pfarrer, sir, I was sent to make sure everything was in order, sir."

"Ja, everything is fine, soldier."

The soldier nodded and saluted again, though he seemed unconvinced. "I will inform the Hauptmann." He turned, snapping his heels together, and strode off.

Friedrich stood for a moment outside the door. He removed his cap and closed his eyes. Discipline would not let him release his tears in public, but he was not ready to re-enter the room either. His stupid choices had *not* been worth it. He'd known it then, and he knew it now—dear God, did he know it now. Greta had not lived many years after their marriage, and after her death, he had thrown himself into his work.

If he had returned to America, he would have watched Frederick grow up. He would have taken him fishing, played ball with him, and taught him to drive. He and Hannah would've had more children. They could have lived in peace. He would not be embroiled in a war that was bound to get worse when France and England decided to play their hand. There certainly would have been no reason for his son to become involved in a European conflict...would there?

The past is gone, but it rests with the Lord. Certainly He would not have brought Frederick all this way if reconciliation were not possible.

He re-entered the room and closed the door gently. Approaching his son, he knelt and placed his hands on Frederick's shoulders. "My son, saying I'm sorry does not bring back the life I stole from you and your mother. Asking for forgiveness does not seem sufficient, though I do ask for it. If you cannot, I understand."

Frederick looked up with tear-stained eyes that still burned with anger and sorrow. "Give me time."

Friedrich nodded. He rose to his feet and went to the door for his overcoat. "Stay here as long as you need, son. I'm going to make my rounds at the hospital and grab a bite to eat."

<hr>

Later that afternoon, Friedrich returned to his quarters. He hung his cap and jacket by the door and looked around the room. He hadn't really expected Frederick to be there, but now, the empty room brought a shock of disappointment.

He bent to pull his riding boots off. Pain and anger welled up inside, and he flung the boots at the wall, dropped to his knees, and finally released the tears he'd been holding in all afternoon.

CHAPTER 22

Ascending the hospital stairs, Frederick swung open the old wooden doors and stepped inside, grateful to leave the cold wind outside. The doctor had declared Heinrich well enough to make the trip home. The only condition was that Frederick make the trip with him.

Had there even been a question?

Frederick's pack and bedroll were secured on his shoulders over his greatcoat. He had bathed and shaved, and his undercut had been touched up just yesterday. He strode up the stairs and arrived at Heinrich's bedside to find his friend seated, legs swung over the side, and fully dressed in his uniform. His tunic had been left open, revealing his loosely-fastened suspenders and white undershirt, the thickness of the bandages evident beneath his clothes. Still, his friend looked more the way Frederick remembered him.

Ilse appeared. "Hallo, Sanitäter. I see you are both ready to go. The hospital will not be the same without you." She glanced around to make sure no one was looking and kissed each of them lightly on the cheek. "*Dankeschön*, my heroes."

Frederick blushed. Heinrich nodded in humble acknowledgement. Ilse turned and retreated to another part of the infirmary.

Frederick stood and allowed Heinrich to lean into him as he rose to his feet. "Let's get that coat on." Heinrich struggled to remain balanced as Frederick pulled the coat over his shoulders and helped him slip his arms inside. "Now. Swing your arm around me, Kamerad. Just lean into me as much as you need, all right? If you feel like you can walk on your own let me know, but take it easy, you hear me?"

"Ja."

"Good. Let's go home."

Heinrich winced a little in pain but they began to move slowly toward the door of the infirmary. They continued their slow walk down the stairs, and Frederick felt Heinrich leaning more desperately into him and gripping his hand harder. "The stairs are the worst." Heinrich groaned.

"We're almost there, Kamerad."

The train was nearly empty when they boarded it a half hour later. Frederick helped Heinrich gently down into a seat toward the back, seating himself on the other side of the aisle. He stretched his legs into the aisle and his arms above his head, then relaxed back into the seat.

"Thanks, Freddie," Heinrich said weakly.

Frederick nodded. "You go ahead and rest if you need to. That's probably more work than you've done in weeks."

"Ja..."

It wasn't long before Heinrich fell asleep. Frederick pulled out a piece of paper and a pen. He had not taken time to write home the entire time he was in Poland. What would his mother think of him, anyway?

He could focus on the good: *I've been saving lives. I've become a Christian. I've made friends...* He could not imagine telling her about his father. At least not yet.

Dear Mom,

Forgive me for not writing before now. I have no excuse, really. I know that you are worried, and by now you may even fear I've been killed in battle. I want to assure you that I am fine. No, I am better than fine. You will be happy to know I have chosen the faith you tried so hard to instill in me in my youth. War has demanded much of my body and spirit, and I now understand that men either find their faith on the battlefield or lose it.

I lost my dear friend Fritz within the first weeks of battle. Two other friends were gravely injured, but as I sit here now, one of them rests nearby, recovering, and is evidence to me that the Lord is near.

We are returning now to Heinrich's home. I only have a few days left of leave before I am due back to the army, so I don't know whether I will be able to visit Aunt Maria and Uncle Werner again, and I do not know where the army will take me next.

Please tell Paul I say hello.

Love,

Frederick

He folded the letter and tucked it back in his pocket. Heinrich stirred.

"You all right, Kamerad?"

"Ja." Heinrich winced in pain as he strained to sit up. "I'm a little thirsty."

Frederick reached for his canteen, leaned over and held the bottle to Heinrich's lips. When his comrade had finished, Frederick took a swig, replaced the cap and said, "I stopped by the kitchen and filled up two mess kits for us. I picked up some extra biscuits, too.

Heinrich shook his head. "Nothing now, Freddie, thanks."

Frederick grabbed a biscuit from his pack, unashamedly devouring it almost instantly. He hadn't noticed his own hunger until that moment.

<hr>

There was no stopping Heinrich when they arrived in Schwerin. Frederick felt as if *he* were suddenly the dead weight as his injured friend struggled toward his mother and two younger siblings.

Frederick steadied the eager young man as his diminutive mother reached up and hugged her six-foot-two-inch son.

"Thank you for caring for my Heinrich," she said, turning to Frederick and grasping his hand. "You have been so kind. Will you be staying with us for a few days?"

"A few days. My leave is almost up."

"Na ja, I am glad you will be staying." She turned back to her son and patted him on the cheek. "I do not think I'd be able to carry him around as you do. I am sure Heinrich told you his father is away serving in the *Kriegsmarine*?"

Frederick nodded, and she glanced down at the younger children. "This is Hilda and this is Georg." A beaming smile spread across her face. "Your brother Hans sends his greetings. He recently received a promotion, you know."

Their journey was over. For now. Frederick helped Heinrich to his room and got him settled before throwing himself down on Hans's vacant bed nearby. Any attempt at conversation was precluded by heavy exhaustion.

He woke hours later, still fully dressed except for his boots, which Frau Schuyler had insisted he remove at the door. The hour was late, so he quietly removed his Feldbluse and pulled his suspenders from his shoulders, then slipped under his comforter.

"Freddie?"

Heinrich was awake. "Ja?"

"Danke. It is good to be home."

"Of course, Kamerad."

There was a pause. Then, "Freddie?"

"Ja?"

Again Heinrich's voice was hesitant. "A lot happened in Poland...Things I didn't expect."

"Ja." He felt stupid giving one-word answers. He was still half asleep. But, this was important.

"Shooting those innocent people..."

"I know, man." He sighed deeply, trying to sink into Heinrich's perspective. Frederick had felt sick enough standing there watching. Heinrich had pulled the trigger.

"If this is the way it's going to be, Freddie, I don't know if I can go back. I didn't sign up to be an executioner."

Frederick turned toward his friend. "Pfarrer Schmidt told me that an order went out, saying members of the army may refuse an order to participate in a firing squad."

Heinrich huffed. "And how do you think that would look to the other guys?"

In the dark, Frederick nodded. "The Pfarrer said it seems like a lot of the noncoms aren't even aware of it."

Heinrich huffed, and they both fell silent for a few minutes. Frederick was still exhausted and in need of more sleep. No weighty questions would be answered tonight.

CHAPTER 23

The next morning was Sunday. After the family left for church, Frederick washed and shaved while Heinrich sat up in bed, finishing off a massive plate of eggs with biscuits and jam. Heinrich's color had improved, and he seemed to have more energy than he had in weeks.

"Freddie, will you help me get to the piano?"

A smile spread across Frederick's face. "You sure you're up for that?"

"Ja. Feeling good."

Frederick removed the tray from Heinrich's lap and helped him to his feet. He could feel Heinrich leaning on him a little less than yesterday. They moved out to the *Wohnzimmer* where the family's old piano stood against the wall and helped Heinrich lower himself onto the bench, then relaxed into a chair nearby, wishing he had had the opportunity to learn to play when he was young.

Heinrich sat stiffly at the piano and tested the keys with a few pieces they'd heard recently on the Request Concert for the Wehrmacht. But then his posture loosened and, to Frederick's shock, his Kamerad launched into a piece by Gershwin.

A smile spread across Frederick's face, and he rose from the chair, leaning an elbow on the top of the piano. He drummed a little with his free hand and started to sing. It was ironic in a way—they grinned at each other, well aware of how that *verboten* jazz could get them in trouble!

The music stopped abruptly. Heinrich gripped his side in pain, though a hint of a smile remained on his face.

"You all right, Kamerad?"

"Ja." Heinrich chuckled. "I guess I better pace myself though."

Frederick helped him into a more comfortable chair and sat beside him. "Thanks, man, I needed that. It's been *too* long."

"Just don't tell the Führer."

They both laughed. "How did you even learn that, Kamerad? I thought jazz was banned here."

"I started learning it before." He tapped his temple. "I'd offer to babysit so Mutti could visit her friends. Then I'd play while Hilda and Georg danced around, and I'd give them candy so they wouldn't say anything when she got home." He snickered again. "It was the woman downstairs who ratted me out."

Frederick shook his head. "It shouldn't be that way."

A key turned in the lock and Heinrich's mother appeared in the doorway, followed by Hilda and Georg. "Hallo, Heinrich!" She placed her things on the table and came to his side. "So good to see you up. Good morning, Frederick."

"Good morning, Frau Schuyler."

Heinrich kissed his mother on the cheek. "I'm sorry, Mutti. I was so tired yesterday I don't remember what you said about Hans. Could you tell me again?"

Frau Schuyler sat down on the sofa close to her son. Her graying hair was done in a bun and she wore a simple green hat with a net veil. Her tired blue eyes sank deep into her caring face. "They've transferred him to Weimar. He'll be working at a camp there."

Heinrich gave a slight nod.

Frau Schuyler stroked her son's hair. "I know you miss him."

"Ja…" Heinrich looked at Frederick, then back to his mother. "I think I better get back to bed."

"Of course."

Frederick stood to help his friend, and the two of them disappeared into Heinrich's room. After helping Heinrich onto the bed, Frederick shut the door, then sat down on Hans's bed, stretched his legs out, and leaned his back against the wall. "You haven't said much about Hans."

The late-fall sun shone through the window, illuminating the little room. Heinrich was lying flat on his back, staring up at the ceiling, his hands folded on his stomach. "Hans is two years older than me. We used to be very close. He's an SS man now."

Frederick nodded. He'd noticed pictures of both Heinrich and Hans on top of the piano, Heinrich in his Wehrmacht dress uniform, and Hans donning the sharp black uniform of the SS. "You look quite a bit alike."

"Thanks," Heinrich said grimly. "It's not as glamorous as she makes it sound. They probably had to increase the number of camp guards once they—once we—forced all those people out of their homes."

Frederick closed his eyes and rubbed his face with his hands. "Heinrich, Kamerad, I'm really sorry."

"Just never pictured my brother as a jailer, you know?" Heinrich continued to stare at the ceiling. "It's like everybody just accepts it. *No. They act like I should be *proud* of him."

Frederick nodded and pressed his lips together. He didn't know much about the camps. "The camps are for political prisoners, right? Trouble makers? Criminals?"

"Yeah. But who decides who is a trouble maker or a criminal?"

Frederick pondered the question while Heinrich continued, "My family has always been religious. My brother and I were altar boys. My father was a lay minister until he was called back to the Kriegsmarine. Now my brother is working at a concentration camp, and I'm a soldier with innocent blood on his hands."

"Concentration camps are nothing new."

Heinrich sighed heavily. "Just never pictured my brother working at one. Having him join the SS to begin with was bad enough. He told us straight off that he and his comrades were warned: *not everyone is going to like this uniform.*"

"Ja...My aunt and uncle didn't like it. I didn't know what to think until I saw what went on in Poland."

"Unquestioning loyalty," Heinrich sneered. "I thought I was nothing like him."

Frederick just shook his head. They'd come full circle, back to their discussion from late last night. "You're not, Kamerad."

Heinrich just studied the ceiling.

Frederick stood and pulled up a chair, settling down at his friend's bedside. "I'm not in a position to judge anyone here in Germany. I feel like an outsider, but I also know I've got a job to do. Bind wounds and minister to the dying."

Heinrich turned to him, an amused smile on his face. "We all ought to be more like you."

Frederick shook his head. "It's easy to say, harder to do. That's why we need each other." His face lightened, and he pretended to punch Heinrich on the arm. "Which means you had better come back to us, ja?"

CHAPTER 24

FREDERICK

The Eifel, Western Germany

November 1939

His leave had ended with an order to report to a village in the Eifel, a hilly, wooded area near the border with Belgium, where he would rendezvous with his unit. Other units had assembled up and down the western border of Germany. However, any planned movement into France or the Low Countries had been postponed indefinitely. Instead of fighting, they found themselves being marched through the woods day after day, drilling in the neighboring fields, and living with local families.

It wasn't hard to grow comfortable. Frederick, Pieter, and Klaus were billeted in a small cottage with a father, mother, and two young children. Pieter and Klaus often escaped to the taverns in town, saying they preferred the company of their comrades to family life. Frederick wasn't sure it was family life that he preferred, but after a few trips to the tavern, he discovered that it didn't suit him any better.

"It's been a few nights since you've joined us, Kamerad," Pieter observed as he buttoned his greatcoat and popped the collar up over his cheeks. He pulled his cap down over his reddish-blond hair and shoved his hands into his mittens. "You just going to sit around here all night?"

Seated by the fire with his feet up, the idea of getting dressed to go out in the cold held *no* appeal whatsoever. "You guys go ahead." He gave his comrades a wave and laughed to himself as they bustled out into the snow, before pulling a book from a nearby shelf and settling back into the soft chair.

His hopes of a quiet evening were soon dashed by 6-year-old Anna and 3-year-old Franz as they scampered into the room. Their father Rolf brought up the rear and settled into his chair, ready for the family's ritual story time.

Anna grabbed a book, and Rolf pulled the two children into his lap. Frederick tried to focus on the page in front of him, but found his eyes wandering repeatedly to the family. He could see their mother beyond them, cleaning up the kitchen after dinner. Alice had dark hair like Frederick's mother, and her belly protruded beneath her apron. In a few months, the family would welcome their third child.

So this is what a normal family is like. No longer interested in his book, he closed it and turned his stare to the fireplace as the familiar ache formed in his stomach. Soon, he rose and escaped to his room.

The Pohl family had welcomed three soldiers into their home and provided beautifully for them with the little they had. Three soldiers was really one too many, but they insisted Frederick stay with them as well, rather than billeting at the inn. It meant sleeping on the floor while Pieter and Klaus slept on the spare bed, but he had graciously accepted their offer. Perhaps that had been a mistake—like self-inflicted punishment.

Someone knocked at the bedroom door.

"Come in."

The door swung open and Alice appeared. "Are you all right?"

He nodded and started to sit up. "Just a little stomach ache, that's all."

She looked at him in the same way his mother would've. "This is the third time since you boys arrived that I've seen you disappear into your room like this. Don't you carry anything that can help you with these stomach aches?"

"No, ma'am," he said, feeling more vulnerable than he was willing to admit. "There's really nothing that helps."

She sat down on the edge of the bed and rested her hands on top of her belly, looking down at him with caring brown eyes as if waiting for him to speak.

"You have a beautiful family. It's nice to see what that looks like."

"You didn't have a good childhood?"

"I grew up without a father, that's all."

"I'm sorry." Compassion flooded her eyes, and she nodded slightly. "I felt that you'd had a difficult life. Perhaps that is what makes you so willing to give so very much of yourself to your comrades."

What does a person say to such a statement?

"Why don't you force one of those other boys onto the floor, Frederick? You need the bed more than they do."

"I'm all right, but thank you, Alice."

"If you're sure." She rose and headed for the door. "Please let me know if there is anything you need."

He nodded and stated his thanks again. She left quietly, shutting off the light as she went. Frederick turned his gaze to the window, where the moonlight was beginning to peek in. His father was probably stationed nearby with the medical unit or commissioned officers.

Sooner or later he would have to break the silence.

———————

DAYS TURNED INTO WEEKS. The winter weather grew more bitter.

Pieter pushed open the cottage door. Frederick and Klaus followed, bringing a burst of ice and snow along with them.

"This has to be the worst winter on record." Pieter hissed, pulling his boots off.

Anna and Franz skipped excitedly into the room, cheering a jaunty, "Hello!" The little girl grabbed as many boots as she could in her little arms and carried them to the fireplace, dropping them to dry and then bounding back for another armload. Franz picked up mittens as they were dropped on the floor and carried them to the opposite side of the fireplace.

"Maybe family life isn't so bad, Petey." Frederick elbowed Pieter in the ribs.

"Ja, the little servants are nice." Klaus laughed. He bowed to the two children. "Danke, Anna und Franz."

"I can't believe they make you boys drill in this weather," Alice said, appearing with some hot tea. "Oh, Frederick, this came for you." She placed the tea on the table and handed him a package postmarked from Sternberg. He reached for it eagerly.

His Bible had finally come from Aunt Maria. Before he could escape to his room, though, Anna bounced in a second time and stood before him. "Frederick, will you help us decorate for Advent? And can Pieter and Klaus stay home tonight too?"

Advent. Was it really almost that time of year? He looked at his comrades. "We're being invited to decorate for Advent, gentlemen. Think you can handle it?"

Pieter and Klaus looked at each other and grinned. "Ja," Pieter said, "I think we can handle it."

Frederick gave Anna a decisive nod. "We will all join you."

Perhaps, in spite of a looming war, he'd finally be able to enjoy a real German Christmas. "I'll be back soon, Anna." He knuckled her cheek and retreated to his bedroom, still clutching the package from Aunt Maria.

It had been too long. He lay back on his bedroll, opened the package and flipped through the worn pages of the old *Lutherbibel* that had traveled across the ocean with his ancestors almost one hundred years before. Here it was, back in Germany again...in *his* hands.

Too soon, though, Alice called for dinner. He set the Bible aside and rose to join the family and his comrades at the table. After the meal, Rolf set down his napkin and said, "Frederick, would you help me gather the things from storage?"

Anna's eyes grew wide, and she prepared to follow her father and Frederick. Rolf gave her a stern look. "I asked Frederick, *Liebling*. You stay out here and make sure his friends don't get into any trouble."

Pieter slapped Klaus's knee. "Ja, Anna, we need constant supervision." Klaus whooped and popped a last bite of bread into in his mouth.

Frederick followed Rolf into a small storage area at the back of the house. "Help me carry these boxes out, bitte."

Frederick picked up a box and carried it into the living room, then returned for another. Rolf was seated on a crate, lighting up his pipe. "Also. You're our *American*."

"Ja."

"Haven't had time to hear your story, son." Rolf gestured. "Pull up a crate."

Frederick obeyed.

"What brought you to Germany?"

"I have family here."

Rolf pulled his pipe out of his pocket and lit it. "Your mother must miss you."

Frederick nodded. He missed her too.

"My wife tells me your father passed?"

Frederick felt ill. "No. I just grew up without one." Thinking it might reflect badly on his mother, he added, "They were married. He left when she was pregnant with me."

Rolf nodded. "I'm sorry, son. From what I see, your mother did a wonderful job raising you on her own. It says something, that you're not out carousing every night like those two comrades of yours." He chuckled. "They're nice boys, but they do come in late."

Rolf's humor lightened Frederick's mood a little, but he did *not* feel like talking. "Did you have any other boxes for me, sir?"

"Ja." Rolf gestured in the direction of a few other boxes, and Frederick rose to carry them into the living room. Anna had already gotten into the first box, and if Pieter and Klaus weren't truly amused by her, they were doing an excellent job at feigning interest as she began to set her treasures around the house. Frederick joined them as they watched the girl and her mother transform the place from mundane to glorious. The Christmas tree itself would not be brought in and decorated until Christmas Eve. Still, the small home was beautiful with pine boughs, shiny glass ornaments, wooden trinkets, and an advent wreath, all of which had probably been handed down for generations. Anna proudly showed off the wooden advent calendars her father had hand-made for her and her brother, as well as the Christmas pyramid. "The candles make the fan at the top spin, and you can watch the people dance!" she explained proudly.

Alice provided drinks and gingerbread cookies, and Anna, thrilled to have an audience, led everyone in a few traditional Advent hymns—or at least, what she remembered of them.

"Ok, little ones," Alice finally said, "it's time for bed."

Pieter and Klaus headed for the kitchen table as the mother herded the reluctant children toward their beds. "Cards, Freddie?"

"Maybe later."

Frederick headed down the hall himself, closing the bedroom door behind him and settling back onto his bedroll with his Bible in hand. He flipped through and shook his head. The thought of his father still gnawed at him.

"What *am I* supposed to do?"

Whether it was God's voice, or the voice of his mother, or his own knowledge of the answer, he heard the words, clear as day: *Have you prayed for him?*

"No." He huffed. "Of course I haven't."

Perhaps it was time. Frederick pulled his knees close to him and folded his arms around them. "I am *angry*, God. Is that wrong? How am I supposed to feel after twenty years? I guess he must be suffering too, and maybe he's been suffering all these years. He's certainly not the man my mother and Paul described to me, that's for sure." His voice trailed off. This was not going to be easy.

EACH EVENING, THOUGHTS OF what his childhood could have looked like continued to flood Frederick's mind as he listened to Rolf read advent lessons to Franz and Anna, and watched both parents interact with their children and each other.

Considering what he knew now, though, he wasn't sure he would have wanted *Chaplain Schmidt* for a father.

Frederick was knocked out of his reverie by the sound of jumping and squealing in the main room of the house. He rose, buttoned his shirt, and threw his tunic on over his shoulders before heading into the living room.

Pieter appeared immediately behind him, grumbling something about *hard to feel like a soldier when this is going on*.

Anna's tiny voice burst through his comrade's groaning. "Look, look!" she cried, dancing around the living room with a little doll. "Look what Sankt Niklaus brought!"

Franz lay sprawled in the middle of the floor, happily playing with a new set of toy soldiers. Frederick gave a tired laugh and retrieved a small gift from his boot. *A package of real coffee. Nothing better in the world.* And paper to write home on. Of course. He tossed a grin to Frau Pohl. "Danke."

"Of course, Frederick. Pieter, you'd better check your boots as well."

Pieter grunted and moved slowly toward his boots. Being billeted with this family was both a blessing and a curse.

Along with a fresh stack of paper of his own, Pieter retrieved a small box of candies from his boot and sat at the table distributing them to the already sugared-up children. Frederick took the opportunity to duck back into the room to shave and finish dressing. Again, he wondered if the inn would've been a better place for him. Every day here brought another reminder that he needed to reconcile with his father.

CHAPTER 25

FREDERICK

Dear Father,

I am sorry I have not been in touch. I am a little surprised that I haven't run into you somewhere around the village, but perhaps that is for the better. Until now, I haven't been ready.

We are very lucky to be billeted with a good family. They have two small children who keep things entertaining. They also gave me this paper as a gift from Sankt Niklaus.

If we are still here by Christmas, would you consider joining us on Christmas Day?

Your son,

Frederick

He wrote the address of the cottage at the bottom of the paper and sealed it. Then he pulled another piece of paper from the stack. The army had been supplied with Christmas cards for soldiers to send home, but he had no desire to send his mother a Nazi-sponsored Christmas card. A simple letter would have to do.

Dear Mom,

I don't know if this will reach you by Christmas. I honestly don't know if it will find its way to you at all. We are staying in the home of a nice family with two children, 6 and 3. I am finding much joy in the traditions of a German Christmas and hope the mother plans to bake Stollen. I have vague memories of Oma making it as a child. Even now, I can smell the butter, spices, and fruits warming the entire house as it baked.

I am billeted with two comrades, Pieter and Klaus. We share a small bedroom, and although they are clowns, I enjoy their company. I do miss having a close friend like Fritz or Heinrich, but I believe Heinrich will return when he is well enough.

I hope you and Paul enjoy your first Christmas as husband and wife. You are always in my thoughts and prayers.

Frohe Weihnachten *and Merry Christmas,*

Frederick

———

FOUR DAYS BEFORE CHRISTMAS, Frederick and Pieter walked together back from the field where they'd been participating in drill exercises.

"You are going to the solstice fire tonight, oder?"

Frederick gave Pieter a look as the young soldier shifted his Mauser from one shoulder to the other and explained, "It's an ancient tradition that honors our ancestors. There will be fires burning across the Fatherland in every village, town, and city."

Frederick's stomach twisted—it sounded like some ancient pagan ritual, something people back home eschewed. Were Germans still into that stuff?

"Come on, Kamerad. Think of how great it will be to participate in the first nation-wide celebration of the winter solstice."

A few hours later, it became clear that everyone else in the household was going. Reluctantly, he buttoned his Feldbluse and prepared to go to the bonfire. At the very least, it would be quite a spectacle with all the villagers and their billeted soldiers together in one place. He pulled on his greatcoat and forced himself out the door, trudging through the snow behind the family. His comrades had gathered earlier for a little pre-fire revelry.

Again, his stomach gave him angst.

"I—I can't go." He stopped in his tracks before the main road that lay between the village and the open field. "I'm sorry, Alice, I need to go back to the house."

She looked at him sympathetically. "Is it your stomach, Frederick?"

He nodded. At any rate, it was a great excuse to remain behind. He returned to the house to the sound of shouting and singing from the field beyond the village. The fire flared in the distance, lighting his final steps to the house.

The flame was to be kept burning until Christmas Eve, when the villagers would return to it and light candles, carry them home, and use them to light the candles on their Christmas trees.

It sounded beautiful, honestly. What was he supposed to think? These were the sorts of questions he would have asked the chaplain—if only the chaplain weren't his father. It begged the question, was his father at the bonfire or a similar one a few villages away? Or did Chaplain Schmidt stay home too, on account of his own reservations?

<hr>

Alice walked into the open door of the room Frederick, Pieter, and Klaus shared and presented them proudly with three freshly washed and pressed uniforms. "You will look your best for your Christmas Eve soiree," she said, laying each one out on the beds. "We are so very proud of our handsome soldiers."

They each thanked her in turn.

Alice turned to Frederick. "Will your friend be joining us tomorrow for Christmas?"

He had received a short telegram from his father saying he would come to dinner the following day. "Ja."

It wasn't that simple. His stomach tensed with anxiety about seeing his father at such an intimate occasion. For the time being, though, he was going to the inn with Pieter and Klaus, to celebrate with his comrades. Young men who, despite their bawdy jokes and great consumption of beer, were much easier to be around than his father.

As they walked out fully dressed into the main room of the house, Franz gasped in awe and Rolf exclaimed, "Well, well. You boys clean up nicely. The Führer certainly knows how to dress his soldiers."

"Will you be home in time to join us for midnight mass?" Alice's question was directed specifically at Frederick, although she gave welcoming looks to Pieter and Klaus as well.

Frederick glanced at his comrades and gave her a smile. "We'll try, ma'am."

Only as a child did Frederick remember a heavily laden Christmas table, filled with turkey, stuffing, mashed potatoes, gravy, squash, cranberry sauce, and an assortment of pies. Funny how those memories brought a twinge of homesickness, even though he *knew* that was not the reality back home. Hopefully his mother and Paul would be going to Mark and Susannah's as they had in the past—half a dozen families, contributing what they could to a meal. It made the leaner years more bearable.

The dishes were different, but he and his fellow soldiers had been well-supplied with a Christmas feast. Wine, beer, and schnapps flowed freely alongside goose, potato dumplings, and red cabbage.

"Freddie." Johann swung his arm around Frederick's shoulder. The boy Frederick had bandaged on the first day of the Poland campaign had quickly become a battle-hardened soldier. His childlike blue eyes had been overshadowed by a furrowed brow, and Frederick knew from the evenings he'd spent with Pieter and Klaus at the inn that Johann also drank heavily.

"Frohe Weihnachten, Kamerad." Frederick patted Johann on the back a few times and slipped out of the young man's grip.

A few men struck up a rendition of "O Tannenbaum" with guitar and accordion. Frederick closed his eyes and leaned back, relishing the sound of their voices, although a few were already at less-than-ideal levels of sobriety. Frederick shook his head in second-hand embarrassment, threw his arm back around Johann, and joined them in a loud voice.

"Sanitäter," someone yelled, "you should come out at night more often, instead of staying in that house of yours. We always have a good time."

Frederick chuckled. "I can see that."

"Freddie's a homebody," Pieter said. "Likes to put his feet up by the fire and read his *Bibel*."

Johann turned to Frederick. "You going to be a preacher or something?"

Frederick shrugged. Not in the short term. He wasn't even good at finding the right words to say one on one, how could he ever speak in front of a church full of people?

Klaus raised his glass and said, "Hey, as long as Freddie's got my back if I get taken down by a French bullet, I don't care what he's reading."

A number of the men around the table nodded in agreement. "To Freddie." They raised their glasses, and Frederick felt his cheeks turn red.

It wasn't long before he tired of the festive atmosphere and longed for the relative quiet of the cottage—two children were certainly less rowdy than a room crammed with drunken Landsers. He excused himself and took the long way home, sucking in the chilly air and watching as it escaped through his mouth and nostrils.

Rolf, Alice, and the children arrived home carrying candles lit by the still-burning *Jul* fire. In the Wohnzimmer, Frau Pohl unveiled the Christmas tree she'd decorated in secret, and the family gathered to light the candles with the flame from the bonfire.

Then, Frau Pohl turned and distributed a few presents to her children.

"I have something for you as well," she said as she approached Frederick.

He took a small box from her hands and opened it. Inside was a chain with a small oval pendant. On one side was St. Michael and on the reverse was the Aesculapius.

"It's Saint Michael the Archangel," Alice said gently. "He is the patron saint of soldiers and medics. My father carried it in the Great War. Those who watch over others need someone to watch over them."

Though saints had never meant anything to Frederick, he was touched by what obviously meant a great deal to Alice. "Dankeschön," he breathed, and gave her an awkward hug.

At that moment, Klaus and Pieter clambered into the cottage. Frederick grinned.

"Did we make it in time for church?"

"Ja," he laughed—a little surprised. "You made it."

CHAPTER 26

The door was opened by a petite woman, heavy with child. Her brown eyes reminded him instantly of Hannah—no. He pushed the thought away and handed her a basket of sausages and cheese.

"You must be Frederick's friend. My goodness"—she eyed the contents of the basket—"these are *lovely!*"

"Thank you for welcoming me into your home."

She stood back so he could enter and indicated a stool. "You may sit here to take off your boots. I will let Frederick know you're here."

"Thank you."

When she returned, she apologized. "I am sorry, I did not ask your name."

He extended a hand. "Chaplain Friedrich Schmidt, but Friedrich is fine."

"Alice Pohl. We are so very pleased to have you." She smiled broadly as Frederick entered the room. "Friedrich Schmidt—sounds so much like your name, Frederick."

The boy cleared his throat and offered a hand. "Good to see you, *Herr Pfarrer* Schmidt."

It had been foolish to hope for a different greeting. Friedrich placed his greatcoat in Alice's waiting hands and walked stoically over to the fireplace. Frederick settled down opposite him and began to stare into the fire.

"Merry Christmas," Friedrich said in English, testing the waters a second time.

"Frohe Weihnachten, Pfarrer Schmidt."

Achso. The boy probably wished he had not sent the invitation. Alas, Friedrich was here now. He looked forward to enjoying Christmas away from the officers who hadn't returned home for the holiday.

Alice seemed to sense the thickness in the atmosphere. With a forced smile, she asked, "Herr Schmidt—Friedrich. What can I offer you to drink? I made a special mulled cider that's warming on the stove."

"Mulled cider sounds wonderful, thank you. It is a lovely home you have here."

"Danke." Her eyes glistened at the compliment.

Two children burst in the back door, chased by two young men of the company, who stopped in their tracks. "Herr Pfarrer Schmidt?"

"Hello, gentlemen," he said, rising and extending his hand to them. "Remind me of your names?"

"Pieter."

"Klaus."

"Achso." Pieter, the redhead. Klaus, brown haired, brown eyed. He extended a hand to each of them while in his peripheral vision Frederick seemed to sink deeper into his chair.

Alice reappeared, carrying a tray with four cups of cider. Behind her, the little girl carried a tray spread with the cheese and sausage he'd brought.

"It was very kind of you to bring this, Herr Schmidt," Alice said. "I'm afraid it is probably nicer than what we have to offer you this Christmas."

Friedrich shook his head and assured her, "Please, Alice, don't worry about a thing. I am grateful to be invited into your home. It has been a long time."

He glanced at his son, who still sat staring into the fire.

"Do you have a family of your own?"

"I was going to dine with some of the officers, but when I received Frederick's invitation, I decided I would much rather enjoy Christmas this way."

Frederick rose from his chair. "Excuse me, I'm not feeling well." The young man walked out of the room abruptly and without further explanation.

"You must know Frederick has some stomach issues," Alice said softly.

"Oh yes, stomach issues."

Again the observant woman seemed to sense something was amiss. "Let me go see if he needs anything."

"By all means."

Alice left, and Friedrich looked from Pieter to Klaus.

"We both kind of thought Freddie had invited a girl." Klaus snickered.

"Mmm, yes." Friedrich sipped his cider thoughtfully. "And what about you two gentlemen? How is *Sitzkrieg*?"

They both laughed.

"It can't be that bad. I've heard the local beer is quite tasty."

"A guy could get used to it," Klaus mused. "Beautiful here too, with the mountains. Not like back home."

"Indeed." Friedrich sipped again. "Quite a bit of snow this year too, oder?"

Pieter shrugged, and Alice returned. "Dinner will be done shortly, gentlemen. Friedrich, you're welcome to go down the hall and visit with Frederick."

She stopped him as he made his way toward the bedroom, adding in a casual whisper, "I understand it is no coincidence that your names are so similar."

He glanced at his feet. "No, it is not."

He felt compassion in her gaze, though he did not look at her. "It would seem you two have a lot to talk about."

"Indeed." She returned to the kitchen, and he knocked on Frederick's door. "May I come in?"

"If you must."

Friedrich entered, closed the door and sat on the edge of the bed facing his son. Frederick lay on his bedroll, his chest rising and falling with each frustrated breath.

"Frederick, why did you invite me?"

"I thought it was the right thing to do."

"You didn't have to. No one would blame you."

"I thought I was ready."

Friedrich came to his son's side, taking a seat next to him on the floor. In spite of his years of experience doing pastoral counseling, as well as the years he'd spent interacting with men under his command, nothing had prepared him for this. "Frederick, this is just as hard for me as it is for you. I feel an immense amount of shame because of what I did to you and your mother. Not only do I feel completely unprepared to be your father, I don't know if I can function as your pastor or even your friend." He pushed his glasses back up the bridge of his nose. "As I said, no one would blame you if you decide you don't want me in your life."

Frederick's eyes remained cast on the floor. "I was fine believing you'd died in the Great War. I had this idea of the man you'd been, a man who was passionate, energetic, loving, and loyal." He huffed at the word *loyal*. "Instead, I find out you willingly chose to break your marriage vows and abandon us. I can't get past that."

"I suppose I deserve that."

They sat in silence until Alice knocked on the door. "It's time for dinner, gentlemen."

Friedrich rose to his feet and looked down at his son. "Are you ready?"

Frederick gripped his stomach and shook his head.

"Na *dann*." He placed a hand on Frederick's shoulder. "I will stop in to say goodbye before I go."

He pulled the door closed. Alice raised an eyebrow but said nothing, instead leading Friedrich to where her husband sat, warming his feet by the fire.

"Rolf, this is Herr Pfarrer Friedrich Schmidt, a friend of Frederick's."

Rolf rose and extended a hand. "Forgive me, Herr Pfarrer Schmidt. I was outside trying to make some emergency patches on the roof. I am sorry I was not here to greet you."

"*Kein Problem*." Friedrich grasped his hand heartily.

"I hear Frederick has stomach problems," Rolf observed. "I hope he is all right."

"He will be."

———

FRIEDRICH MADE HIS WAY back to the bedroom hours later, after dinner, dessert, and an impromptu performance by Anna and Franz.

"Frederick?"

"Ja, come in."

Again Friedrich took a seat on the end of the bed. "You missed a nice meal. Alice made the most delicious duck I've tasted in all my time here in Germany."

Frederick inhaled deeply.

"I'll be going soon."

His son only nodded. Friedrich shook his head. "Look, Frederick, we both know God would not have brought us together if he didn't have a reason for it. I've asked both you and God for forgiveness. Please stop judging me for my past mistakes."

He waited to see if Frederick would respond. When he didn't, Friedrich stood to leave. As he stepped into the hallway, he heard Frederick's voice, barely audible from behind him. "I do love you, Father."

Friedrich cast a glance over his shoulder. "I love you too, Frederick."

CHAPTER 27

May 1940

After spending six months with the Pohl family, Frederick tied up his bedroll and threw his pack over his shoulders. Pieter and Klaus waited by the door, and Alice sat quietly in a chair by the fireplace, her three month old son wrapped and sleeping in her arms. Frederick approached her and placed a hand on the baby's head. "Thank you for everything."

"It has been our pleasure," she whispered. "You boys are welcome here any time."

It had not been all roses. After Christmas, the house had seemed to grow smaller. Family and soldiers got in each other's way and on each other's nerves. Pieter and Klaus spent more time at the inn, and Frederick even began tagging along, although he never stayed late. Klaus and then Pieter began volunteering for guard duty, rather than waiting to be assigned. Once the baby was born, no one was sleeping anyway.

Frederick gave Rolf's hand a firm shake, and ruffled Franz's hair. When he came to Anna, she threw her arms around his legs. "Promise you'll write, Freddie. Please?"

He chuckled and patted her head. He wasn't even good at writing letters to his own family. "I'll try, Anna."

She stomped her foot. "Not good enough."

"Anna, dear, you have to let the soldiers go now," Rolf chided. She released Frederick's legs and ran to her father, who pulled her into his arms and walked with Frederick to the door and out into the morning light. "God be with you."

As he said a final goodbye, he heard a familiar voice from behind him.

"Freddie!"

Frederick turned around. "Heinrich!" He grasped his comrade's shoulder as the two met in the road that was already filled with soldiers heading to the assembly point beyond the village.

"I just got in last night. I sure am glad to see you," Heinrich said.

The tall, slim blond had put on weight from months of his mother's good cooking. His cheeks were rosy, and his skin was no longer pale.

"Likewise, Kamerad." Frederick slapped him on the shoulder and jerked a thumb at Pieter and Klaus. "I've been living with these two clowns for six months."

***

TANKS AND PIONEER UNITS had already cleared the way for them as they marched through the thick forests between Germany and Belgium. Aircraft flew overhead and Frederick couldn't help but be transported by the sound of his comrades voices as they sang song after song, waving at girls as they passed, and meeting only a few small pockets of resistance, as if victory had already been attained.

The air was charged with energy and pride until the company came to a halt. Exhaustion slammed into Frederick, and his roiling stomach reminded him it had been neglected during the grueling march.

He reached into his mess kit for the pills that had been given out along with his food supplies. Coffee was supplied regularly, but this worked better. He liked how it made him feel.

He moved the tube from his mess kit to the pocket of his Feldbluse and lay back on the ground, curling onto his side in the hopes that his recently re-emerging stomach pains would ease.

"Up, men!" A Feldwebel marched by barking orders. Some men jumped to their feet, others rose more slowly. Were they really going to march again so soon?

"On your feet, Sanitäter," Pieter joked as he walked by. Frederick pulled himself into a sitting position and tossed a lazy salute in Pieter's direction.

"You feeling all right?" It was Heinrich who came to his side.

"Ja, I—" the pain sharpened as he tried to stand.

Heinrich cursed. "You don't look so good, Kamerad. Stay here. I'll see if I can get someone to give you a ride." A few moments later, Heinrich reappeared with a smile on his face. "The medical supply truck is coming soon. They can probably give you a lift."

"Danke, Kamerad." Frederick watched as Heinrich marched off to rejoin the unit. Soon the medical truck rumbled up and pulled to a stop. Two orderlies jumped down and came to his side.

"Sani? You all right?" One of them looked Frederick over. "You're looking pretty pale, Kamerad. Can you walk?"

With some effort and the help of the orderlies, Frederick stood. "I think I just need to rest for a while." They helped him up onto the passenger seat of the truck and circled back around. Once they began rolling, Frederick leaned against the seat, closed his eyes, and fell asleep.

THE NEXT MORNING HE awoke in the shady interior of an army field hospital. The light shone through a few openings in the tent, stinging his eyes. His father sat quietly next to him.

"Dad, what are you doing here?"

"Making my rounds," Friedrich said. "I couldn't just leave with you lying here. What happened?"

Frederick shook his head and tried to sit up. *Nope.* His abdomen was still too tender. He lay back down and groaned. "I don't know. I just felt really ill. We marched nonstop for days, sat down to take a short rest, and when they announced we were moving on, I tried to stand up but doubled over in pain."

"I've never seen anything like it." Friedrich sighed and rubbed his temples with his thumb and forefinger. "Everyone's been moving at breakneck speed."

"That's *Blitzkrieg* for you."

"Ja, but this is like nothing I've seen before, even after all my years as an officer." His expression became one of concern and he asked, "Are you taking care of yourself?"

"Of course."

Friedrich grasped his son's hand in both of his. "May I pray for you, son?"

Frederick nodded, and his father prayed. As he closed the prayer, Friedrich squeezed Frederick's hand. "Frederick?"

"Ja?"

"Is there anything you can think of that might be making your stomach issues worse?"

His father seemed to be hinting at something, but what? "Nothing I can think of."

Friedrich simply huffed.

"Thank you, Father."

"Of course...son."

CHAPTER 28

FREDERICK

France

June 1940

"I'm out of bandages!" Frederick cried to one of his stretcher bearers. He tore his wounded comrade's undershirt and wrapped it around a heavily bleeding head wound.

Until this moment, much of the so-called war had been a waiting game. Now, he'd barely helped one young man when two more were brought to him.

"Don't forget the bandages," he yelled as the stretcher bearers marched off toward the bandaging station farther back from the line. "If you see Pfarrer Schmidt, tell him I need help!"

Machine guns rattled, and artillery exploded all around him. Apparently, the French had used the lull in fighting to strengthen their supply lines...and their resolve.

"Sani! Hilfe!" Multiple voices shrieked in discordant melody. Bullets whizzed and dirt flew up around him. He landed on his knees and ripped his helmet off, sweat falling in great drops as he bent over his next patient. "Hey," he breathed, "you're going to be all right."

Soon, bandages and fresh cloths landed on the ground beside him. He glanced up long enough to see his father staring down at him. "Danke. I need help with these wounded." He jerked his head in the direction of the men lying nearby and turned back to his patient, wetting a cloth and wiping blood from the young man's temple. "You'll be ok. Can you walk?"

The soldier nodded. Frederick helped him to his feet and sent him on his way. *Another head wound...* He glanced around for his helmet.

From meters away, his father called for him. In dire circumstances, chaplains served alongside medics, but Friedrich's medical knowledge was limited. Frederick rose to his feet, swiped up his helmet, and strapped it back on. "I'm coming," he cried. "There are just so many."

Hours later, he collapsed onto the ground, his chest heaving as he gasped for breath. The French had stopped their bombardment...for now. The following days could look much the same as German forces pushed their way farther into France. He curled up on the ground and fell asleep for the first time in two days, too exhausted to find a more appropriate place to sleep.

The next day's battle began almost before the sun had fully risen over the tops of the trees. When the Germans seemed to have the upper hand, fewer injuries meant less adrenaline to keep him going. He reached for his tube of pills, dumped a few in his hand, and tossed them in his mouth along with a swig of water.

"Sani!"

Already feeling refreshed, he rushed out of his foxhole to the scream-ing comrade.

"Freddie." The soldier gasped as he approached. Frederick signaled a nearby comrade to help him carry the injured man behind the lines.

Johann approached, slung his Mauser over his shoulder, and came to the young man's side. Together they lifted him, each with an arm behind his back and the other under his legs.

"Johann," the injured solider gasped.

"Gebi." Johann's eyes shone down on the boy in recognition.

Now Frederick recognized him too—*Gebhardt, Johann's cousin.*

Johann helped lower him into the foxhole, lingering as Frederick began to attend him.

"He'll be all right," Frederick insisted.

Johann nodded curtly and darted back into the fray.

Frederick tore open Gebhardt's tunic, muddied and covered in blood. Nausea washed over him—he paused to catch his breath, then forced the young man's undershirt open. It was difficult to stem the bleeding as his hands trembled and his stomach lurched.

He had just assured Johann that Gebhardt would be fine. *God help me.*

The young man gasped for breath.

"No, no, no, man, you're going to be all right." Frederick pressed his hands into the wound, only to realize he was about to be violently ill. He twisted and retched, wiped his mouth, and returned to his work, shaking and sweating.

Pressing into the wound again with one hand, and reaching for his forceps with the other, he repeated his assurance to Gebhardt. "You're going to be all right."

Gebhardt shook his head and reached for Frederick's arm. "Freddie, I just want my Mutti. Can you get my Mutti?"

Frederick stopped fumbling through his medical kit and spoke through the ill feeling that clung to him. "Your Mutti loves you so much."

Gebhardt nodded. His breathing slowed. "Pray for me, Freddie."

Frederick grasped the young man's hand and prayed. Gebhardt's breathing evened. A peaceful expression spread across his face and then he stopped breathing completely. Frederick reached a hand out and closed his comrade's eyes. He'd learned to accept death, but had the side effects of the drugs prevented him from saving a comrade who could've been saved?

Frederick scraped a hand over his face.

"Sani!"

He shot to his feet. *No time to worry about that now.*

FREDERICK FOUND HIMSELF FUMBLING for his tube of pills more often as the division pushed west tirelessly. It made everything so easy, and he needed to press on.

The pills gave him loads of energy, but did nothing to ease his stomach aches. Deep inside, he wondered if they were actually making things worse.

A cry came from the machine gun position. Frederick sprang from his foxhole and ran, bent double, to Pieter and Klaus.

"Klaus, you ok?" Frederick went to his knees, gripping his stomach with one hand. Klaus rested with is back against the wall of the dugout, clutching a balled, bloody fist against his chest.

"Hand got clipped," he explained through a few gasps.

Frederick took Klaus's hand in his and reached into his medical belt, only to be thrown into Klaus as a shell hit meters away. Pieter retook his position with little more than a few choice words, but the sound of the battle pounded in Frederick's head. He pulled himself up and tried to continue cleansing and wrapping Klaus's hand.

"Freddie, man, you don't look so good."

"I'm fine."

"No man," Klaus raised his voice, "wrap me up quick and get yourself to the medical station."

Frederick shook his head and tried to continue his work, but Klaus pushed past him and repositioned himself next to Pieter, where he proceeded to finish wrapping the bandage himself. "If you don't go, I'll take you myself."

He didn't honestly think he could *make it* to the medical station. He leaned back against the dirt wall. Klaus glanced back at him a few seconds later, then cried, "Sani! Hilfe!"

Soon Frederick's father appeared. "The medics have their hands full. Can I help?"

Klaus motioned curtly toward Frederick.

"Dear God," Friedrich groaned. He lowered himself and swung his son's arm around his shoulder. "Just lean on me, son." He rose and proceeded to walk him to the medic's station. Even against his father's shoulder, Frederick could hardly keep his balance. Another wave of nausea rushed over him, and he bent down to throw up.

His father pulled out a clean handkerchief and wiped his son's mouth, then reached for Frederick's canteen. He removed the cap and lifted it to Frederick's mouth. "Rinse."

His father's stony blue eyes grew tender beneath the brim of his cap. "My dear Frederick," he whispered. "Herr Jesus, please help my son."

———

Frederick lay again on a cot beneath the medical tent. His father had promised to return, but it was night by the time he finally did.

Friedrich removed his cap as he walked into the tent. He nodded to a few of the wounded, stopping to greet a couple of them briefly. Finally he made his way over, pulled up a stool, and sat down next to Frederick's bed. "Feeling any better?

"Not really."

"Do you know what's causing these stomach problems?"

"Nein. I've had them for a few years now. Nothing really seems to help."

"You had them back in America?"

"Not so much."

"Achso, what about in Poland? You never said anything."

Frederick shook his head. "Not this bad."

"Frederick, this war is hard on all of us, and it affects you in ways it might not affect your comrades because of your role as a Sani. You're a man of faith, and I know you're also still wrestling with your feelings about me." He leaned in and took his son's hand. "Anxiety can cause stomach problems, but I want to make sure there's nothing you're doing that might be causing your illness to become more violent."

"Like what?"

Friedrich glanced around and began speaking English in a low voice. "Please tell me you're not taking the pills they've been handing out."

"I have to."

Friedrich sat back in his chair, sighed heavily, and rubbed his temples with a thumb and two fingers. Leaning back in, he continued, "Frederick, this drug is still in experimental stages. They tested it on some of the troops in Poland and saw good results, so they handed it out en masse before sending you all into France, but they still don't know what the long-term effects are."

He knew the pain in his stomach wasn't simply being created by his anxiety, yet he resented his father for confirming what he already knew. It was not Friedrich's place...but was it the place of a chaplain? "Look, Dad, I can't keep up with my unit if I don't take it. I need to be able to do my job."

"Is this what you call doing your job?" Friedrich gestured around him at the infirmary.

"No, of course not."

"Have you prayed about it, son?"

"No, I haven't." He stared up at the dark canvas roof of the tent. "Look, I'm not ready for this kind of father-son stuff, all right?"

Friedrich nodded. "I understand." He replaced his cap and stood to his feet. "Get some rest, Frederick."

CHAPTER 29

LISOLETTE

Nantes, France

July 1940

Lisolette watched the German soldiers as they milled around outside her apartment. This subtle ritual had brought her joy ever since the young men had arrived in town.

She grasped a few locks of her wavy, dark hair and twisted them around her fingers. The boys reminded her of her father. She could still hear him singing her to sleep—in French when Mama was listening, in German when she was not.

"Lizzie," hissed her older brother Stefan, "stop staring."

She turned away from the window and rose, seating herself between Stefan and Jacques, who lived across the hall. Two other young people had also arrived, Nancy and Gaspard.

Gaspard had called the meeting. At 23, he was the oldest of those present. "They may seem peaceful now, but you know what they've done in Czechoslovakia and Poland."

"What have they done, Gaspard?" She tipped her chin up in defiance.

"They can't be trusted. We must begin to organize ourselves immediately."

"You didn't answer my question. I'd like to know what's been done in Czechoslovakia and Poland. What about Austria? A peaceful transfer of power?"

Gaspard shook his head in condescension. "Lizzie, Lizzie. You're too young to understand."

"They shot thousands in Poland," Nancy added.

Lizzie pursed her lips. "Yes, but, my father told me—"

"Your father had his biases," Gaspard snapped. He turned to the rest of the group and reiterated, "We need to begin to organize."

His voice faded into the background as she began thinking of the young soldier she'd met the other day. He'd held the door for her as she stepped out to go to the market for her mother, and had still been standing there when she'd returned. His eyes were blue, just like her father's. Blond hair. Tall. Slim. Kind.

She had no doubt that some of these Germans were not to be trusted, but as far as he was concerned, she was willing to take her chances.

They were billeted at the local school—an excellent reason to go out for fresh air. She imagined herself walking arm in arm with him, scandalizing her people by falling madly in love.

Should he leave the German army and join Gaspard's resistance? Or could he whisk her away, back to Germany with him?

"Lizzie!"

She shook herself back to reality. "Yes, Gaspard. I agree."

"You agree they are our friends?"

"*Non*, I agree they are *trying to be* our friends."

Gaspard nodded and eyed her as he continued his speech. She would probably join the resistance, but right now, she was determined to follow her heart.

As soon as Gaspard and Nancy left the apartment, she rushed to the bathroom, combed her hair, pinched her cheeks to make them rosy, and put on a little of her mother's lipstick. Then she slung a small leather bag over her shoulder and slipped out the door before anyone could stop her.

On the street, she strode casually in the direction of the local gardens. Her hair was tossed by the breeze, and she walked confidently, her brown eyes searching for the tall German boy on whom she'd set her heart. He was always around at this time, and he wouldn't be hard to find.

There they were, loafing around the pond. A few of them had unbuttoned their shirts and loosened their suspenders. They were fit and handsome, every last one of them. But him? She breathed deep and took a seat on a bench opposite the walkway from the young men. A willow tree swayed in the breeze behind her, and a fountain spouted nearby. She opened her satchel, pulled out a book, and pretended to read it.

The weather was perfect and the garden in full bloom. Colors of every kind burst around her, birds sang, and water from the fountain splashed down in a pleasant sound like rain. From behind her book, she continued examining each of the young men to see if he might be the one—then he stood. Her heart leapt with joy as he began walking toward her.

"*Bonjour*," he said, taking a seat on the other end of the bench.

"Bonjour." She placed the book in her lap.

He appeared to be thinking, probably trying to figure out what to say to her in French. Rather than reveal that she knew his native language quite well, she gave him a moment. He was quite cute, after all.

Finally, he managed, "*Comment vous-appellez vous?*"

She laughed and revealed her secret, saying in German, "*Wie formell*! My name is Lisolette. Lizzie, for short. And you are?"

He was clearly relieved. "Heinrich."

She smiled, "Freut mich, Heinrich. May I call you Henri?"

He smiled and relaxed against the bench, swinging his arm around the back. "Ja, I like that."

FREDERICK

"Heinrich, be careful, man."

It was the third night in a row Heinrich had been out with Lisolette. The blond slid down onto his bedroll and leaned against the cold stone wall. He removed his cap and smiled. "It was no big deal. We just met up with some of her friends."

As if that was better than a quiet *rendezvous*. Frederick put down his Bible. He actually appreciated that most of his comrades had been going out in the evenings because it gave him much-needed time alone. The time was worth being picked on a little—one of the boys who knew a bit of American history had even called him a *holy roller*. It was worth it. Still, he worried about Heinrich. "I know a lot of the guys like to get to know the girls in town—"

"Hey, man," Heinrich said, a bit defensively. "I told you, we've been with her friends."

"Sorry, Kamerad." He opened his mouth to say what was on his mind, but a few other Landsers clambered in and threw themselves on their bedrolls, Pieter and Klaus among them. "Hey, Heinrich." Pieter pulled his cap off, revealing his fiery hair. "What's your girlfriend's name?"

"Lisolette." The name lingered on Heinrich's tongue. "She's half German, speaks Deutsch perfectly."

Frederick rolled his eyes. He'd never seen his normally level-headed friend act like this. Pieter chuckled and elbowed Klaus. "Sounds like a match made in heaven, ja?"

Klaus sat up, gave a tug on his suspenders, and looked hopeful. "Maybe she has a friend? I'm tired of hanging out with Pieter here."

Pieter pulled Klaus into a side hug. "Sorry man, we're a match made in heaven too. Two eternal bachelors, just like Freddie but a little more fun, right Kamerad?" He shot a teasing glance at Frederick.

Frederick rolled his eyes a second time and looked back at Heinrich. "You be careful. We're not going to be here forever."

"No, we're not." Heinrich lay back on his bedroll and shut his eyes. Something in his voice was *not* reassuring.

CHAPTER 30

Stefan paced back and forth before her. "Lizzie, you're only seventeen. You don't see what's happening. Since they've been here, the value of our currency has dropped to nothing. We can barely afford bread and milk while they parade around with fine cheese and wine and—"

"Heinrich is not like them, Stefan. Just the other day, he brought us those delicious pastries."

"I don't care if he brings you the Eiffel Tower itself. He's a German."

"So are we!"

"We're not German, we're French! Father came to live *here*, remember?"

Lizzie shook her head. "He would've taken Mama back to his village if she'd been willing to go."

Stefan growled.

"It doesn't matter. Heinrich is not like those *Nazis*. The invasion broke his heart." She'd been seeing Heinrich for two weeks, and had easily broken down his guard with her young but sophisticated feminine ways. It wouldn't take much to win him completely to her side. Stefan would understand—if only he'd listen. "Perhaps you could—"

"No!"

She rose from the sofa and walked toward the door. "I will have him."
She grabbed her satchel and left before Stefan could stop her.

FREDERICK

With a heavy sigh, Frederick opened the large wooden door to the
church. He let it close behind him and walked into the nave, pausing
reverently to observe the stained glass windows and flickering candles
before the little altars along each side.

The building was quiet and empty, save for a few worshipers. His
father was likely among them. He'd seen Friedrich go in from time to
time, and now he understood why. The presence of God lingered here.
Neither he nor his father were Catholic, but the peace of this place
transcended whatever brand of worship the faithful carried in with them.

He made his way slowly up the aisle, tossing apologetic looks to worshipers who were disturbed by the sound of his hobnailed boots on the
floor. *Is it the noise itself or my uniform?*

When he reached the third row from the front, he found his father, kneeling, his brimmed cap sitting on the wooden pew beside him.
Friedrich's eyes were closed, his elbows resting on the pew in front of
him, and his folded hands partially covering his face.

Frederick removed his cap and slid into the pew next to him.

Friedrich opened his eyes and turned, a look of surprise flashing
through his eyes before his features turned stoic again. He gave Frederick
a nod.

Frederick knelt beside him and spoke as quietly as possible. "I knew I
would find you here. I—I need your advice."

Friedrich sighed, rose from his knees, and slid back into the pew. "How can I help you, Frederick?"

"Has Heinrich been to see you?"

"Once or twice."

"I'm worried about him. He's fallen in love with a local girl."

"Well, even though it's discouraged, it's not so unusual."

His father's gaze weighed on him, but Frederick wasn't ready to meet it. "I know, but he's fallen hard. I never see him anymore."

"Frederick, have you ever been in love?"

His gaze drifted from his boots up to the high ceiling of the church. "No. I haven't."

Friedrich nodded. "I thought as much. Frederick, what are you worried about? That he will have to leave her when we're removed?"

"That's part of it, but I'm more afraid that he"—Frederick returned his focus to his boots—"I'm more afraid he'll defect, Father."

"What makes you say that?"

Frederick checked around the sanctuary, relieved that the other worshipers had cleared out, though he hated knowing it was likely his fault. "I think shooting those civilians really upset him. After his injury, he lost all his resolve as a soldier. I think he's *searching* for a way out."

"Where would he go?"

"That's just it. I think this girl is involved in something."

"Have you talked to her yourself?"

"Not much. I hardly see him to begin with. He's at roll and drills and stands guard when it's his turn, but that's about it. Otherwise he's with *her.*"

Friedrich rose and straightened his tunic. "I will take care of Heinrich, son. You talk to the girl. Perhaps that will help allay your fears a bit."

An ache coursed through Frederick's stomach. He didn't want to remind his father what fraternization with a local girl had ended up costing their family. Still, he had no better ideas, so he followed his father out of the building, and together they made their way to the park where Heinrich and Lisolette often spent time together.

It was a warm, sunny midsummer's day, but Heinrich and Lisolette weren't on the bench, so they continued past the fountain into the gardens. Frederick stayed a few steps ahead in an attempt to avoid further conversation with his father.

Gunshots echoed from behind. Frederick and his father stopped, glanced at each other, and hurried back to the street where a German soldier lay writhing on the ground. Not far from him, blood pooled around the body of a young Frenchman. Two other soldiers lay wounded, while another pair stood by with Mausers drawn. Policemen raced onto the scene, shouting and forcing the gawkers back.

Frederick dropped to his knees beside the soldier and checked him over, listening in as his father questioned the nearby soldiers.

"What happened here?" When necessary, his father's voice reclaimed the sharp, authoritative edge it must've had when he'd commanded his own troops.

The boys snapped to attention and answered with the respect he was due. "Herr Pfarrer Schmidt, that Frenchman opened fire on us with an illegal weapon."

Friedrich folded his hands behind his back and stared the young man down. "You say he opened fire?"

"Jawohl, Herr Pfarrer Schmidt."

Sirens approached and an ambulance screeched to a stop. Two medics got out and began tending to the wounded soldiers. As Frederick glanced at the dead Frenchman, his eyes flashed in recognition. He had seen him briefly before and from a distance...with Heinrich and Lisolette.

Two officers walked over. Friedrich nodded to them in deference and took his place at Frederick's side.

"Father," he whispered, "that young man was the brother of Heinrich's girlfriend."

At that moment, the couple in question rounded the corner, no doubt drawn by the commotion. Frederick looked to his father for help. Friedrich nodded, and father and son headed toward the young lovers.

"Freddie, what's going on?" Heinrich asked. Frederick glanced at his father for direction, but it was too late. Lisolette had recognized her brother's body. She broke into a run, shoving a few soldiers out of her way as she fell at his side. She crumbled upon his chest, pounded the pavement, and then sat up, shooting angry glares at the men around her.

The soldiers gripped their Mausers, but no one moved. "Get this woman out of here," a Leutnant snapped.

Frederick moved forward. "I will walk her back to her apartment."

The Leutnant nodded and jerked his head to another soldier, indicating that he was to accompany Frederick and Lisolette. Heinrich moved to follow but was waylaid by Friedrich's firm grasp.

Once inside her apartment, Frederick helped Lisolette to the sofa, then looked at the comrade who still stood behind them, gripping his rifle. "I'm just going to make sure she's all right, comrade." He touched his medical belt to indicate he was on official business. The soldier nodded and backed into the hallway but took a guard's stance. *Fine. Stay.*

Frederick returned to the sofa and sat beside Lisolette. She glared at him through swollen eyes. *Lord, help me. I know I'm the enemy here.* He sighed and began, "Lisolette, I am so sorry."

She only stared at him. After a few minutes, she finally asked, "Why?"

Frederick closed his eyes and prayed again for the right words. He was thankful she spoke German. "I wasn't there when your brother was shot." He opened his eyes and directly met hers. "I came on the scene a few minutes afterward. I was told your brother drew a gun and shot a few of our men."

Lisolette narrowed her eyes. "Why would he do such a thing?"

Frederick shook his head. "I don't know." Was it a moment of hot blooded rage, or had Stefan planned this? If he had, he *must* have realized he might be killed. "Lisolette, I may wear a German uniform, but my job is always to preserve life, on every side. I want to help you." He cautiously put his hand on her forearm. "I know you're in love with my friend Heinrich. Would you be willing to let me look around your brother's room for a moment?"

"What? *Why?*"

He shrugged. "Call it a hunch. If your brother planned this, he might've left some clues as to why."

She narrowed her eyes at him again, but nodded and rose from the sofa. Leading him down the hall, she opened the door to Stefan's room. It wasn't long before they found what they were looking for. A note addressed to *Lizzie* lay on his pillow.

Lizzie grasped it and ripped it open, dropping the envelope to the floor:

My dear sister,

If you're reading this, it is because I have been killed in the line of a duty I felt I had to perform. If we are to stand against them, we must all be united. I have given myself to unite my people against them, starting with

Lisolette closed her eyes as tears fell afresh. Frederick put an arm around her and led her back to the sofa, sat her down, and took a seat next to her. After a few minutes, he reached for her again. "Lisolette, where is your mother?"

She wiped her eyes and spoke through her tears, "Mama's gone to the country to stay with my aunt. She couldn't bear it here with—"

He knew what she would've said if two sets of boots hadn't arrived in the room at that moment. He turned, not surprised to see his father and Heinrich.

Heinrich rushed to Lizzie's side, and she fell into his arms. Frederick looked at his father and grimaced.

Stefan's plan had failed.

CHAPTER 31

FREDERICK

Frederick laid his Bible down on his lap and closed his eyes as the words of Song of Solomon echoed in his mind:

Love is as strong as death.

Rather than driving Lisolette out of Heinrich's arms, Stefan's death had only driven the two fated lovers closer together.

Frederick had been questioned at length about Heinrich's whereabouts. At his suggestion of the aunt's house in the country, a team had been sent out, but the search turned up empty.

Heinrich had been looking for a way to escape the army. Lisolette had given him one. They could be anywhere.

The words did not go away. In fact, more of Solomon's words weighed on his mind, reminding him of another man who had done something foolish for love. *His father.*

Love is as strong as death...
If a man would give for love

All the wealth of his house,
It would be utterly despised.

Yes, Frederick despised him for it. He'd always believed his parents had been very much in love, and that only death had separated them. Perhaps he had been wrong…But that would mean his mother had been wrong as well.

The familiar ache rumbled in his stomach, but a knock at the door distracted him. "Smith?"

"Ja."

"Visitor. Pfarrer."

Frederick rose and pulled his suspenders over his white undershirt. Grabbing his Feldbluse and cap, he headed to the vestibule of the school building where his father waited. "Hello."

"Hello, Frederick. I figured you'd be here. It's a nice night, would you like to join me for a walk?"

Frederick shrugged. "I guess."

Friedrich held the door for him and they walked together out into the warm summer night. A few clouds obscured the stars, and a slight breeze blew. He placed his cap on his head and put his arms through his tunic, mostly to maintain his appearance. It was honestly too warm.

"Any news about Heinrich?" Friedrich asked.

"I was going to ask you the same thing."

"I don't suppose they'd let us know if they did find out anything."

Frederick shook his head. "Hey, Dad, is there somewhere we can talk privately? I mean, without my comrades around?"

"Of course, son. Would you like to go to my quarters?"

"It has been a while."

"Since Poland."

Friedrich was again billeted at a hotel. The room was nice. Not terribly fancy, but it had a sitting area and a sleeping area which could be closed off by French doors. He had a small desk and a bookshelf on which his Bible and a few prayer and theology books were stacked, along with obligatory reading material from the Wehrmacht and NSDAP. Friedrich motioned to his son to have a seat on the sofa opposite the desk and sat down, facing him. "So, what did you want to talk to me about, Frederick?"

Frederick inhaled deeply. This was the only person in the entire company who really understood him. In spite of the past, he *needed* this connection. He forced himself to look his father in the eyes. "I need you, Father. I need the friendship we had in Poland. I'm just afraid. Very afraid. It's like scar tissue, you know? Like a wound that has healed, but if something were to rip it open, it would wreck me with pain."

Friedrich leaned forward, rested his elbows on his knees and clasped his hands together. His hardened exterior always softened when the two of them were alone. "Frederick, even if you and I spend every day together for the rest of our lives, which I hope we do, you still have to find your healing in your relationship with God, not in your relationship with me. Do you understand that?"

"I guess."

"Some people have to find healing without any real resolution, yet I'm here trying to prove to you how very sorry I am. I know I did the wrong thing. I can't change the past, but I'm asking you to forgive me and to take a chance on having a relationship with me. God has provided us with this opportunity. I think we'll both live to regret it if we throw it away."

Frederick rose from his chair and walked to the window. They were on the first floor of the hotel, so the view wasn't exciting, but he could watch the people walking by. Most were Landsers, their sharp Feldgrau uniforms illuminated under the street lights. Some were in groups, others strolled casually with a lady friend, trying to feign obedience to the rules. He sighed and looked down at the windowsill.

"Frederick?" His father rose from his chair.

He couldn't stand it anymore. "Father," he said, making a dash across the room and throwing his arms around him.

FRIEDRICH

Relieved, Friedrich embraced his son, inhaling his scent and smiling broadly. For a moment, he felt like the man he'd been twenty years prior. A man who dreamed passionately and loved deeply. "My son, Frederick," he said. "I love you."

"I love you too, Father."

He was beaming. This young man was an exact imprint of what God had wanted him to be so many years ago, but he'd willfully turned away. Lost love and fallout from his poor choices had hardened him infinitely more than military discipline, and he knew it. Perhaps the kind of compassion Frederick exhibited was rare in a man, but he saw no weakling in his son. He saw someone whose strength surpassed that of any soldier or officer he'd met in over twenty years in the military. This strength came from within and yet outside of Frederick himself. It drove him to forget about himself and serve those around him to the point of exhaustion. He saw someone whose indignation against the evils of humanity made him sick at times, but also birthed in him a determination to do what was right no matter what the cost. God had worked behind the scenes, helping Hannah raise their son, and He had worked things out for good.

Releasing Frederick, he stared at him proudly, his hands still on the young man's shoulders. "I am incredibly proud to call you my son."

Frederick gave him a humble, almost embarrassed smile, and they took their seats back on the sofa. Friedrich stretched his legs, still beaming with pride at his son. Dark brown hair, worn in an undercut like so many of his comrades. Energetic yet compassionate blue eyes. A warm smile. "How has your stomach been lately?"

"Not too bad. The pains come and go, but they are nothing like they were before."

"Have you always had them?"

"At least since I arrived in Germany. That's when I first noticed."

Friedrich raised his eyebrows and nodded. Folding his hands in his lap, he looked inquisitively at his son. "You don't know what causes them?"

With a shrug, Frederick explained, "It usually starts when something's bothering me. Either I'm conflicted about something, or angry, or worried. Sometimes it just comes to me when I know something's wrong."

His father nodded again, and gave a small chuckle. "It tells you to stay off the Pervitin."

"Yup."

"We've yet to see how addictive and harmful that substance really is. I don't have to tell you that I have my reservations. I know it helps you all perform beyond your means and deal with the horrors of battle, but God wants you to be fresh and available to Him, not flying through your days in a state of euphoria." He gazed at his son with unreserved pride. "Your comrades need the real you, Frederick, and Christ working through you, even in your weakness." He pushed the foot of the small coffee table with his foot. It was a meaningless gesture but served to signal the changing of subjects. "Son, have you been baptized?"

"Pretty sure mom had me baptized as a child," he said after some thought.

"Of course." Friedrich looked more intently into his son's face. "You know, in the Bible, people were baptized as adults, as a public confession of faith."

Frederick chuckled. "Pretty sure my comrades already know I'm a Bible-thumper."

"Now there's a term I haven't heard in a while." Friedrich joined his laughter but then added, "There's a healthy respect there, though, I've seen it. Don't think you're not having an influence on them."

"I'd like to think that."

"Anyway," Friedrich continued, "if you'd like to go out into the country sometime, I would be honored to baptize you myself. I know a beautiful spot on a tributary of the Loire."

Frederick nodded. "Tomorrow afternoon." After a moment, he added, "I'd like Klaus and Pieter to be there, too. Would that be all right?"

"Of course. I'll come for you with my driver tomorrow afternoon."

CHAPTER 32

FREDERICK

"Thanks for arranging this, dad." Frederick looked through the car window at the sunny countryside. His father's longstanding service and respected position had its perks. This was meaningful, and his father had offered, so he didn't feel guilty about being driven out of the city into the countryside with two of his best friends for the afternoon.

Friedrich sat in the front seat with his driver, Erich. "It is my pleasure, son."

Seated between Frederick and Klaus, Pieter chuckled. "Freddie, why didn't you tell us that Herr Pfarrer Schmidt was your father?"

Frederick shook his head. "It's a long story, fellas."

"We've got time," Klaus said, his eyes fixed out the window.

"Ja." Frederick stuck his arm out the window and let the air stream between his fingers. "I wouldn't even know where to begin." He didn't want to make his father uncomfortable, or revisit the past on such a beautiful day.

"Sometimes families are more complicated than we want to admit," Friedrich observed. "Because of one person's selfishness, life doesn't always look like it's meant to." He removed his glasses and polished them on a cloth. Frederick detected subtle emotion clouding his face. "I think what you boys need to know is that Frederick and I were separated for a long time. When we met, we didn't know it ourselves. When the Lord wants to show you something"—he replaced his glasses and touched the chaplain's cross that hung around his neck—"He'll make sure you don't miss it."

"But, Freddie, you're American."

"*German*-American," Frederick reminded them.

Pieter raised his eyebrows and nodded, as if he finally made the connection. "Your Mutti fell in love with a German boy."

"Ja," Klaus said, running his fingers through his hair and straightening himself in the seat. "Natürlich. Who wouldn't?"

Frederick reached over and punched him playfully as Erich pulled the car to the side of the road. "We're here, Herr Pfarrer." Amusement sparkled in the driver's blue eyes and at the corners of his mouth.

It was a glorious afternoon, warm and sunny. Frederick breathed deep as he stepped out of the car. "Wow, Dad, this is really fantastic." A sandy bank stretched out into the water, which ran slowly by under some willow boughs. Some local boys fished from an old stone bridge not far from where Erich had pulled off the road. The appearance of Germans seemed to alarm the locals at first, but when it became obvious that the men had just come for a swim, they resumed fishing.

"Pieter, Klaus," Friedrich began, "I am sure it means a lot to Frederick that you've come with him today. I know he values your friendship, and that's why he chose you to witness his baptism. Frederick, son, are you ready?"

Frederick nodded, and soon he and his father were both waist-deep in the warm, gentle current.

Pieter, Klaus, and Erich removed their outer clothes and made themselves comfortable on the sandy beach, stretching their legs out and leaning their elbows back on the sand.

"Frederick Karl Smith, my son, my comrade, and my brother in Christ," he began, his voice loud enough to be heard by the soldiers on the bank and the young men fishing on the bridge. "We've come today to witness as you make a public declaration of faith in Jesus Christ, to honor and obey him by being baptized before your peers. Your devotion to him is already evident to those around you, but this act of baptism symbolizes and celebrates your identification with Lord's death, burial, and resurrection, and the washing away of your sins by His blood."

His father drew near and whispered a few words that were meant for him alone. Then Friedrich pressed his son's nose between his thumb and forefinger. With tears forming in his stony-blue eyes, he said aloud, "Buried in the likeness of the death of our Lord Jesus Christ." He guided Frederick backward into the water. As Frederick was pulled gently back up, his father concluded with the words, "Raised in the likeness of His resurrection."

Soldiers and locals cheered as Frederick pulled his father into a wet embrace. Klaus brought out his harmonica and played something that sounded like a hymn as Frederick walked back onto the shore. Pieter tossed him a towel and grinned. They didn't often show interest in his religion, but they didn't disparage him either. Their presence today meant more than he could say.

"What are you waiting for, Klausey?" Pieter rose to his feet and kicked sand toward his comrade. Klaus tossed the harmonica toward the place he'd piled his uniform, stood up, and chased Pieter into the water. Erich followed while Frederick sat next to his father on the beach. "Thanks

again, Dad. I just wish Heinrich was here. We could've done this together."

"I know, son."

Frederick picked up a stone and skipped it over the water. "I hope he
doesn't do anything stupid. Violence isn't going to do anything to help
the situation."

"He's in God's hands," Friedrich stated. "He may have plans for
Heinrich that we don't know about."

A spray of water flew across their faces and Klaus ran back up the hill,
chased by Erich and Pieter. "It's good to see that young man laugh,"
Friedrich said of his driver. "He's pretty reserved most of the time."

Frederick nodded and watched his friends as they chased each other
up and down the beach. Soon, the young men who had been fishing
appeared on the beach with a soccer ball, and they took up a game of
three on three.

"Frederick, I'm hoping to take leave in a few weeks. Why don't you
see if you can come home with me? I'd love to spend some time with you
away from all of this."

Frederick nodded and reached for his Feldbluse as a cool breeze blew
across his skin. "I'd really like that, Dad."

CHAPTER 33

It was the end of September before they were finally able to board a train headed east, towards Berlin via Paris.

Friedrich unbuttoned his tunic. "I saw a few people staring at me in the station," he chuckled. "Forgot that people occasionally mistake chaplains for SS."

"You're kidding." Frederick gave his father a funny look.

"*Nope.*"

Frederick eyed his father. "Na ja, if you were twenty years younger, they would've snapped you up, Dad."

"I like to think so..."

"Would you have gone?"

"If I had wanted in, I could've made it." Friedrich gazed out the window. "Plenty of men my age in the SS officer corps."

"Ja, I guess." Frederick would *never* have wanted in, but what gave his father pause?

Friedrich seemed to sense his question. "It demands a level of loyalty I just couldn't give."

"Because you're a Christian?"

Friedrich shrugged. "I know some men who still practice their faith. Himmler actually *requires* belief in a higher power. If that's Christ, so be it. Just keep it to yourself."

Frederick shook his head. "You can't do that."

"Nope."

<hr>

The French capitol didn't look much different than any other city they'd been in since the occupation. A somber mood hung in the air as French civilians went about their business and uniformed Germans sauntered through the streets.

The bed, on the other hand, was the softest thing he'd felt in a long time. He was actually sorry to have to leave it and continue on to Berlin.

"Too much walking. You're used to marching. I'm not." Friedrich sat down on the edge of the bed and began to massage his foot. "I hope you've enjoyed Paris."

"When you described Paris, you described an entirely different place."

"So I did." Friedrich sighed and switched feet. "Of course they resent us. I've seen the other side of the coin, Frederick too. The town I lived in with Greta was under French occupation at one time."

"So what? Tit for tat?"

Friedrich shook his head. "It's not like that...well, maybe a little." His father's mood began to take on the appearance of the French civilians outside. "You and I have talked about how difficult it is for you to understand. Here you see another facet of the German-French conflict that seems foreign to Americans. I myself couldn't understand the situation from the German point of view until I'd spent some time in Europe.

Even then, opinions were so varied—interpretations differed, and each circumstance was unique, although we all suffered."

"So you're saying it's all right for us to just come in and take over?"

"I'm not saying that at all."

Frederick pursed his lips.

"All right, son, what's on your mind?"

"I just want someone to convince me we're doing the right thing."

"Sometimes *the right thing* can't be measured. Only God sees the whole picture—that there are good deeds and evil deeds on both sides. Certainly you know of Robespierre, of whom Louis Blanc wrote: *Vanquished—his history is written by the victors.*"

"Paul Strauss said as much."

"I'm sure he did, once the Allies recanted of their propaganda campaigns." There was a hint of bitterness in his father's voice.

"You are bitter at the U.S."

"Not bitter. Grieved. And not just for the U.S." His father rose and went to stare out the giant window into the city. "What we're fighting for goes back a long way, son. A lot longer than the French occupying the Ruhr or Versailles or even Sarajevo." He paused, as if inviting his son to a response. "If you really get beyond politics, son, I think we're here because of decisions made hundreds of years ago."

Frederick chuckled. "I had to know you'd go philosophical on me."

"It's not philosophy, son. It's just me, sitting alone in my apartment, reading and thinking and praying over these things. It's me, having lived here since 1918 and having worked in both military and theological circles. It's me, having fought to reconcile my own American upbringing with my twenty-some years in Germany."

"Fair enough."

Friedrich ran a hand over his graying hair. "I know man believes he can bring about peace and harmony. That the warrior will one day disappear as we live in perfect equality, perfect unity. It doesn't sound so bad, but in reality, there will always be people out there who seek to harm women and children. Who seek to destroy the family. There will always be evil. There will always be an adversary. What if someone doesn't stand up?" Friedrich's words fell away, and he sighed. "What kind of world will we have?"

Frederick felt incredulous. "And you think these"—he waved a hand in the general direction of Berlin—"are the men to do it?"

"There are always going to be people who want to use positions of power and influence to their own advantage. They will declare that we follow age old and holy principles by which they themselves can't abide." He shook his head again. "And what of the average man like you and me, who are seeking to do the right thing?" He gazed out the window. "I can only pray that God sees our good faith."

Frederick huffed. "The only faith many people seem to have is in the Führer."

"Hitler *never* claimed to be the savior of the world. Savior of Germany, perhaps. He does not claim to be able to save their souls."

"Doesn't change the fact that they've followed him as if he does."

"Frederick, I cannot speak for anyone. I can only speak for myself, and what I see in the world beyond these borders is not the world I want. I cannot stand idly by and let it overrun my homeland."

"By your own admission, the political system or ideology is not going to save us."

Friedrich sighed with resignation. "Let's not think about it anymore, Frederick. Let's enjoy our time here in Paris. We have a long journey back to Berlin tomorrow."

Frederick closed his eyes and exhaled. *Back into the epicenter.*

———

"It isn't much," Friedrich apologized as they entered his apartment. The room was sparsely decorated with old wooden furniture and off-white walls. "It's just me here. I'm not home often, and I don't need much. There's an extra bedroom down the hall if you want to put your things in it." He pointed the way, and Frederick headed for the room. A bed in need of bedding, a small desk, a bookshelf. Not surprisingly, the shelf contained old Bibles, theology books, and war memoirs, interspersed with a few books on science, poetry, and classic novels, written in both English and German.

A series of leather-bound volumes on the bottom shelf caught his attention. He pulled one out and flipped through the pages.

Arrived in France today. How I long for Hannah. To hold her, inhale her perfume, run with her in the open fields. I have already been separated from her for too long. My fellow soldiers are little comfort, though they amuse me to no end...

Constant bombardment. Fought off a trench raid at 0300. Lost Timothy. Shame...

Friedrich's feet sounded in the hallway, drawing to a stop just outside the door. "Didn't take you long to find those."

He looked up, startled. "May I look at them?"

"Of course, if you think you'll find anything interesting in them."

"Interesting? Dad, this is amazing!" Frederick pulled a few volumes out of the stack and brought them into the Wohnzimmer, placing them on the coffee table next to a well-worn copy of *Storm of Steel*. He grinned. "If Jünger had things to say, maybe you do too."

"Na ja. Don't give me too much credit. I was a corporal, remember?"

"So? You outrank him now."

Friedrich held up a hand. "Don't spread that around."

Frederick chuckled and opened the first of his father's volumes again. It was smaller than the rest, only pocket-sized.

After the raid, Paul was returned to us with his leg split open by shrapnel. The medics were busy attending to other wounded, and I tried to stem the bleeding, wrapping his leg myself. He was screaming in pain, and I wanted to knock him out just to shut him up. Now I regret his absence. He's been my companion for twenty years.

The entries ended abruptly a few pages later.

"That was my war journal," Friedrich said, then added, "My *first* war journal. Greta kept it safe for me while I was in the hospital. She gave me a new, larger journal when I was well enough to sit up and write."

Frederick picked up the next volume and opened it.

Today, I received this as a gift from the nurse who has attended me for the last few weeks. I believe I am falling in love with her.

Frederick swallowed hard and reminded himself that these things were in the past. Still, he wasn't ready to read that particular chapter of his father's life. He reached for the third, and here, he noticed that his father had begun to write in German. It was dated a few years later.

Greta's father has secured me a spot in the Reichswehr. I would like to believe I have merited this appointment. They only accept the best candidates, and I hope it is my reputation that has preceded me, not my connections. Still, having a father-in-law in the service of a member of the General Staff means I have strong connections. All the more reason why I must prove myself, so that in the end, no one will say this has been handed to me.

"Dad, this is fascinating." Frederick flipped through further, glancing every so often to see if anything grabbed his attention.

We buried my Greta today. I could not perform the service. My throat was clenched tightly, and I could not speak. I have no love left in my heart for the Lord after He's taken the one thing I hold dear from me. Was it punishment for my sins? Perhaps. Today, I hung my pastoral garments up for the last time. I can now give my attention to becoming an officer in the Reichswehr.

Frederick closed the book and placed it on top of the stack. "Dad, these are priceless. What do you plan to do with them?"

Friedrich looked up from his book again. "I don't know, son, I really haven't thought about that."

"May I have them?"

Friedrich considered the request. "When I wrote those, I had no idea I would have any posterity to give them to. I suppose you may have them, I just ask that you keep their contents to yourself as long as I am alive."

"Of course."

Frederick pinched his lips together. He'd read about a British air raid on Berlin one month prior. "Do you think they might be in danger if they stay here in Berlin?"

"In danger?" Friedrich shrugged. "I don't think they're of any real value."

"No Dad, they are." He smiled. "If only for me. Is there a place they could be kept safe?"

"Yes, son, I think I know a place we can send them that they will be safe."

PART III

CHAPTER 34

HANNAH

Upstate New York

June 1941

Where is he?

Hannah sat bolt upright in bed, her heart pounding. Had she not just been with Frederick, only to see him stray from her into a fiery cauldron?

"Hannah?"

Paul's gentle voice greeted her. She curled into his side and tried to find comfort, but fear clung to her. "I'm so worried about Frederick."

"Of course you are."

"No, Paul, I'm *very* worried about Frederick. I feel like he's walking into danger." She trembled, and Paul pulled her close, speaking a prayer over her.

She knew God knew where Frederick was, what he needed, and what lay ahead, yet she found no comfort in the knowledge. She lay awake for another hour, alternately pushing out her fears of what could possibly be happening to her son and allowing herself to imagine the worst. She envisioned the German soldiers marching in perfect formation in the newsreels. It brought her little comfort that he was a noncombatant, and in her weakest moments, it only caused greater fear.

In the morning, she rose and pulled a letter from between the pages of her Bible. Dated back in September, it was already nine months old.

Dear Mom,

I have enjoyed two weeks leave with a dear friend, an older man who has taken me under his wing. He is the battalion chaplain, and the father I never had. This summer, he baptized me while we were stationed in France. I have included a picture from that day, which he took. Some of my comrades are with me, as well as a few younger local boys, all of whom witnessed my baptism.

I do not know what lies ahead, but I continue to feel called into God's service. When the war ends, I must explore my options—as you know, I don't have a history of faith, but at this point, I cannot imagine doing anything else with my life.

Give my regards to Paul, and thank him for standing in my stead to be sure you are loved and cared for.

All my love,

Frederick

Hannah pulled the picture out from the envelope, glanced quickly at the group and then fixed her eyes on his face. One could believe he'd grown up amongst the young men on either side of him, running barefoot over the foothills of the Alps, laughing and joking in the German language. Had he ever been hers? The two and a half years he'd been gone had stretched into an eternity. Again, she felt the breadth of a chasm she could not cross.

PAUL SIPPED HIS COFFEE and unfolded the morning newspaper. "Oh."

Hannah sat down beside him with her tea and tried to look around the paper at her husband. "Yes?"

"Germany has invaded Russia," he said simply.

She set her teacup on its saucer and gave a shaky breath, fighting back the images that had plagued her for two days. It was bad enough that no soldier should ever tell their loved ones details about where they were being sent. The only information she ever received about her son's whereabouts was from the newspaper, and with that she could only speculate at best.

CHAPTER 35

Dizzy with fatigue, Frederick marched on beside his comrades, fighting his way through exhaustion as his fellow soldiers battled the Soviets. He bandaged wounds with shaky hands and a pounding heart, and knelt over dying men, praying the few words he could manage in his exhaustion. More and more, he relied on his father's help as he felt his sanity slip from him.

Finally, a rest. He did not need to force his eyes closed—heavy as they were, they fell shut on their own as he removed his Stahlhelm and rested his head against the trunk of a tree. He sighed and reached into his medical kit. He still kept a bottle of Pervitin there, though he hadn't thought much about it since last summer. His hands shook with weariness as he held the small red, blue, and white tube in his fingers. How else could he keep up? How many of his comrades would die if he didn't?

Then he remembered lying in the hospital bed. Twice. The severe pains in his stomach—which he was prone to anyway.

I can't do it.

He sighed heavily, dumped the contents onto the ground and crushed them beneath his jackboot. *All right, God. You're gonna have to get me through this.*

Could it really be that simple?

He rested his head back on the tree again. The tingly, dazed feeling of exhaustion began to melt away as peace spread through his body like a friend resting their hand on his shoulder.

He lay down on his side and slid a hand beneath his cheek. As long as this lull in the fighting continued, he was determined to get some sleep.

———

LITHUANIA AND LATVIA. A thousand years of German heritage, heavily contested after the Great War. You can still see the German influence in the cities. I wasn't in the Freikorps but my cousin Ernst was. Boy does that man have some stories. His father's stray thoughts had come out in increasing number as they made their way through the Baltics. It was becoming real now. This church, like so many others, had been shuttered by the Soviets twenty years ago.

Frederick mounted the steps and shielded his eyes from the sun to gain a better view of the edifice. Behind him, Pieter settled down on a step and took a swig of watered-down, tepid coffee from his canteen. "What have they done to this place? It looks like it used to be beautiful."

"It still is," Frederick breathed.

The facade, once brightly painted, had faded and chipped over time. Window panes had fallen out. The steps were crumbling and the wood rotting away.

Klaus came up alongside Frederick and stuck an elbow into his comrade's side. "Feeling adventurous, Freddie?" He walked toward the large wooden doors and gave one of them a pull. "Come on," he called from inside a moment later. "Looks like they've been using it for a warehouse or something."

Frederick looked down at Pieter who had turned his face to the sky and closed his eyes, letting the warm summer sun beat against his skin. "Coming Petey?"

"Nein, you two go. I need a break."

Frederick swung the door open and walked inside. "Klaus?"

A crash came from a few yards away and he heard Klaus's voice. "I'm all right Freddie, don't worry."

Frederick rolled his eyes and ran a hand down one of the pillars, glancing around at the ornately decorated walls and ceiling. "This is really sad."

Klaus emerged from behind a pile of crates. "I think we need to get this place cleaned up so your father can have services in here. Do you think he would go for that?"

He smiled broadly. "Ja, Klaus. I do."

The door creaked open and Johann, Pieter, and a few other Landsers walked in and began inspecting the old Orthodox church that had become a Soviet warehouse.

"What are they even keeping in here?" Johann peered into one of the crates. It was unlocked, but empty. He let the top slam down with a crash, and a cloud of dust puffed into the air.

"Whatever it is, no one seems to care much about it." Pieter coughed and pulled a blue patterned handkerchief out of the pocket of his Feldbluse and held it over his mouth. "It's really dusty in here, gentlemen. Stop moving stuff around so much."

Klaus gave a few fake coughs. "Your hay fever acting up, comrade?"

Pieter picked up an abandoned glove and threw it at him.

One of the men who'd come in with Pieter climbed up on some crates and pulled a sheet down from a window. Brilliant light flooded the room, bringing color to the darkened corners and reflecting off faded gold. He climbed down, found another stack of crates, and repeated the process. More and more light shone into the sanctuary until, eventually, the entire room was illuminated with a dusty light.

Klaus pulled his own handkerchief out of one of his pockets and began to polish some of the glass on a ground-level window. "Fellas, don't you think we ought to get this place cleaned up so Herr Pfarrer Schmidt can have services here?"

Pieter nodded, still holding his handkerchief over his mouth and nose.

Johann nodded enthusiastically as well.

A throat cleared. "What have we here?" The Leutnant had appeared out of nowhere. The Landsers turned to salute, their boots snapping in unison.

"At ease," he said, glancing around the beautiful interior of the building himself. "Quite a place you boys have found."

"Herr Leutnant," Johann said nervously, "we would like permission to restore this building and use it for our religious services, sir."

The Leutnant nodded thoughtfully. "We will be stationed here for the time being, until supply lines can be established. I don't see any harm in devoting some time to this." He paused. "But it must be approved by the chain of command, as you know."

A chorus of "Jawohl" was accompanied by a ripple of curt nods.

"As for right now, however, I suggest that you begin finding your billets."

———

Under Friedrich's direction, a number of eager young Landsers came daily after drills to clear the sanctuary of old, empty crates and other things that had accumulated there. Windows were washed, and inches of dirt were scrubbed from the walls. Locals came regularly to see what was going on and offer their help.

"I've never seen so much dirt," Johann exclaimed. He wiped a wet cloth across the wooden molding of one of the interior doors, thrust the cloth into a bucket that lay at his feet, swished it around, and wrung it out, then he repeated the process.

Frederick was wiping down the door from the other side. "Ja," he said.

Their faces were filthy, but their eyes betrayed how much they loved every minute of the work. As soon as the doors and the floor around them were cleaned, they could reopen the sanctuary for worship. And since the next day was Sunday, they'd determined to finish the work before dinner. A few other soldiers worked at the far end of the sanctuary, polishing the templon, and Klaus leaned against the wall for a moment's rest, playing softly on his harmonica.

"Excuse me, bitte," a hesitant voice spoke from behind Frederick. An older Russian couple, probably in their late sixties, stood there. The man beckoned, asking if they might follow him outside.

Frederick nodded and gestured to Johann. They tossed their rags into the water and wiped their hands on their trousers before following the couple outside where a teenaged boy sat on a horse-drawn cart, holding the reins.

"My son, Evgeny," the older man said.

Frederick extended his hand to Evgeny, who grasped it firmly. "I'm Frederick. This is Johann."

Johann gave him a nod. Evgeny nodded in return, hopped down from the driver's seat and came to his father's side.

"Please, gentlemen," the older man said, gesturing to the veiled contents of the cart. Together Frederick and Johann pulled the linen sheet off of the cart, revealing a large wooden chest and golden lamp stands.

"These must have belonged to the sanctuary," Frederick breathed. His heart warmed as he reached to open the chest, revealing golden censers, cups and plates for Holy Communion, smaller candlesticks, and other sundry items. He ran his fingers over the accoutrements of worship. *Gott mit uns.* "Johann, run and get my father."

Johann obeyed, and Frederick turned to the man and his family. "You have hidden these all these years?"

The man nodded, his eyes filling with tears. "We never thought we'd be allowed to worship again," he said in broken German. The woman, too, was silently weeping. Too young to have experienced worship in a church, Evgeny looked on, mystified.

Soon, Friedrich appeared, tall and formidable in his perfectly-pressed uniform, cap, and riding boots, but he smiled and extended his hand to the family. "I am Chaplain Friedrich Schmidt," he said. "This is truly wonderful, thank you."

The older woman continued to weep, and Friedrich extended a hand to touch her shoulder. Joy sparkled in his eyes, beneath his composure. "You and your people will join us tomorrow, oder?"

She looked up at him through her tears and nodded, grasping his hand and thanking him repeatedly in Russian.

"Come, Nadia." Her husband put his own hand on her shoulder. "We must let them bring these things into the church."

———

THE NEXT MORNING, FRIEDRICH stood to the side of the altar in the sanctuary of the newly restored church, watching as soldiers and locals streamed inside, along with a number of officers of the battalion. Sunshine permeated the colorful sanctuary.

Frederick came up alongside his father. "It's time." He took his place at the side of the altar as Friedrich stepped forward and raised his hands to quiet the congregation.

"Welcome, everyone," he began. "Let's sing a hymn of praise to our God, who has given us victory over the foe and allowed us to work together to restore this house of worship."

Mouthing the words quietly, Frederick listened as the congregation sang *Ein feste Burg ist unser Gott – A mighty fortress is our God*. The locals may not have known the song, but they seemed caught up in the moment, once again able to come into the house of God and worship with their neighbors. He had also never seen so many of his comrades gathered for a worship service. Some were faithful in their attendance at field services, striving to maintain their devotion amidst the wartime difficulties. Others acknowledged God but didn't actively pursue Him. Still others didn't seem to have any interest in religion. And some adhered to Nazi doctrine as if it *were* religion, and Hitler was their savior.

Frederick smiled to himself that morning, recognizing even some of the latter group in the midst of the congregation. Perhaps they had only come out of curiosity, but it wasn't his place to judge. He was just glad to see them.

Friedrich called him forward, and together they served bread and wine to the congregation. There was no distinction between German and Slav, and Friedrich had mentioned in passing that he was willing to take the backlash if criticized. For the time being, it didn't seem necessary.

After the service, as soldier and civilian filed out the door, they greeted Frederick and his father, expressing hope that they would continue to hold services weekly, or possibly, even more often.

CHAPTER 36

FREDERICK

Klaus hefted a wash bucket onto the altar they'd set up in a grove next to the church. Frederick and a few other young men brought water, filling it almost to the brim.

A crowd of soldiers and families had gathered, and on steps of the church, Friedrich and the Catholic chaplain stood chatting. His usually serious face bore a wide grin as did the priest's, and they seemed steeped in enjoyable conversation as they made their way down the stairs to the altar.

Frederick greeted them and then took a few steps back, taking his place behind his father as had become his custom. He folded his hands behind his back and looked out over the crowd. Generations of Russian families had come with their children, none of whom had ever been baptized. At the back, a few of his comrades stood with some of the younger children on their shoulders.

It was a hot, sunny day, but the shade was pleasant. The crowd quieted as Friedrich and Father Burkhardt took their places together behind the makeshift baptismal. Friedrich gave a slight nod to the priest who said a few words of welcome, highlighting the joy of the first baptism in over twenty years. He then blessed the water of the font and appealed to the crowd to continue to renew their own faith in God. As responses in various languages rang out from amongst them, the priest nodded with satisfaction. Then he invited the children to come forward. The sunlight that filtered through the leaves of the trees cast a picturesque light on the scene as older children came on foot, followed by soldiers bearing the younger ones on their shoulders. A few young mothers approached with infants in their arms.

A smile spread across Frederick's face as he observed the uniformed men who had come forward with the children. They were not the ones he would've expected. Heinz, who had always been a little brash with Frederick, came forward carrying a little girl with curly brown hair on his shoulders. The man bent down and lifted her off, hugging her as he placed her on the ground. *Does Heinz have a daughter back home?*

As each child was brought before him, the priest sprinkled them with water and spoke of the cleansing blood of Christ. Friedrich stood beside the priest, anointing the forehead of each child with chrism oil after the sprinkling. His stony expression softened as he touched the children's foreheads with the sweet-smelling fragrance. Frederick inhaled deeply as the scent drifted on the breeze to where he stood behind his father.

Pfarrer Burkhardt said a final blessing and dismissed those in attendance, though most stayed in the cool, shady grove. A number of families had packed baskets with bread, cheese, jam, and fruit, which they spread out in the churchyard to share their picnic with the soldiers who were billeted in their homes.

Friedrich approached his son, still holding the oil. "I'm not sure you know how much your service means to the battalion, to the Lord, and to me."

Frederick shook his head. Honestly, it meant nothing. He was just doing his duty—to the army and to God.

"Take this as a symbolic gesture of the future I see in you, son." Friedrich continued:

"Every place the sole of your foot will tread upon I have given you. No man shall be able to stand before you all the days of your life. Be strong and of good courage; do not be afraid, nor be dismayed, for the LORD your God is with you wherever you go."

Shots rang out in the distance, shattering the confidence instilled by the biblical words. Soldiers jumped to their feet and ran for their rifles, which rested in pyramids near the perimeter with a few men standing guard. Frederick ran his hands over his forehead to disperse the oil and retrieved his medical belt from where he'd stashed it beneath the altar.

No one had seen the *Einsatzgruppen* roll in. An all-to-familiar trench was being dug on the outskirts of town by a few townspeople Frederick hadn't expected to show up at the baptism anyway. Local miscreants...or were they Bolsheviks? In support of the partisans? *Jews?*

Frederick had thought nothing of their absence.

The SS leader approached Hauptmann Becker and spoke a few words. Becker turned around as his men snapped to attention as one. "Men, this is Hauptsturmführer Jäger," he announced. "I know many of you had requested permission to attend special religious activities and were not aware of his unit's arrival. It is now time to return to your duties as soldiers of the Reich. At the Hauptsturmführer's request, you will assist his men with any and all tasks regarding the local population."

Frederick felt sick to his stomach, and the rest of the Hauptmann's words faded into the rushing of blood in his ears. Of course, the peace of the preceding days could not have lasted.

<hr>

WANDERING THIS CLOSE TO the edge of town was foolish. Frederick stopped abruptly as a couple of the recently-arrived SS men rounded a corner a few meters ahead.

"What's wrong, Kamerad?"

"We have to turn around, Klaus. I can't watch them do this like I did in Poland."

Klaus shook his head. "It's war, Freddie. They've gotta do what they've gotta do."

"Na ja. I can't watch."

Jäger rounded the corner at that moment. "*Gefreiter.*"

Klaus snapped to attention.

"One of my men is laid up in the nurse's station." He sized Klaus up in one glance. "I need you to take his place."

Frederick touched his friend's arm subtly and whispered, "Don't do it, man. They can't make you."

"You are under orders, soldier."

"Jawohl." Klaus saluted. "I have no weapon, sir."

"One will be provided for you."

Klaus cast his eyes briefly at Frederick before following Jäger around the corner.

Frederick swallowed and broke into a run back toward their billet, his pace only slowing as he approached the door of the isba. He burst into the wooden hut without acknowledging the couple who sat at their small table drinking tea, and threw himself onto his bedroll.

It wasn't worth asking how this could be happening. He already knew. Beauty and ugliness stood juxtaposed, intertwined in this crusade fought by Germany.

I can only pray that God sees our good faith. Was there any *good* in what was going on outside the town limits?

His Bible lay on the thin pillow the kind old woman had given him. He grasped the book and threw it against the wall.

Boot steps sounded in the isba's main room, and Friedrich appeared. "Son?" He approached his son and sat down next to him.

Frederick sat up and moved beside his father. "I thought we were doing the right thing."

Friedrich sighed and rubbed his temples between his thumb and two fingers. His hair seemed to be graying more rapidly, and the lines of sadness and worry deepened at the corners of his eyes. "We were, Frederick." He shook his head. "It doesn't mean that every decision and every order given by the leadership is right." He turned and stared out the tiny, dirty window. "Many of the men truly see this as a *holy war*. They are acting on orders. Orders they believe are going to cleanse the evil from around them."

Frederick shook his head. "By killing civilians?"

Again his father rubbed his temples. "I don't have an explanation, Frederick. And no, I don't agree. The young men come to me broken over what they've done. All I can do is offer them God's forgiveness. Help them understand that they are not the sum of their crimes."

"The SS just comes in here and stacks up bodies."

"They are suffering too, Frederick."

Frederick huffed.

"Would that I could do something to ease their suffering. Himmler can only offer them booze and diversions." Friedrich sighed. "What you do not see, Frederick, is the many millions of men who were killed in the years prior to this war—tens of millions killed off when the communist revolution took place. You yourself saw evidence when we entered Russia. In the minds of these young men, they are stopping that Red tide from reaching Europe, their homes, and their families."

"But innocent civilians?" Frederick reiterated.

Friedrich shook his head. "I cannot make this okay for you, Frederick. But I ask you—are those back home who stand against us *unwittingly* supporting something far more sinister?"

"What kind of question is that?"

"I'm afraid it's the question many of your comrades have asked themselves. It is a question I am still asking myself." He shook his head. "You saw for yourself the destruction communism brought to Russia. We just reopened a church that has been closed for twenty years."

Frederick shuddered. Friedrich put a hand on his shoulder. "Sometimes, it is not as simple as we want it to be. Do you remember when I told you I've been mistaken for a member of the SS?"

"Ja." The idea had been funny at the time. Now it was disgusting.

"When I see those young men out there in the killing fields, it reminds me that my Savior was hung on the cross between two criminals, one of whom in the end would turn to Him and accept God's grace and mercy. We too hang between crimes of two natures, both of which overstep the bounds of human decency. Our own German men have been ordered to do things no man should ever have to do. They are being led into a dark place in the name of saving civilization, and I've no doubt that God will call the men who led them there to account. I can't influence them. But when our young men need someone to extend God's forgiveness to them, I am going to be right there waiting."

237

CHAPTER 37

FREDERICK

Demyansk, Russia

February 1942

Frederick shivered and rubbed his hands together. His grey knit gloves weren't sufficient against the cold that threatened to blacken his fingers with frostbite. He pulled the collar of his greatcoat up over his bearded cheeks and bundled his head in a scarf and balaclava, but it still wasn't enough. Multiple times a day, he prayed they would be supplied with warmer hats, but to no avail.

They were encircled, trapped with five other divisions after an unsuccessful attempt on Moscow. The orders were to hold. Completely cut off from their supply lines, they were forced to rely on air drop. The two small airfields were frozen over, too slick for the planes to land.

The cold didn't stop the Russians as easily. For two weeks, the temperature lingered at nineteen degrees below zero. As soon as the bitter cold had begun to relent, the Russians had renewed their attacks.

Some units sat in the comfort of the towns within the pocket, but Frederick's unit was now stationed near the front. More were entrenched even further forward. In rotations they would come to the shelters, gather around the small stove, play cards, and sleep.

If there was a lull in the shelling, no one believed the Russians would be silent for long.

Frederick pulled his Bible out of his coat and fingered through it, hoping to get a few minutes of encouragement, but *Ivan* started up again. The moment was lost. He pocketed the Bible, rose from the bench, and pulled on his helmet on his way to the machine gun position. Pieter, Klaus, and Johann—now their number three—sat bundled in the nest.

"Hey Freddie," Klaus whispered. Pieter's eyes were fixed on the slot through which the machine gun was pointed.

"Shh!" Pieter hissed. "And put that harmonica away, Klaus. They've moved up, I can tell." Klaus obeyed, tucking the small instrument into his greatcoat.

A shell whizzed overhead and landed in the shelter Frederick had just left. He nodded to his comrades and ran back to the shelter, which had been hit dead-center. The stove had been knocked over, and two men struggled to put out the flames that threatened to engulf the entire structure. Frederick pulled his balaclava over his mouth and began to look for signs of life. Another soldier appeared, and together they began carrying survivors from the wreckage.

Machine guns chugged up and down the line as volleys of rifle fire came from the other side. He glanced at the comrade who'd helped him carry the wounded. Beneath the head wrap, beard, and Stahlhelm, he recognized a dirty, sleep-deprived face. "Josef. *Vielen Dank*. Help me make them comfortable."

"Ja." Together they knelt and began checking wounds. Frederick took the more serious injuries, and Josef bandaged those who could be treated more simply. Removing his gloves, Frederick exposed his fingers to the bitter air. If it was difficult to work with the bulky wool gloves, it was nearly impossible to work as the feeling left his fingertips. *But the injured are suffering even more.*

Fierce shivers shook their bodies. He couldn't expose their skin long enough to treat them. "These men need to get to a hospital," he finally said. "Go see if you can get help."

Josef nodded and took off at a run, leaving Frederick alone. Voices called for him from every side. He closed his eyes and sent up a silent prayer that help would come quickly, then assured them help was on the way.

More voices called for him. Bent double, he fought his way toward his comrades, vaulting into the fray and onto his knees before a soldier who'd received a chest wound and was losing blood fast.

Heinz.

"Please take this." The man gasped. With difficulty, he handed Frederick a folded piece of paper. "My daughter. Tell her Vati loves her."

Frederick shook his head. "No, man, you're going to tell her yourself."

The man feigned a laugh. They both knew the truth. "God's vengeance," he said through shallow breaths, "for what I did to other men's children."

Bullets sailed over Frederick's head as he bent down closer to his comrade. "It's not too late."

The man shook his head. "It's my fate. Just following orders. The men who gave the orders, they're the real criminals." He fixed his eyes resolutely on the sky.

Frederick felt a wave of grief wash over him, grasped the man's hand, and breathed a prayer in his heart. There were others who needed him.

THE FRONT HAD QUIETED. Frederick and his comrades were relieved, and Friedrich appeared, bundled in a heavy greatcoat with a thick collar and Russian-style fur-lined hat, to perform a memorial for the dead.

With an uncharacteristic twinkle in his eye, Friedrich approached and offered an identical hat for Frederick.

"Whoa, Dad." Frederick received it with a smile and exchanged his thin knit cap for the new prize. "Thank you."

Friedrich embraced him firmly. "I wish I could have been here to help you."

Frederick shook his head, knowing his father's constant prayers for him. "You were."

They walked side by side toward the burial place. The frozen ground had been softened by days of shelling and rising temperatures, and the men were finally able to dig graves for the fallen.

Called into God's service or not, Frederick did not envy his father the task of performing funerals.

It is an honor to die for Germany.

Sure.

Frederick had always wondered at the respect his father received from the officers of the battalion. As Friedrich worked through his memorial address, his voice grew more authoritative as it still did from time to time. He sounded more like a commander than a chaplain, though his message was inspired by heaven, not the High Command.

"For all have sinned," Friedrich declared, "and fallen short of the glory of our God. The greater the sin, the greater God's mercy toward us. Is it weakness to confess our need for mercy? By no means. Indeed, real strength comes from admitting that by ourselves we cannot do what God asks of us. Perhaps it is by real strength that we bring ourselves before Him and ask for mercy." Friedrich paused and looked at his son. "Perhaps real strength is doing what is right in the face of great evil."

Frederick prayed the men would understand the appeal his father was making. From time to time, comrades still came to him expressing remorse over their war crimes. Even if the army had been granted the right to say "No" to the SS when ordered to assist in shootings, it meant little in the field. The same young men who were afraid to pull the trigger against innocents feared reprisals from their supervisors, and more immediately, shaming from their comrades.

But who was doing the shaming? Those who had seen the Soviet crimes against their own people? Those who had seen the way Russians handled Germans who had been separated from their unit?

It was bitter out here—like nothing he'd seen in France. Not even Poland compared.

This is war.

Is this what his mother and Paul had warned him about?

Those selected to place the bodies in the ground came forward, and a trumpeter began to play. The voices of the gathered men sang, and he raised his voice along with them. *Ich hatt' einen Kameraden.*

There were no coffins available. The dead had been carefully wrapped and were placed in the earth. Friedrich lifted a shovel, sank it into the fresh dirt, and sprinkled the earth on the bodies of the fallen men.

CHAPTER 38

FREDERICK

April 1942

Winter cold gave way to spring. Runways thawed, supplies arrived, and so did the longed-for letters for many of Frederick's comrades.

A care package for Klaus.

A love letter for Johann.

Two letters from Heinz's wife...written before she'd learned he'd been killed.

Frederick sat alone on his bunk as the letters were distributed.

"Smith?"

Frederick sat up in his bunk. "Ja?"

"Letter for you." The courier chuckled. "Looks like it's been through the ringer."

He shook himself and slid off his bunk. Was it possible?

A few of his comrades looked up from their own letters in amazement as he tore open the envelope. It was dated months ago, and the writing on the outside envelope was nothing he recognized. There were a few blacked-out portions, but it was his mother's handwriting. How had she managed to get a letter to him now that the United States was fully engaged in the war?

My dear, dear Frederick,

I am taking a chance on this getting to you. A friend shared that there was a way...I could not pass up the opportunity.

I want you to know how proud I am of you...I beam with pride when I think of you over there, fulfilling your calling...I know that you are right where you need to be.

If you are able, son, I would love to have a photograph of you in your uniform. I would display it as proudly as any mother here displays her son's photo...

Paul sends his love and admiration...Praying for your safety, and longing to one day see your face again.

All my love,

Your "Mutti"

Frederick folded the letter and tucked it away, along with the fear that his mother was ashamed of him. "Klaus?"

His comrade looked up from a small package of homemade gingerbread. "Ja?"

Frederick shuddered to think how long the care package might've been waiting to be delivered. *He'll be asking for something for his stomach in a minute...* "Do you have any photos on you?"

"Natürlich." Klaus sat up and rifled through his kit, eventually pulling out a small pile of photos and handing it to Frederick.

"Danke." He hadn't bothered keeping his formal photograph, but Klaus was sure to have something suitable. He began flipping through

Klaus's stash, most of which had been taken in the Eifel or Nantes, back when soldiering life had been glorious and simple. A sad smile crept over his face as he spotted Heinrich. They both leaned against a high brick wall. Heinrich had stolen Klaus's harmonica and was making a lousy attempt to play.

This must have been before he started seeing Lisolette.

He set the memory aside and flipped through a few more pictures. *Me and dad on the Loire before my baptism.* It was a nice picture, but he still wasn't ready to explain that the man in the picture didn't just *look* like her late husband...

Flipping through a few more pictures, he found a photo of himself in the uniform Frau Pohl had so proudly cleaned and pressed for him, ready to go to the Christmas party of Sitzkrieg two years earlier. "Can I keep this?" He held the picture up to Klaus, who gave him a nod.

"Thanks, man." Frederick tucked the photo into his Bible. If his mother could get a letter sent to Germany, he had to at least try to get one back to her.

Dear Mutti,

I received your letter a few days ago. Thank you for your kind words. I admit I needed to know that you stand behind me. Enclosed is a picture from Christmas 1939. It is all I have. I wish you could see the gray-green of my uniform. It is a handsome color. We call it Feldgrau—*field gray.*

You might not want to see a picture of me now. My skin is dry and chapped from the cold, and until recently, I donned a beard—a necessity here in the Russian winter.

It is difficult to work in such conditions, when so much of my job requires my fingers to be nimble. Thankfully, things are improving now that the weather is better.

I feel a little embarrassed saying this, but along with my medical duties, I find myself being something of a therapist as well. I wish I had more wisdom to give, but I can offer a listening ear and prayer. Occasionally I encourage them to sing hymns as we sit around our bunker, along with our beloved military songs. I'm not much of a singer, but Klaus is, and he also plays a mean harmonica. One of the men in a nearby bunker has an accordion, and he visits us from time to time.

I hope this letter finds its way to you. My regards to Paul.

Love,

Frederick

FREDERICK'S UNIT REMAINED AS others were pulled from the pocket. As numbers dwindled, so did morale. It was hard enough to fight off his own misgivings—listening to the woes of his comrades made it worse.

How did his father do it?

July brought news of a new offensive, far to the south in Stalingrad. Enthusiasm awakened the sleepy division as marches blasted from the radio with renewed vigor, accompanied by glowing reports of German successes. Yet as the battle continued to rage months later, Frederick's misgivings returned, more foreboding than the foul weather that ushered in another Russian winter.

CHAPTER 39

FREDERICK

Demyansk, Russia

December 1942

By Christmas, there was still no victory at Stalingrad.

Gathering in a stone church building that was badly in need of repair, Friedrich stepped forward and began with a prayer. "Dear Lord, we think tonight of our fallen comrades, who are not here to celebrate with us. We honor their sacrifice. We also pray for those who are fighting desperately across this vast white wasteland, especially those in Stalingrad. As this battle wages on, we ask that you surround them as a shield."

His father paused. Frederick could almost hear him swallow back tears. Or was he weighing what to say next? "Lord, we confess that we have sinned and have not done what is right in Your eyes, yet you will follow us to the ends of the earth to offer forgiveness. Well, here we are, scattered across the ends of the earth. Grant us the joy of your presence, and visit our comrades on every front this Christmas. Remind us that our hope is not in our might, but in You. In the name of our Lord Jesus, Amen."

Friedrich looked out at the young men gathered in the blown-out church. "Perhaps you boys know—or perhaps you don't—that I was born in America. I was raised in the church and married young, before I made my way to Germany.

"My wife's favorite song was *Steh mir vor Augen*. It has become one of my favorites too."

Frederick smiled. *Be Thou My Vision. Of course.*

"In fact, it is almost one thousand years old, and is one of the Western World's oldest and most beloved hymns, with dozens of verses. I would like to draw your attention to a verse we don't often sing in America:

Be Thou my Battle Shield, sword for the fight
Be Thou my dignity, Thou my delight
Thou my soul's shelter, be Thou my high tower
Raise Thou me heavenward, O Power of my Power

"There are some spheres in which it is not popular to talk about God, yet out here, even atheists are driven to their knees." He paused for effect. "I believe our comrades in Stalingrad would agree. As this struggle continues—and as our own struggle continues—let us remember that our fight is not against flesh and blood, ultimately, it is a fight of the spirit. We do not fight for Germany alone, we fight for Your Kingdom, which will last forever."

A chill tingled over Frederick's shoulder. So that's why his father had hesitated.

"Tonight, faithful Christian soldiers, let us take stock of our own hearts, our own thoughts, who we worship, and what we trust to save us here in this wasteland. We all want the same thing: the best for our nation and our families. But let us not forget that our hope lies outside of time and space, even as we struggle within those boundaries."

Friedrich glanced at Frederick and continued. "Let us hold fast the confession of our faith...for He who promised is faithful."

A few heads bobbed around the room. Friedrich stepped back only slightly. "Now boys, he continued, it is Christmas Eve. Let us rejoice in the birth of our Savior, Jesus Christ."

———

IT WAS TWO MONTHS later that they received news of the surrender at Stalingrad. Friedrich held a piece of paper in his hand.

"Dad?"

"I received a letter today," Friedrich stated, "from a fellow chaplain. He must have sent it with the last group airlifted from Stalingrad."

Frederick gazed at his father's stony face. In an instant it softened, and a deep sadness spread across his eyes as he began to read aloud:

My Comrade,

When the final judgment comes, I cannot imagine it will be more fiery than the one in which we now find ourselves. The men come to me as little more than skin and bones, starving in their filthy uniforms, and ask for prayer. Repeatedly they ask what will happen to them when they die. They say when, Friedrich, when. They already believe they will not make it out alive—and I would be lying if I told them otherwise. A few come right out and pray for death to come to them quickly—the bravest among them only add that it might be honorable.

I have never seen more desperation amongst these once formidable warriors. The wounded at the hospital ask for one thing: a Bible. Even a page.

If we have been in a fiery cauldron, Friedrich, it is a purifying one. Perhaps God has pursued us all this way simply to win our wandering hearts. In our darkest hour, he continues to stand with open arms, like the father to the Prodigal Son.

I have chosen to remain with them until the very end, Friedrich. I do not believe I will see you again this side of eternity.

Your brother,

Alois

Friedrich folded the letter and tucked it back into his pocket. Frederick's fingers touched the sacred reminder on his belt buckle: *Gott mit uns.*

A volley of shots fired back and forth. Father and son rose to their feet, grabbed their helmets, and thrust themselves into the fighting outside. Through the dust and smoke, someone cried for a Sani. Frederick ran toward the voice, diving to his knees as a bullet scraped his helmet. He whirled around to find that the already-injured comrade had received the shot intended for him. With a shaking hand, he reached for his pistol, pulling it from its holster as another shot tore through the sleeve of his uniform. *No mercy for medics.* He tried in vain to locate where the shots were coming from. Could he even fire?

Even as he hesitated with his finger on the trigger, shots rang out behind him and a body dropped. He turned to see his father tucking a pistol into his belt. "Let's get this fellow to safety."

———

FREDERICK SAT IN THE bandaging station, staring blankly at his bandaged arm.

"Thank God that partisan was such a bad shot." Friedrich sat down next to him.

Thank you for saving my life...even though it meant you had to take one.

"Our unit will be removed from the pocket soon," Friedrich continued. "We've been offered leave, too. When I spoke to Hauptmann Becker, I requested that you be allowed to return to Berlin with me for a week."

Frederick felt a rush of relief flow over him. He wanted nothing more than to have a real bath and to sleep in a real bed.

After another minute's hesitation, he said simply, "Thank you for saving my life, Dad."

CHAPTER 40

FREDERICK

Berlin

March 1943

"I hope you enjoyed tonight's performance," Friedrich said, checking his appearance in the bathroom mirror.

Frederick stole a look at his father. Freshly shaved, hair slicked back with Pomade, uniform perfectly pressed—Friedrich looked young again.

*They must have made a perfect couple, him and mom...*Frederick pushed the thought out of his mind and finished adjusting his own tunic.

In spite of the constant threat of Allied bombing raids, films and concerts continued to play in Berlin, with plenty of officers and soldiers in attendance. *Along with plenty of Party members who probably don't even know there's a war going on.*

That evening, they had enjoyed pieces by Wagner, Brahms, and Beethoven and had given the Philharmonic a standing ovation with three encores.

"Would you like to walk around a bit?"

"Why not?"

They stepped out onto the street. "Dad, do you ever miss jazz?"

Friedrich sighed. "I've missed a lot of things over the years...but other things took their place."

Frederick thought about the implications of that, trying again to imagine the handsome image of his father in the mirror alongside his mother. "Do you still love my mother?"

Friedrich slowed to a standstill and looked up at the sky. It was a warm evening for that time of the year. Moonlight and stars mixed with patchy clouds. "Of course I do, Frederick," he sighed deeply, and sat down on a nearby bench. "Especially since you came into my life, I think about her all the time. And yes, I regret my choices. If you hadn't told me she had remarried, I would have already contacted her in the hopes that she would have me, and if so, I would return to the States as soon as this war is over. But a man has to accept the consequences of his decisions and move on, not imagine what could've been."

As they gazed upward at the sky, the air filled with the hum of engines. Soviet planes appeared overhead. Bombs crashed around them. Friedrich shot to his feet and grabbed Frederick's arm, dragging him toward a nearby building. They crowded inside and merged with others on a stairway that led to the basement. Friedrich didn't release his arm until they reached the bowels of the cellar. "I'm sorry," he panted, giving a sharp shake of his head.

"Sorry for what?"

"Dragging you in here like a child."

Fredrick chuckled. "It's okay, Dad." Someone lit an old oil lamp, and his eyes swept the room for injuries. "Is anyone hurt?"

People glanced at each other in the dim light. "I think we're all right, soldier."

Only then did he remember he was dressed for an evening at the Philharmonic, not combat. His medical belt lay back at his father's apartment with the rest of his gear.

The door at the top of the stairs flew open again and a hysterical woman cried, "My husband's been injured! He needs help."

Frederick and his father rose as one man and headed for the stairwell. The woman darted ahead of them, falling on her knees at her husband's side. Frederick knelt beside her and gave him a quick once-over before motioning for his father to hook one arm behind the man's knee and the other behind his back, while he did the same.

The planes approached again from the other direction—a second pass.

"Get inside!" Frederick yelled. They hefted the man between them and moved as quickly as they could toward the door. A bomb exploded nearby, shattering a lamppost and ripping pieces off the corner of the building next door. Friedrich let out a gasp as splinters of glass and metal drove into his back and side.

"Dad!" Frederick cried, attempting to slow his pace.

"Move!" His father's voice was both pained and authoritative. Together they hustled the man into the building and down the stairs, laying him in the space they'd previously occupied. Frederick moved toward his father, but Friedrich pushed him away. "Take care of your patient, Sanitäter."

Frederick nodded and turned to the man. "I have no supplies," he explained. His voice was firm but gentle. "Your leg."

"Ja. Something exploded. Got me good in the leg. Then I tripped. I think my ankle is broken."

"I need bandages," Frederick barked to the people crowded in the basement. *Bandages, and forceps, and painkillers...* Locating two castoff pieces of wood, Frederick set the ankle and wrapped it with a few strips of clothing. After making sure the gentleman was comfortable, he moved to his father, who sat on the bottom step, leaning against the cold stone wall. Friedrich's breathing was labored. Anxiety welled in Frederick's stomach. "Can you lie down?"

"Freddie, there's not much you can do until we can get to a hospital. I'll be OK."

"No, Dad. Please, let me take a look." He helped his father onto the floor and knelt before him, unbuttoning his tunic and ripping open his undershirt. The splinters had torn open scar tissue from twenty years earlier. Frederick gasped. Treating comrades—even Fritz's death—hadn't prepared him to see his father like this. Without tools, he could do little besides trying to control the bleeding. He rose to his feet and looked at the people gathered in the cellar. "Does anyone have any first aid in their apartment? Pain killers?"

"Frederick, what are you doing?" His father's voice was weak, but weighty with authority.

"I'm going to go upstairs to get some supplies."

Friedrich rose slightly and, in one motion, grasped his son's hand and pulled Frederick back to his knees. "No. This is not the time to try to be a hero. You don't know what it's like up there or if the bombers will be back."

"Dad, you need help. That other man would probably like something to numb the pain too."

"I've always believed the Lord would tell me when it's my time." He pulled Frederick closer. "Tonight is not my time."

"Dad—"

"Don't you dare make me pull rank."

Frederick felt a grin spread across his face. His father released him, and he settled down on the other side of the step.

A man scoffed from the back of the cellar. "A *Kriegspfarrer*, oder? If the only man in this building who gets hit is a man of God, I guess that tells us something, doesn't it?"

Frederick's insides burned. His jaw tightened.

"Let it go, son," Friedrich warned.

Frederick leaned back and closed his eyes, awaking suddenly to find medical workers standing above his father. Swiping away the sleep, he rose to his feet. "This man is my father. Please. I'm a member of the medical corps. Perhaps I can be of some assistance."

The men, both older with graying hair, exchanged a glance. "All right, Sanitäter," one conceded, "Help me transport him. Horst, check the other gentleman."

His partner nodded and knelt before the gentleman with the broken ankle. "Nice work," he said as he examined the makeshift splint Frederick had constructed.

<hr>

THE HOSPITAL OVERFLOWED WITH bombing victims. Frederick was put to work cleansing and bandaging wounds, removing shards of glass and metal, and offering encouragement. He worked tirelessly until a nurse bumped into him. "You have quite the bedside manner. I haven't seen you before."

"I'm actually on leave."

"And yet you're here, working hard."

He had to laugh at himself. "What else would I be doing?"

"Relaxing?" The corner of her mouth pulled up, and her eyes twinkled. "As much as one can with all these bombs falling."

"I'm headed back to the front tomorrow anyway."

She pouted a little. "That's too bad. I'm off duty tomorrow."

Frederick shook his head and turned away to examine his next patient. "How are you feeling?"

"Been better," the old man tried to quip, "I fell last night trying to get out of bed in the dark."

The man's effort demanded a response in kind. "Those Russians have some nerve running their bombing raids after bedtime." Out of the corner of his eye, Frederick saw the nurse walk away.

"You may have a good bedside manner, son, but you're terrible with the ladies."

Frederick smiled. He was right, after all. "I'm far too busy."

"A handsome soldier like you? On leave, no less?"

Frederick shook his head. "I've got my hands full."

He finished his examination and wiped his hands as another nurse approached and said, "Frederick Smith?"

"Ja?"

"Your father is asking for you. Next floor, second room on the left." She moved toward the older gentleman. "I will take over here."

Frederick gave the patient one last nod and left, taking the stairs two at a time and nearly slamming into a doctor as he rounded the corner toward his father's room. Catching his breath, he slowed and entered. "Dad?"

"Frederick." Cleaned, bandaged, and dressed in a hospital gown, his father sat up in bed.

"Dad, are you going to be all right?"

"Yes, son, of course. It's not as bad as the last time. I should be able to return to the front in a couple of weeks."

Frederick clasped his father's hand in his. He wasn't ready to lose him.

Friedrich pushed him away gently. "Frederick."

"Yes, Dad?"

"As I have been lying here, something occurred to me. Hard to believe it's never come up before. It might help you understand your comrades."

There was something ominous in his words. Frederick grew uncomfortable but grabbed a nearby chair and took a seat beside his father anyway.

"Two generations of German men have now been involved in bloody wars, and there are many like me who have been involved in both of them." He lowered his voice. "You must understand that some of these men are fighting simply so their sons will not also have to fight in a third war."

Frederick considered his father's words. Even if he hadn't come to Germany, he might have ended up being sent to fight in Europe anyway. Drafted, just as his father had been drafted into the Great War.

Instead, they served side by side. *For Germany.*

PART IV

CHAPTER 41

FREDERICK

Belorussia

June 1944

"When you cease plundering,
You will be plundered;
When you make an end of dealing treacherously,
They will deal treacherously with you."

Frederick closed his Bible and looked at the small group of men sitting around him on the grass in the center of camp. Four years ago, he might've had a different reaction to the scripture from the Book of Isaiah.

"I came into this greener than green," he chuckled. "We all come in green, but I was an American. I had no idea what Germany was fighting for when I set foot in Poland in 1939." He glanced around and bit back the words he wanted to add. *To me, the invasion felt unprovoked—I felt like an aggressor.* "I understand a little better now, but I can't help but wonder how often we've crossed the line and whether our sins haven't come back on our heads."

He laid the book down and scanned the small group of men who'd begun listening to him preach during his father's long absences. Klaus had settled down outside the circle, just inside the door of the tent they shared—but Frederick noticed when his friend turned toward him attentively.

He waved a hand to the great Russian steppe. "A lot goes on out here, things some of us would never write home about."

He saw a few nods.

What would his father say? "It's easy enough to say we're at war, but the Lord demands our fidelity—to Him, even before Germany." *Dangerous words depending on who's listening.* "Ask yourself honestly: what do you think this warning means?"

"The Bolsheviks have no God, Kamerad."

"I don't deny that."

"Didn't they teach you about the Crusades in school, *Ami*?"

Klaus piped up from beyond the circle. "All right, fellas. I think he gets your point. Did you catch his?"

"The *alter Hase's* speaking." One of them chortled.

"Old Hare"—Klaus spit—"I'm twenty five."

"Oh, my aching back..."

Klaus's dark eyes shot into the heckler. "Have you ever had to shoot down a line of women and children, Kamerad?" He snorted and continued. "Sometimes I think God allowed us to be left out here at the ends of the earth to *die* because we've turned our backs on Him."

"Hey man, speak for yourself." Someone hissed.

"I am, comrade. I've got more innocent blood on my hands than any of you jokers." Klaus rose to his feet and pulled on his boots. "Freddie, can I please talk to you?"

"Ja, Klaus." He turned to a young man he knew to be a preacher's boy. "Bart, can you finish this up?"

"Jawohl." Bart took Frederick's place as he followed Klaus out of the circle.

They passed through the tents to the perimeter of camp and sat on the edge of a broken down stone wall. "What's going on, comrade?"

Klaus stared down at the ground. "Too much has happened out here, comrade." He cursed. "I keep seeing the faces of those men, women, and children, even the POWs in my dreams. I wake up at night, still feeling my Mauser kick against my shoulder and seeing the blood run from their lips as they fall to the ground..." His voice trailed off and he grimaced in pain.

Frederick put a hand on his friend's shoulder.

"It's impossible to disobey these orders. You know, it's kind of bred into us. *We follow orders.* The other guys have all lined up and aimed their rifles. How am I going to stand there and say no?" His eyes flashed black with anger. "We went too far, Freddie. War is war. Butchery is something else." Klaus shook his head and repeated, "We went too far."

Frederick understood, but Klaus wasn't finished. "I've watched your life for years now, Freddie. You were this conflicted American kid. If anyone was going to fall apart, it should've been you. *Und doch...*"

"It's not that easy, comrade. I've wanted to turn my back a thousand times."

"And yet you didn't." Klaus shook his head. "I quit going to church *years* ago. When everything around me gave me reason not to believe, I believe now because of what I see in you."

The sentiment made him uncomfortable. What could he say? "Nothing out here is easy."

"*Absolut nichts.*"

"You ever pray, Klaus?"

"Na." He shook his head. "Seems pointless."

"It's never pointless." Frederick squeezed his shoulder. He understood the sentiment: *we all know we're doomed.* Und doch...

CHAPTER 42

"You wanted to see me, Herr Hauptmann?"

"Friedrich." Formality gave way to familiarity as Ludwig Becker rose from his desk to shake Friedrich's hand. "My old comrade. Have a seat."

The captain offered him a chair and then sat back down himself, straightening the edges of his tunic. "Friedrich, I know this is not what you want to hear, but we've received orders that our chaplains are no longer considered noncombatants."

Friedrich could not stop the grimace from spreading across his face.

Unfazed, Becker continued, "We both know the Ostfront has been difficult on our ranks. I believe the men could use your experience and wisdom on the battlefield."

"I'm not much good to them if I die," Friedrich stated.

"You were at the top of our class and commanded great respect as an officer."

"During peacetime."

"That is true." Becker sighed. "Still, I know you, Friedrich. I have no doubt you will be of value to them both as a *man of God* and a fellow soldier."

"Ludwig—"

Becker held up a hand. "Friedrich, I have orders I must obey as well, and this has come down from the OKH." He turned and reached for the rifle leaning against the wall behind him. "I hope this small token of our friendship will help make your adjustment easier."

Friedrich held out his hands and took the Mauser from the captain. He slid his hand along its smooth wood and held it to his shoulder, aiming at the far corner of the room. "It's been a while, Ludwig."

"Ja," the captain agreed. He produced an ammunition belt and cartridges. "It was mine, many years ago. I trust it will serve you well."

"Thank you, friend."

Ludwig nodded. There was slight hesitation on the Prussian's stoic face. "There is one other matter, Friedrich."

Friedrich set the butt of the gun on the floor and leaned it against the chair. "Yes, sir?"

"This is difficult for me because I still see you as a friend. Were we to speak of rank, you and I both know you would outrank me if you had not given up your authority to put on that Pfarrer's tunic." The captain stood and came around to the front of the desk, sitting back down on the edge of it and looking gravely at Friedrich. "I have tried to be very tolerant of your outspoken religious views," he continued, "however, I have been asked to see that you are reigned in. They don't want to see your words damage the morale of the men."

Friedrich inhaled deeply and prayed for wisdom. "May I speak off the record, Ludwig?"

His friend nodded.

"The men's morale might be greatly improved if their duties were not bound up with"—he sighed, still searching for words—"duties beyond what is right and proper in warfare."

"These things are not uncommon in wartime."

Friedrich nodded. Ludwig pursed his lips. "You also know that the war out here is not like the war we knew in the West."

"Yes."

"Friedrich, I respect you, and I appreciate your feelings about the brutal warfare we face out here on the steppe. You must remember what they have done to their *own* people and understand that I cannot sit idly by while they plow westward toward my wife and children. What kind of future would my unborn grandchild have if we were to allow Bolshevism to penetrate our homeland?" Ludwig shook his head, rose from the table, and strode to the window. "I will gladly give my life for that."

"My prayers are always for the wellbeing of our people, Ludwig. You know my past."

"Yes, Friedrich, I do. Still, you cannot allow your *religious convictions*, born out of an American upbringing, to cloud your understanding of the need for merciless warfare."

"A crusade."

"If that is how you would like to think of it."

"I wish I did not have to." Friedrich rose to his feet. "Ludwig, I fear for our nation, and I understand your point of view. If I had a wife and family back in Germany, my fear would be even greater. However, if we push too far, I have heard it said that by what we are doing to them, we are teaching them what it will be acceptable to do to us."

"You and I both know Ivan does not need to be *taught* brutality."

Ja. Friedrich closed his eyes and swallowed hard before slinging the Mauser over his shoulder and clicking his heels. "All the best to you, Ludwig."

The Hauptmann turned. "Until we meet again, Friedrich."

CHAPTER 43

FREDERICK

July 1944

For months, the only action they'd seen had come from partisans. Now, the Red Army itself pursued cobbled-together German units through the wilderness and sweltering heat.

More and more of Frederick's comrades fell, and the smattering of men who replaced them were old men and teenaged boys—some of whom could not even handle a gun.

Like fish taken in a cruel net
Like birds caught in a snare,
So the sons of men are snared in an evil time...

The words from Ecclesiastes could not have been more appropriate.

His father had been coming and going for months, spread too thin over hundreds of kilometers and dozens of battalions. Frederick worried his father would fall in battle as the other chaplains had, but that did not stop Friedrich. He knew his father's heart. *Serve as many as you can—for as long as you can.* Still, he longed for days gone by when they had seen each other almost daily.

Frederick took a seat by a few comrades who'd claimed a spot of soggy ground behind a fallen tree. A few boys opened their mess kits only to shut them in disappointment. The rest lay back in the leaves and tried to catch a few minutes of rest.

At any second, the quiet forest could erupt with enemy fire.

Frederick handed a few biscuits off to the boy on his left, a mere kid who'd only joined days earlier.

"Danke, Sanitäter."

The only evidence he was still a Sani was his medical belt. In France, the Red Cross insignia had been a badge of honor. Out here? It was like the Wild West.

Along with his sidearm, he now carried a Mauser.

Wild West, indeed. This was far worse.

"Name's Frederick, but most of the boys call me Freddie. Where are you from?"

"South. Bavaria. I'm Walther."

Frederick chuckled. "Bavaria. Of course."

His unit now boasted multiple Wehrmacht divisions, men from the Luftwaffe, and apparently, Hitler Youth from Bavaria.

The Wild West.

"How about you?"

Frederick chuckled. "Volksdeutsch. United States."

"That's funny."

Frederick nodded, "I'm serious, man. Ask anybody."

Walther folded his lips into a line. "I just thought you spoke one of those funny dialects from up north."

Again Frederick gave a laugh. "Well, I probably do that too. I polished my German in Sternberg."

"Where the heck is that?"

Frederick shook his head. "Never mind."

Walther took a long look at their surroundings. "You regret it?"

Frederick considered the question, fierce loyalty stirring in his heart. "Not for a minute."

Shots rang out from the forest. They grabbed their guns and dove for the ground. "Man, these Russians just don't let up." Walther hissed.

Bullets whistled overhead. Down the line, Klaus knelt at the machine gun with Johann beside him. Shells burst behind and before them. Trees crashed to the ground, and mounds of earth and leaves burst around them. Filth clouded their vision. Bullets ripped past Frederick, grazing his helmet as he crawled toward the wounded.

With every engagement there were more. More Russians. More wounded. More killed instantly.

More needing my father's prayers.

There was no time for that now.

A shell burst into splinters in his periphery. Klaus and Johann flew backward.

"No!" Frederick wrapped bandages around the man who lay before him and darted toward the machine gun position.

The memory of Fritz's final moments crashed on him as he saw Klaus and Johann's torn bodies and blood-soaked uniforms. Their stunted breathing reached his ears above the tumult. *Still alive.*

Pulling air into his lungs, he forced himself to work, fighting to save his friends though he knew there was little chance. The wounds, especially Johann's, were too severe.

"We've had it, Kamerad." Johann gasped.

Klaus shook his head faintly and panted. "We're gonna be all right."

"I'm not ready to go, man."

"I am." The gurgling of blood in Klaus's throat didn't prevent a slight laugh.

Frederick swallowed the emotions welling up in his throat. "If it's your time, Klausey, but not a moment sooner."

Klaus forced himself onto his side as Johann's breathing continued to slow. Frederick opened his mouth to speak, but Klaus raised a bloody hand to silence him. "It's my turn, Freddie."

Frederick leaned back against the fallen tree that had not provided enough protection for his friends and watched Klaus offer comfort and prayer for their dying comrade. His eyelids grew heavy as he listened to the muted conversation and the sounds of battle as they drowned into the distance. His eyes began to fall closed when a series of explosions jerked him awake. *Landmines.* Heart racing, he flew to his feet and took a few disoriented steps, only to have his foot slip from beneath him. His arms flailed and he careened backward. His head smacked the tree, and the world went black.

CHAPTER 44

He awoke and sat up, touching the sore spot where his head had hit the tree. Relieved to find no blood, he tried to collect his thoughts. What had happened? Explosions. Mines. What else?

The bodies of his two close comrades lay nearby, peaceful beneath the sunlight that danced between the leaves of the trees. A fresh wave of grief coursed through his body. Klaus and Johann were gone. Along with Pieter's disappearance a fortnight ago, not one of his original group remained.

He sighed and moved to Klaus' body, pulling the chain with Klaus's ID tag from beneath the bloody fabric. A quick snap broke the disc in two. Similarly, he reached for Johann's, and placed them in his bread bag. Klaus's pack lay beside the machine gun. He dug for Klaus's photos and pocketed them. One more look revealed his comrade's harmonica. This he placed in his pocket as well. *Something to remember you by, Klausey.* He patted his comrade's shoulder and whispered, "*Wir sehen uns.*"

Rising cautiously from the bodies, he considered the angle of the sun and which direction was most likely to connect him with a German unit.

The mines were a factor he would have to reconcile with along the way.

———

THERE WAS NO SIGN of a medical station. They had also been pushed west by the Red Army. Or had they? A faint glow shone in the distance, and for better or worse, he moved toward it.

The remains of a small village stood in a clearing. Some smoke still rose, a few embers glowed, but it was mostly still.

Except for the angry voices.

One isba was still standing, a light in its window. Around the corner, he could just make out the silhouette of a half-track.

He drew near and listened—*Germans.*

Releasing a silent breath of air, he started forward again, only to stop as he reconsidered the tenor of their conversation. *Are they rogues?*

He slipped the Mauser noiselessly off his back and clutched it to his chest, cursing himself for not picking up Klaus's machine gun. Then again, he didn't even like carrying a rifle.

Preserving life means protecting innocents.

He crept forward and peered in the window. "Dad," he breathed.

Three men in SS camouflage stood in a semicircle around his father. Beyond, a family huddled together in a corner.

Did this have something to do with his father's lengthy absences?

Frederick stiffened his jaw, lifted his Mauser and shot into the air. The captors exchanged glances, and one of them motioned with his chin to a beefy blond comrade. Frederick slipped around the corner and steadied himself, his back against the wall of the isba, clutching the Mauser. The door opened, and hobnailed boots stalked toward him. Frederick prepared himself. He would do what he could to avoid killing this man. The soldier appeared, carrying an MP40 submachine gun. Frederick spun his rifle in his hands, smacking the man square on the head with its butt.

A perfect hit. The soldier crumpled at Frederick's feet, unconscious.

Frederick removed his Y-straps and bound the man's hands tightly around a nearby fencepost. Then he retrieved his Mauser, slung it over his shoulder, and grabbed the man's MP40, praying he wouldn't have to use it. He inched back around the corner until he was close enough to hear the conversation inside. His father's voice was steady. "I will come with you. Let these go."

"Come with me? What good would that do?"

Frederick flattened himself against the wall and tried to peek in with one eye.

The officer had one comrade left.

"Certainly Reichsführer Himmler will not smile upon your murdering an officer of the Wehrmacht." His father's voice continued, calm and collected. "We have not always gotten along, the Wehrmacht and the Schutzstaffel, but do we not play for the same team?"

"*We* do," the officer asserted. "But I am not convinced that you do, *Judenhilfe.*"

This guy is off his rocker. This is what happens when you send decent young men out to do the dirty work.

Frederick turned his head the opposite direction and peered through the small, dusty window. His father had moved, positioning his body between his captors and the family. Frederick swallowed hard.

Footsteps neared. Frederick lifted his gun. The second soldier emerged, eyes locking onto the barrel of the MP40. "Inside," Frederick demanded. The man raised his hands and backed into the house.

Using the wall for cover, Frederick leaned into the room. "Put it down. Now."

The officer—tall, brown-haired, and blue-eyed—laughed. "I kill them, you kill me, what does it matter? We're all dead. The war is over."

Frederick focused his eyes sharply on the officer. "Don't tell the Führer that. Even if it ends tonight, you may yet have your own piece of land, a wife, children. Do you have them already? Are your children at home praying for their Vati to come home safely?"

"My children do not need to pray."

"Don't they?" Frederick shook his head. "Na ja. If you ever want to see them again, you need to let these go. Give your weapon to the Jew, or I will open fire on you and your *Schütze*."

The officer chuckled sardonically. "Isn't your job *saving* lives, Sanitäter?"

"That's what I'm doing. Give it to him, bitte."

The man lay his weapon down and raised his hands. Frederick nodded toward the door. "Both of you. *Raus*."

The two men exited, followed by Frederick and his father. Frederick motioned toward the halftrack. "Everybody in." Flicking the gun at the officer's underling, he added, "You. Take us west. *Schnell*."

Friedrich grinned at his son and whispered, "You are enjoying the tough guy act."

"I'd do anything to save your butt, Dad."

The driver stepped on the gas. Frederick gasped and grabbed onto the side of the vehicle. "Slow down man, this terrain is too—"

The vehicle sped up and the driver headed for a nearby cliff. Frederick looked at his father and screamed "Bail!" Together they dove into the brush and watched as the half-track careened over the cliff.

281

CHAPTER 45

FREDERICK

Frederick picked himself up off the ground and dusted off his Feldbluse, though there was little point. The thing was filthy and torn to the point of being almost unrecognizable. The entire left side of his body hurt from the impact—which had apparently happened hours earlier.

He bent down again and felt around for his weapons. In the dim morning light, he could see nothing, but he heard voices. He stopped to listen.

"My Kamerad died bravely, trying to do away with you two traitors to the Reich."

The voice of the SS officer.

Noiselessly, Frederick crept closer, staying hidden behind the brush.

"*You* are the traitor to Germany." Frederick heard pain in his father's voice. "As is every man who ordered his men to do that which was dishonorable."

There was a smack. Frederick looked up just in time to see his father fall to the ground. The officer's voice rumbled low. "Your Germany is not my Germany."

Frederick cursed inwardly. How could he have forgotten to check the man for a sidearm?

"Nein." Friedrich gasped, clutching his side.

How many beatings had his father already taken?

"I would not want your Germany. Not for all the riches in the world."

The towering SS man took another swipe at his father. Anger coursed through Frederick, and he dove toward the officer, knocking him onto the ground. The pistol flew out of the man's hand and into a tangle of weeds. He chuckled, as if the whole thing was a game, and swung Frederick back to the ground, clambering on top of him. "You have no combat experience, do you, Sanitäter."

"No. I don't." Frederick breathed a prayer though no sound came out. *Blessed be my Rock, who trains my hands for war.* He grasped the man's smock and forced him onto his back, straddling him with his legs. Still the officer cackled and thrust him back onto the ground, regaining the upper hand. "Keep praying, Sanitäter. See if God helps you."

Frederick flipped again, throwing the officer onto the ground and diving on top of him, finally pinning his wrists to the ground. He cast a glance in his father's direction. Friedrich was still dazed. Blood poured from multiple wounds on his head. The officer's hands broke free and pummeled Frederick's temple, sending him flying into the thicket. Thorns tore at his skin and clothing. As he struggled to free himself, the officer grabbed hold of his pistol and strode toward Friedrich, taking aim as he sneered, "We've no place in the Reich for people like you."

"No!" Frederick tore himself free of the thicket and broke into a run, crashing into the officer and pushing him full-speed toward the same drop-off the half-track had gone over the night before. Arms locked, they tumbled down the rocky embankment where the busted half-track had disappeared among a vast array of other wreckage. Rocks pounded into their bodies and finally their hands broke free—the officer tumbling backwards and smacking hard against the burnt-out shell of a Panzer.

Bruised and bloody, Frederick pushed himself up onto his hands and knees. He couldn't sense any injuries, though his bones hurt like he'd just crashed down a hill...which he had.

The SS officer lay a few meters away, gasping for breath but still chuckling, his eyes gleaming with one more taunt. "Well, Sanitäter, your God came to your rescue after all. I'm afraid you have me."

Frederick looked around. The Luger lay about five feet behind him.

"Go ahead, Sanitäter. Grab it. Shoot."

Frederick shook his head and rose to his feet. Slowly, carefully, he approached the man. "May I examine you?"

The officer flinched as Frederick reached out a hand.

"Please."

Reluctantly, the man relaxed. Frederick sliced open his camouflage smock and the shirt beneath it. Bloody and bruised—a stream of red trickled freely from the man's head wounds. "You hit this tank pretty hard, Kamerad," Frederick said. He continued the examination. "You are badly hurt all over. Broken bones. Lacerations. Your head appears to have gotten the worst of it." The man must've fallen harder than he'd realized—and broken Frederick's fall in doing so.

"I will not live."

Frederick inhaled. "I will do whatever I can, Kamerad. You want to see your family again."

The SS man panted. "It is an honor to die for Germany."

Frederick shook his head. "Not this way."

"How would you have me die, Sanitäter?"

"Old and full of years."

"If I had wanted that, I would not have joined the SS."

"You do care for your family, don't you?"

"Of *course* I do."

Frederick prepared a syringe. "You said your children do not pray."

"Doch. I said they do not *need* to pray."

"I am sure they are praying for their daddy to come home."

"I have no doubt." He chuckled. His countenance began to soften. "My wife is a woman of strong faith."

"Is she?"

The man nodded. "I couldn't shake it out of her no matter what I did."

"I can't imagine being out here without faith in God."

"I never said I do not believe in God." He gave a sardonic laugh. "Though I am not sure how much He cares." The officer was silent for a minute as Frederick administered the shot. Then, he gave another chuckle, lighter than the last. "You know, I used to count myself among the faithful. Grew up quite active in the church, actually."

"What happened?"

"Gave it up." The man struggled to move—to no avail. "Many of us did."

Frederick offered him a drink. "You chose National Socialism over God?"

"No." He huffed, then added, "Not at first, anyway."

"The two are not mutually exclusive?"

"No, not really."

Guess it depends on who you ask. Frederick poured some of his scarce water supply on a cloth and wiped blood from the man's face. He was handsome, with brown hair and blue eyes—just like Frederick and his father. It was hard to tell his age—he could be only a few years older than Frederick, yet the lines on his face testified to years of pain and fighting off his conscience. "What happened to the rest of your unit?"

"Can't say."

"I heard rumors about a few SS men going rogue. I'm sure that wasn't you guys, though." He wondered if the officer would take the bait.

Instead, the man changed the subject. "You never told me your name, Sanitäter."

"Frederick."

"*Freut mich*, Frederick. Name's Helmuth"—he paused abruptly—"Na ja. *Jakob*."

Frederick stopped cleansing Jakob's wounds and settled down beside him, resting his head against what was left of the tank. "I take it there's a story there?"

"Ja, there's a story."

"We've got time."

Jakob chortled. "I once composed hymns for our church."

"You are a musician?"

"I was..." Jakob's eyes grew sad.

"Is this where the name change comes in?"

He attempted to shrug, but ended up grimacing in pain instead. "Sort of. I changed. A lot of things did."

"Germany."

"Ja...that was part of it." Jakob sighed. "I didn't want to be remembered as this weakling kid, you know?"

Frederick chuckled. "Understandable."

"The name Jakob was too attached to who I *used to* be. Helmuth—now Helmuth had power, you know? And by that time, no self-respecting German wanted such a Jewish name anyway."

Frederick nodded.

Jakob waved a hand as if to dismiss the subject of his name. "As far as the Church, it didn't have much to offer me anymore, either."

"The Hitlerjugend did?"

"Jup...it wasn't all fun and games. There were some real pieces of work in my unit. I got beat up a few times"—he pursed his lips in thought—"but it taught me to be a man. Stand up for myself. Not get pushed around."

Instead you just push others around? It wasn't an appropriate time to ask such a question, though he wanted to.

"Look, Kamerad, don't think it was easy for me to give up my religion. I wanted to grow up to be a church musician." He shook his head. "Life just dealt me a lot of bad hands."

"How so?"

"My father was a drunk. Turns out he was the product of an affair. I got close to my older cousin—a preacher, no less—and he ditched me too. Like I said, I got bullied for a few years and even my wife gave me a hard time. In fact, joining the SS almost cost me my marriage." He huffed. "It may still."

"Na, man. You're going to make it."

Jakob cursed. "Fella, you've got no idea what I've done."

"Care to tell me?"

"What, like a confessional?" His lingering scorn for religion was evident.

"No. Just Kamerad to Kamerad."

Frederick followed Jakob's gaze down to his broken, bloody hands. "You know, Frederick, I was once taught that God was forgiving and merciful, but that was before all this."

"God didn't change just because we did."

Jakob's breathing was becoming more labored. The bleeding from his skull soaked through the bandages and trickled down to his filthy white undershirt. "I should've seen it coming."

"How could you?"

"It was 1934 when I learned to kill in cold blood." Jakob stared weakly into the distance. "We've all done some crazy stuff out here, but my whole life is marked by stupidity, selfishness, and violence."

Frederick slipped an arm around him. "All the more reason you've got to believe what you were taught as a kid."

Jakob drew in a shuddering breath and began to sing softly. It was a song Frederick had heard his father sing. No one else in the world seemed to know it. "How...how do you know that song?"

"The Pfarrer—" he choked. He released his head into the crook of Frederick's arms, unable to finish his sentence. A gurgling came from his throat. He stared blankly out at the broad blue sky. Gasping, he made one more attempt at speech. "Kamerad."

The gurgling was growing more pronounced.

"Ja, Jakob."

"Tell my children...their father...died singing."

Jakob's body went limp in his arms. Tears forced their way out of Frederick's eyes and down his face. *Dear God, will this war ever end?*

Minutes passed as Frederick let the tears fall. The sun peeked around the edge of the wreck and began to warm his face. He turned his eyes to the embankment. *Father!*

He slid his arm out from behind Jakob and grasped the young SS man's identification tag, snapping it and thrusting the bottom portion into his medical belt. Then he started up the embankment at a bound, grabbing the Luger as he passed it, and hefted himself up onto the plateau above.

His father's body rested peacefully on the ground. With hands trembling, Frederick felt for a pulse. It was faint but there. He sat down and pulled him into his arms. "Father?"

Friedrich's eyes opened. "Frederick," he whispered.

"I love you, Dad. You can't leave me. *Tell me you're not going to leave me.*"

"I have run my race, son."

"This is not time for religious clichés, Dad." He grasped a handful of his father's tunic tightly in his hands, as if doing so could keep him bound to earth. "We haven't had enough time. You're only in your forties. You could get married again, have more children. When this war is over we can—"

"Frederick, I told you God would tell me when it's my time." He chuckled lightly. "It's my time."

Frederick shook his head. With one hand, he reached into his medical kit, searching desperately for something that would give his father a few more hours.

"Don't." Friedrich put his hand on Frederick's cheek. "I'm just glad He gave me one more moment to look into your eyes."

Friedrich's head dropped back. A soft wind blew, like the spirit leaving the body. Where Frederick had expected a sense of desolation, peace fell all around, strange, but calming. *We will see each other again.*

He buried his father and Jakob together in a narrow grave at the top of the hill, forming one cross and placing their two caps on it. He knelt before the grave long into the evening, whispering hymns and songs of mourning.

Jakob. Friedrich.

Had they known each other?

Had that been the cause of the scene at the isba?

There is so much I still don't know about you, Dad. I'll never know now.

CHAPTER 46

Frederick lay face down in the dewy grass before his father and Jakob's grave, completely alone and unsure of exactly where he was.

They'd been in Russia, but what had seemed like constant wandering in the woods made locating their precise whereabouts impossible.

West. He could only keep pressing *west.*

He gathered what he could from the half-track and checked a few of the other vehicles for provisions, managing to procure for himself a fully-stocked pack, including a bedroll, binoculars, a second canteen, and the submachine gun he'd lifted off the burly SS man the day before...*Is that guy still tied to the fence post?*

Dear God, I hope I don't run into him out here.

With the addition of his sidearm and medical belt, he felt ready to go—although he could only resupply the medical belt with some extra bandages. He looked to the sun to determine which direction to go, and with a deep breath, made his way across the vast steppe. The sooner he found shelter in a forest, the better.

He walked all morning until he found a stream where he removed his filthy, bloodstained uniform and washed it. The thought of walking in a soaking wet uniform didn't appeal to him, but he had no other choice. He bathed with the small amount of soap he'd obtained and sat on the river bank eating a pack of dry biscuits to give his uniform as much time to dry as possible. The warm June breeze helped, but he still trudged along that afternoon feeling itchy from the damp fabric.

He occasionally saw villages outlined in the distance. Most were abandoned, cleared out, or burnt to the ground, but he wasn't ready to take chances. As night began to fall, however, he needed shelter.

Another cluster of small log houses appeared. He raised the binoculars to his face and scanned for movement. In the twilight, he made out some smoking ruins but no signs of life. If he waited until night had completely enveloped the village, he could investigate further. Perhaps he could find a place to tuck in for the night.

He leaned against a tree and whispered a prayer, although he wasn't sure what difference it would make. Even if he did manage to find lodging for one night, what were the chances he would still be alive the next night? And if he was, would he be able to find another place to rest?

The Red Army remained on both sides of his path back to Germany. Would they find him first? Or would it be the partisans? He swallowed hard and wondered if he preferred death or being taken as a prisoner of war.

A third but equally unappealing alternative came to him. He might be picked up by the *Kettenhunde* and sent to a penal battalion.

He huffed and prayed for the unlikely possibility that he'd make it back to Germany safe and sound.

After an hour, when it had grown dark enough to proceed, Frederick took a few hesitating steps. His confidence grew as he strode forward, sticking close to the tree line until he was forced to move into the clearing.

Nothing moved around him. He was surely alone. He darted behind a cart and peered over the side, examining the few standing houses left. Doors stood wide open, revealing darkness inside. Moonlight shone into one of them, as if inviting him into the safe, quiet darkness of the home.

He crept closer and stepped inside, struggling for a pack of matches he'd scrounged up that morning. With a snap, the match illuminated the small room, and he scanned as quickly as he could before the light went out. He lit another, and then a third, before finally locating what he'd been looking for: a candle. It had been knocked over along with the kitchen table in some kind of struggle, but it hadn't broken.

Without lighting another match, he approached the table and bent down, groping in the darkness until he felt the hard wax of the candlestick and the iron holder with the tips of his fingers. He stood it up and lit one final match, illuminating the room instantly with a faint, warm glow. He righted a chair and set the candle on it, then hefted the table up onto its four legs. One of them was cracked, but it hadn't broken off, so he shored it up against the wall and straightened the weakened leg.

It was then that he heard a slight moan from the corner of the room.

His heart began to race. Hardened through five years of war, hearing shells explode on all sides of him, the roar of tanks, and the constant drill of machine guns, he couldn't believe such a small noise could chill his blood. Slowly, he turned around, afraid to breathe. Another soft moan drifted from the corner. A small form, no bigger than a child, lay under a filthy wool blanket.

As his eyes gradually adjusted, he saw a mess of dark hair at the top where the blanket ended. His heartbeat slowed a little as he approached.

The form twisted slowly and a small, dirty, but strangely beautiful face appeared from beneath the mass of curls. Dark eyes cracked open, then shot fully wide in terror. The little body darted like a cat farther into the corner, pulling its knees up into a fetal position, and grasping the blanket tighter to its chest, trembling frantically.

A terrified little girl glared at him from behind the blanket. Filthy and thin, she could not have been more than eight years old. Slowly, he raised his hands and took a step backward, but her pleas for mercy did not stop. How old was she? What was she doing here? Who would leave a little girl in a burnt-out village all alone?

As he took another step backwards, his leg knocked the table and sent it crashing to the floor. Setting the candle on the chair had been a good move. It flickered but continued to burn securely a few feet away.

He held up his hands again and gave her an embarrassed smile. *If this doesn't show her I'm harmless, nothing will.*

He slid to the floor and pressed his back against the fallen table. Maybe, if he just stayed here for a few minutes, she would settle down. Again, he wondered who would leave a child in an abandoned village. Where had everyone gone?

Frederick and the girl sat uncomfortably in their respective positions for long enough that her body visibly relaxed. He straightened his legs and folded his hands in his lap, but he made no move toward her, and she made no move toward him. Eventually, they both drifted off to sleep.

CHAPTER 47

FREDERICK

Soft footsteps woke him the next morning. The little girl stood over him, holding a heavy-bottomed iron pan with both hands, poised to whip him in the head with it. He dove out of the way just as the blow came, and the pan hit the table, further damaging the wood. The impact sent the girl flying backward into the crude wooden wall of the kitchen. She slumped to the ground and cried.

Instinctively, he inched forward, but then stopped, unsure whether she would sense another threat. Once again, he raised his hands, palms facing her, and greeted her with a gentle, "Hey."

She stared at him through a mass of wet, tangled black curls. With one hand, he reached down to his medical bag and pulled out the Red Cross armband that he'd tucked away some time ago. He unfolded it and held it out for her to examine, hoping she'd recognize the Red Cross as a sign of peace.

She eyed him cautiously, then reached out her small hand. He placed the armband in her palm, and she smiled. Gauging her reaction, he scooted closer until he was kneeling directly beside her. She leaned forward, and he examined the back of her head, touching her with gentle fingers. A goose egg, nothing more. If only there were an ice box or something with which he could reduce the swelling. Instead, he could only check her pupils and remain vigilant.

He helped her up and guided her back to the bed, easing her gently onto it in a sitting position and covering her legs with the musty blanket. She made a face and pointed to her throat. *She's thirsty.* He looked around until he found a bucket and then headed out the door in search of a stream or well.

In the daylight, Frederick could see the extent of the damage that had been done to the village. At the far end lay the remains of a building that had completely burned to the ground. A few homes had suffered the same fate.

A few sets of hobnailed boot prints were easily visible in the mud. Was this the work of Jakob and company? Or a legitimate unit in retreat? Or by the Russians themselves?

Did it matter? The girl was waiting, parched. Any attempts at investigation would have to wait.

When he arrived at the stream's edge, he plunged the bucket below the surface. If helping this child could make up for some of the evil that had been done to her village, he would do everything he could.

Returning to the one-room house, he knelt beside her on the floor and checked the back of her head again. The swelling seemed to be reducing on its own, and she smiled at him. He smiled back and wondered how she had possibly managed to survive whatever had happened. She was dirty but uninjured, except for the bump she'd acquired that morning.

Frederick's stomach growled, reminding him that he hadn't eaten anything since the day before. He scanned the room, then turned back to her and patted his stomach. He felt guilty asking her for food, but he figured she was probably hungry herself. Perhaps there was some grain or some potatoes in the house. If possible, he would save his remaining biscuits for the road.

The girl pointed to a small room off the kitchen area and said something. He couldn't understand her words, but her intention was clear. He obeyed and, after poking around, managed to find a few potatoes. There was a small place for a fire and an iron pot in which he boiled some of the water he'd brought from the stream. He dropped the potatoes in the water and hoped for the best. "I'm not much of a cook," he explained.

She smiled again, and he relaxed.

While they waited for the potatoes, he sat nearby and gestured to himself. "Frederick."

She sat up taller on the bed. Pointing to herself, she said, "Mischa."

He grinned...But what was he going to do with *Mischa*? He couldn't leave her there, and he couldn't possibly take her with him...Could he? It was dangerous enough for a lone German soldier traveling through Soviet forests. What would they do to him if they found him with one of their own?

What would they do to *her*?

"Frederick?"

He realized she was staring at him with a curious look on her face. "Ja?"

She pointed to the pot that was boiling away on the fire.

"Oh." He hurried over and grabbed the dipper hanging next to the fire. Pulling the potatoes out was challenging, but he managed to collect them and place them in a couple of small wooden dishes. She laughed at him when he tried to pick up the still-hot potato with his hands and dropped it immediately.

His heart warmed. He wouldn't leave her here alone, yet he certainly couldn't stay here. There was only one answer.

He spent the rest of the morning and early afternoon planning his next steps while cleaning up the house and the little girl who lived in it. After finding a clean dress for her in a trunk, he gathered more water from the stream, warmed it on the stove, and poured it into a basin, leaving the room so she'd have a few minutes to bathe. When he returned, he tried in vain to pull his own comb through her thick, dark curls. She laughed at him and pointed to a small shelf above the bed where he found what must have been her mother's comb. It was much better suited to untangling her long, thick, wet hair.

He decided it would be best if he replaced his uniform with civilian clothes before continuing his journey west. Returning to the trunk, he found a man's shirt and coat. Perhaps they had belonged to her father? He grasped them and pulled them close to his chest, gesturing to ask whether he might don her father's things.

She paused, then nodded. Did she have any idea what he was plotting? How easy would it be to convince her to come?

He couldn't worry about that now. He would rise early tomorrow, dress for his departure, and insist she come along. It was all he could do. He tried not to think about whether either of them would make it back safely to Germany.

Frederick and Mischa spent the rest of the day in relative silence. They ate a few more potatoes and some grain that he discovered next to the potatoes. He laid out his bedroll and found another blanket that was less disgusting than the one she'd been using, gave it to her, and took the filthy blanket for himself. He would tie both blankets up and pack them for the journey tomorrow morning, along with the rest of the grain and the few remaining potatoes that were stored at the house.

He briefly considered whether he should check some of the other houses for provisions. No. He didn't want to risk her following him and reliving the horror she'd already been through.

As darkness fell, he sat on his bedroll, back against the wall, arms clutching his knees close to his chest. Mischa played with a little hand-sewn doll. He wished more than ever that he could speak to her.

Rising from his place on the floor, he strode over to her and took her arm gently. "Mischa?"

She stopped talking to the doll and looked at him with her big, dark eyes. "Frederick?"

He prayed silently that she would understand him and pointed to his things that were already packed by the door. "Tomorrow morning, I'm going to *go.*" He pointed in the direction of Germany. "I want you"—he pointed to her, then to himself, and then back to the door again—"to come with me."

She looked from him to the door, then back to him. "With—you." Then she did something that surprised him. She pulled her doll close and snuggled into his side, a hint of a smile forming at the corners of her mouth. "Frederick."

Warmth burgeoned in his chest. He was determined to bring her safely to Germany...if Germany was even safe anymore. Certainly it was safer than living alone in a burned-out village in Belarus. If indeed that's where they were.

Frederick lay awake long after Mischa fell asleep. With his tunic draped over his shoulders, he reviewed his plans, alternating prayer with rumi-nations. He truly did not know what to expect when he returned to

Germany. Every time someone had returned to the front from leave, their reports had grown a little dimmer—a little more hopeless. Jakob had said it himself, but no one in the high command would ever admit that the war was already lost.

He contemplated the men he'd interacted with over the years. If others commended him for going above and beyond the call of duty, he felt like he hadn't done enough. Hadn't worked fast enough to save a comrade. Hadn't been honest enough about his faith...

Or maybe he'd been too honest.

Regardless, he began to sing. He didn't feel his voice grow louder, but Mischa stirred on her bed. "Frederick," she whispered, smiling.

He was relieved when she rolled over and went back to sleep, still clutching her doll. He removed his Feldbluse, blew out the candle, and lay down, pulling the musty blanket as far up on his chest as he could bear.

If God had protected him from enemy fire all these years, was it so hard to believe that He would deliver them safely to Germany, and provide for them no matter what they found there?

CHAPTER 48

Sunlight filtered into the home through the small window in the kitchen. Birds sang as if all was right in the world. Frederick sat up quickly and rubbed his jawline.

He hadn't shaved in days. With the exception of the harsh Russian winters, he'd always tried to maintain a clean appearance, as the rest of the boys did, and he chafed at the stubble that was becoming thick on his jawline. He considered shaving with the little water that remained from the night before, but a beard might provide a little more protection from suspicion as he traveled through the Russian-controlled countryside.

He changed into Mischa's father's clothes and carefully folded his uniform, burying it deep in his pack. If he managed to reconnect with a German unit, he'd be required to fall back into the ranks. What would happen to Mischa then?

He'd have to make sure he delivered her to safety first.

He strode over to her bed, sat down beside her, and whispered her name. Nothing. A strange instinct moved him to stroke her cheek. When he did, she stirred and smiled. "Frederick." She seemed to love repeating his name. He internally whispered another prayer that he could get her to safety. She was beautiful and not altogether unlike him, except her dark eyes. She could easily pass for his daughter. Somehow, in spite of their language barrier, anyone they encountered would hopefully see them as such.

"It's time to *go*," he said, with an emphasis on the word "go" because she seemed to have understood yesterday when he gestured toward the door. Half asleep, she rose to a sitting position and swung her legs over the side of the raised wooden platform covered with straw.

He gave her some grain and a cup of water, then looked around the house to be sure there was nothing else they should bring on their journey. He gathered her doll from the bed and folded the tangled blanket along with the musty one he'd slept under.

When she finished eating, he motioned for her to put on her pants and helped her with her boots. He shouldered the pack of supplies and opened the door. Sunlight flooded the house, and they stepped out into it.

Mischa looked around and started to tremble. She threw her arms around Frederick's waist and pushed her face into his side. He gently loosened her arms so he could kneel down before her. "I'm so sorry, Mischa." He wrapped his arms around her. "You're safe now. I won't let them hurt you."

He let her cry a bit longer and then picked her up and carried her out of the clearing into the woods. He was not only eager to begin his journey home, he was eager to get her away from whatever memories the village held for her.

They walked throughout the day and into the evening before finding an appropriate spot to rest for the night. It was little more than a hole in the ground, but a fallen tree sheltered it.

He didn't start a fire, despite the growing chill, for fear of it drawing attention from scouts or nearby troops. Either army might cause trouble for him—even his own. He unpacked his bedroll and the two blankets, putting the musty one down first, between them and the ground. He gave her his bedroll and wrapped himself up in the other blanket.

In the night, she snuggled into his side, waking him from a deep sleep. It was all so strange. Just days ago, he'd been in the heat of battle with men fighting and dying all around him, guns bursting and shells crashing as he crawled from one broken body to the next. Now he was here in the dark, quiet woods somewhere between Russia and Germany with a tiny child snuggled into his side. *A girl, of all things.* He was surprised at how quickly she had attached herself to him, a man who had first appeared in her kitchen wearing the uniform of an enemy.

He put his arm around her little body and whispered a prayer before settling back to sleep.

By the fourth morning, the grain and biscuits had disappeared. Frederick had grown used to a meager food supply, and Mischa didn't eat much, but when she did complain of hunger, it never seemed to be enough.

After finishing the last of the raw potatoes, they resumed their trek. Frederick tried to steer clear of routes that might have been used by the armies, though they occasionally came across evidence of skirmishes.

Around noon, he heard a snap behind him. Gunshots rang out. He grabbed Mischa and dove behind a large rock. "Stay here," he snapped, gripping the MP40.

He peered around the rock. In a cluster of trees, eyes watched from beneath two pea-dot-camouflaged helmets. Maybe taking off his uniform hadn't been such a good idea. At least, if he'd been in uniform, they might've asked questions before opening fire.

He eased back behind the rock, his heart racing. Mischa cowered at the base of the rock. *God just help me get her to safety.* With a deep breath, he raised his MP40 and slipped far enough to fire off a few rounds in their direction. Shrinking back, he gasped for breath as their weapons responded, bullets ricocheting off their shelter.

The guns fell silent. He checked again, ready for any movement. Shots exploded from the opposite direction, and one of the SS men slumped to the ground. His comrade peeked out from behind the tree, and Frederick took his chance. A moment later, the second man fell, but now Frederick was even more worried.

He moved cautiously to the other side of Mischa, who was curled up in a ball, crying softly. He tried to see if he could determine where the shots had come from. Two young men emerged from another cluster of trees wearing red and white armbands over German camouflage. One of them had a beat-up submachine gun, the other a Mauser.

Armia Krajowa. Had they really made it to Poland? He prayed and placed his MP40 on the ground, raising his hands in the air. The two men approached. One patted Frederick down, finding his sidearm and setting it on the ground next to the MP40. The other one pushed past Frederick and knelt down before Mischa, who continued to cry. He addressed her in Polish, then Russian. The two communicated briefly, and the young man yelled to his comrade. Then he questioned Mischa again. Glancing in confusion at Frederick, he spoke in broken German. "She says you are her father and you only speak German."

A shock swept through Frederick. She was lying to protect him! Shaking himself out of his shock, he nodded.

The young man spoke in halting German. "I am sorry. We must be careful. No one is to be trusted. I am Jan." He nodded to his comrade. "That is Andrzej."

Frederick nodded at each in turn.

Jan barked to Andrzej and gestured in the direction of the two dead SS men. Andrzej took off, returning shortly with their weapons. "We have to leave. Now. In case there are any more."

CHAPTER 49

FREDERICK

With Andrzej bringing up the rear, Jan led the way to a field about a half kilometer away, where they'd hidden a beat-up car that looked as though it had also been stolen from the Germans. Frederick didn't know much about the Polish resistance, but this pair of homegrown soldiers clearly had some experience.

Jan allowed Frederick and Mischa to get in the backseat before slipping into the driver's seat of the cabriolet. Andrzej tucked the pilfered weapons in before vaulting over the side into the passenger seat.

Experienced soldiers—not very good drivers. Frederick found himself gripping the side of the car with one arm and Mischa with the other. Neither young man could possibly be his age—they were boys in comparison, just like the greenhorns the army had been sending over for almost a year.

They were both tall and clean-shaven—if they could even grow facial hair yet. Jan was muscular with hair so dark it was almost black, and Andrzej was slimmer with lighter, longer hair. They laughed and joked in Polish as if they'd forgotten their passengers.

Jan parked the car at the back corner of a piece of property with a cottage and a few small out buildings, threw blankets over the car, and led the way toward the house. Andrzej brought up the rear as his brother burst in ahead of them, announcing something akin to "Mama, we've got company."

An older woman came out, wiping her hands on her apron. "Jan," she scolded. Then her eyes lighted on Mischa. "*Kto to jest?*" She placed her hands on Mischa's small shoulders. A few more words of explanation were exchanged, and then the woman greeted Frederick. He smiled and nodded, wishing he could understand and be understood. The few Polish words he'd learned in 1939 had not stayed long in his memory.

It didn't take long for Jan and Andrzej's mother to get Mischa into the bathtub. Four days in the woods had returned the girl to the same condition she'd been in when Frederick had first laid eyes on her—though a little less fearful.

Jan and Andrzej sat with Frederick in the yard. Andrzej's German was slightly better than Jan's, and he began asking questions. "Your daughter speaks Russian, but you speak German. Where were you two coming from anyway? It is dangerous to be in the woods like that."

Frederick ran his fingers through his hair, considering his options and thankful Andrzej had not asked *why* Mischa spoke Russian and he spoke German. "I am not Mischa's birth father," he said at length. "She was orphaned in a German attack in Belorussia. I came to her village and found her alone. I could not leave her there."

Andrzej glanced at Jan, who pursed his lips, and then said pointedly, "You are German yourself then."

Frederick could only nod. It was the truth.

"How are we to know you are not using her as a sort of—human shield?"

Frederick raised his arms in innocence. "I guess you can't."

The brothers exchanged looks again. "Our sister was mistreated by a German in 1939. I suppose we don't have to tell you what happened to him." Jan fingered the pistol that he still concealed beneath his armpit.

Frederick understood. Mustering all his courage, he said, "Do with me what seems right. But please take care of the girl."

Mischa burst out of the house at that moment, freshly washed and dressed in a loose white dress that fell just below her knees. She ran to him and climbed on his lap as if she'd known him for her entire life. Grasping the skirt's fabric with her hands, she lifted it as if to say, "Look!"

He raised his eyebrows kindly and smiled. "*Schön.*"

"Schön," she repeated, practicing the word. The love between them was genuine. He hoped Jan and Andrzej could see that.

A young woman arrived behind Mischa. She was slightly plump, with joyful eyes, a beautiful smile, and long, dark hair pulled back into a braid.

"Ah, my sister." Jan eyed Frederick before continuing, "She was out when we arrived home earlier. Krystyna, this is Frederick."

The woman smiled, curtsied, and began speaking in near-perfect German. "Your daughter is beautiful."

Frederick smiled in relief. Jan immediately began jabbering to his sister in Polish. She nodded as he spoke, stealing curious glances at Frederick. He felt self-conscious under her stare, embarrassed when their eyes met, and grateful for the excuse to turn his attention toward the little girl in his lap.

When Jan quieted down, Krystyna turned back to Frederick and began speaking in German. "You are kind, and very brave."

He smiled weakly, looking up at her, outlined against the summer sun. *Beautiful...*

She turned back to Jan and began instructing him, gesturing to a hayloft above the barn where they'd stashed the car. Frederick's eyes followed her as she turned and headed back to the house. Why had he never taken the time to notice a woman before? Especially as so many of his comrades were veritably preoccupied with them? Krystyna had captivated him instantly. The warmth in his heart could only be identified in one way: *This is love.*

It brought the realization that he hadn't had an opportunity to bathe yet. He tapped on Mischa's knee, rose to his feet, and set her down in his place. "I'll be back. I promise."

Entering the house, he found Krystyna in the kitchen, beginning to prepare supper. This was about to be the most awkward conversation of his life. "Excuse me."

"Yes, Frederick?" She turned and again he averted his eyes when they lighted on hers. She giggled a little. "Would you like to bathe as well?"

"Ja, bitte."

"I will prepare it for you," she said. "Wait here a moment."

While she was gone, he retrieved a razor from his pack. He pushed his uniform down farther into the bag, making sure it stayed hidden beneath the other items he'd brought along. Krystyna returned shortly and said, "I have laid out a towel and some of Jan's clothes for you."

"Danke," was all he could manage.

He bathed, shaved, and put on the clean clothes, but it did nothing for his confidence about meeting Krystyna again.

THE ATMOSPHERE AT THE evening meal was warmer than he'd expected. Jan and Andrzej seemed satisfied enough with his explanation of how he came to be in the woods. Perhaps his battle with the SS was enough to prove he wasn't an enemy.

Krystyna spoke to Mischa, and then explained that the girl was seven years old. Mischa believed her father had sent Frederick to rescue her. "She believes you are her *guardian angel*."

With those words, Krystyna's eyes lingered on Frederick. Approval melted into warm curiosity, accented by a shy smile. He tried to return it, but could only succeed in glancing away again and excusing himself shortly after dinner. *Mischa is a child and has been walking for four days. She needs to rest.*

They rose and made their way to the door. Krystyna followed. "Please, let me know if you need anything."

This time, when their eyes met, he forced himself to hold her gaze until she turned away, giggling softly and retreating into the kitchen.

He lay awake long into the night, wishing he could be near her. He wanted to hear her voice and stare into her joyful eyes.

Then a thought pierced through his joy, reminding him he was *indeed* still part of the German Army. If he were discovered here, they would assume he'd deserted. He turned and tugged the blanket over his shoulders. Was there really any chance of them finding him?

He couldn't think like that. He had accomplished his goal of bringing Mischa to safety. Now, loyalty bade him to return to Germany, even if it meant fighting a losing battle.

In the dim moonlight, he could just see Mischa's face. She was close enough that he could reach out and curl a lock of her hair around his finger. He loved her. He loved Krystyna too. He closed his eyes and envisioned the three of them as a family, skipping stones across a stream, holding hands, praying together around a well-laden holiday table.

The thought was more than he could bear. His stomach folded, and tears formed at the corners of his eyes. Such things were not meant to be. Not yet, anyway.

Still, could he wait a few more days before returning to Germany if it meant earning Krystyna's trust?

He twisted Mischa's hair around his finger one more time before releasing the strand and pulling his hand underneath the blanket. *Lord, give me wisdom.*

CHAPTER 50

FREDERICK
Poland
August 1944

A few days after his arrival, Jan and Andrzej disappeared inexplicably. It was all right. The less he knew about their whereabouts the better. He'd be an enemy again in a few days.

For the time being, their absence gave him greater access to Krystyna. Whether it meant helping her wash dishes or gather eggs, he found a way to be in her presence—usually with Mischa in tow, though he longed for a few moments in which they could be completely alone. He *had* to tell her the truth.

With Mischa curled up asleep under a tree, Frederick looked at Krystyna. *Finally.* "Would you like to go for a walk?"

"Where?"

He honestly didn't know. He wasn't keen on leaving the property. Not yet. "I—I don't know. I just want to take a walk with you. Talk a little."

She smiled and set down the basket in which she'd been gathering laundry from the line. "Ja, Frederick. I will walk with you. There is a stream not far from here. We can talk there."

The stream lay at the far end of a field, in full view of the house. Frederick was relieved—he was chivalrous, but also human and in love for the first time.

They sat down on the bank and dipped their feet in the water. Could they communicate well enough to have such a serious conversation without her becoming either terrified or angry, or both?

"There is something I need to tell you," he began. *Ugh. Anyone who hears those words knows that whatever follows can't be good.* Indeed, when she looked at him, her eyes evidenced both curiosity and concern.

"Krystyna, you know I came from Germany, but in truth, I am American. I was born there. I came to Germany in 1938." He glanced back toward the house where Mischa still slept peacefully under a tree. *This is going to be the hard part.* "I was—I am—a medic in the German Army." He cast his eyes onto the ground, expecting her to gasp or find a stick big enough to hit him with before she ran away screaming. When nothing happened, he peered up cautiously. Her brown eyes stared into him, begging him to go on.

"I volunteered before the war ever got started. I thought it would be fun, you know? *Adventure.*" He pressed his lips together. "As a medic, I've seen many men die, but I've never killed anyone until days ago when the SS were shooting at Mischa and me." He shook his head. "I was too afraid to tell your brothers."

KRYSTYNA

Frederick was wonderful, inside and out. His words surprised her, but they didn't anger her. He was just some American kid who'd gotten caught up in something he'd never imagined, and currently, he was dying inside, afraid of what she thought of him.

He needn't be. From the moment she'd laid eyes on him, even in his soiled clothes, with unkempt hair and a bearded face, she'd known there was something special about him. The fact that he'd arrived on their property because he was trying to bring an orphan to safety said all she needed to know about his character. At the very least, it was enough to make her want to get to know him more.

Then he'd bathed and shaved.

She could not deny the ingrained hatred her people had for the Germans. There had been atrocities on both sides—her people were not guiltless. The Germans had come in and dealt with Polish transgressions with transgressions of their own.

She had been a victim of one of those excesses.

In response, her brothers, little more than boys at the time, had joined the Home Army almost immediately.

"Krystyna." Frederick placed a hand on hers, drawing her back to the present. "I'm sorry. I—I can't stay. I have to return to the army."

She swallowed hard. Of course he had to return. "What about Mischa?"

"That is what I wanted to talk to you about. She would have starved to death in that village. Perhaps she would have tried to make it to a neighboring village on her own, but I don't want to think about what might have happened to her on the way. I had to take her myself."

"She sees you as a gift from her father."

He nodded. "You told me." He ran his fingers through his hair. "I will come back for her. I will find a way."

She shook her head. "You can't promise such a thing."

"I know." He looked at her, a question obvious in his eyes.

"You want me to care for her, don't you?"

"Ja…" He shifted toward her and took her hands in his. "I hope to come back to you as well."

She couldn't help but smile. "Is that what you call a proposal?"

"Would you like it to be?"

Reality hit. She shook her head. Her voice became serious. "You will need to talk to my father."

Frederick released her hands and looked back toward the stream. "I will say nothing now. I will come back after I've finished serving."

She could not allow herself to hope. But, she could do the thing placed in front of her in the hopes that, somehow, it might truly bring him back to her. "I will take care of Mischa."

Frederick nodded, satisfied. He pulled a slip of paper from his pocket and pressed it into Krystyna's palm. "These are addresses. My Great Aunt and Uncle live in Sternberg, Germany. My mother lives in America. There is also a fellow in the Rhineland who knew my father. You must keep this in case you ever need me. I will do everything I can to come back." He leaned closer and said, "If for some reason I can't reach you, you must try to reach me."

That night, Frederick requested that Mischa sleep in the house, making the excuse that the mice frightened her. Krystyna knew the truth.

He was gone the next morning.

CHAPTER 51

FREDERICK

Leipzig, Germany

April 1945

"This is nothing but the final judgment," Frederick whispered, peering through a hole where a window once stood.

He'd returned to Germany only to be placed in command of a platoon of old men and young boys. There had been no point in trying to explain that he'd never been anything more than a medic.

You are a veteran of both fronts. Five years. And you are still standing.

His command duties overshadowed his ability to treat the wounded. They dropped like flies. More stragglers were sent, only to fall in their own turn. Each one seemed older or younger than the last.

Volkssturm. The title made it sound like something to be proud of.

The last of his men, Arno, could not have been a day over 14. Frederick had held him back until there was no one left...but the boy wanted to fight.

Was it really fair to drag him all the way out here only to make him cower in a corner?

If something happens to me, he'll have no one else...

He glanced at the boy behind the broken cabinet and gestured toward the window. Thrill and terror flashed in the boy's eyes as he unearthed himself and darted forward, readying his weapon.

"*Amis* in the storefront." Frederick flicked his chin. *Amis. It would be funny if they weren't shooting at us.*

Arno clutched a comrade's submachine gun and glanced over the side. The gun, too, might have seemed comical in his small hands, *und doch…*

He motioned for Arno to duck and continued to watch as the smoke cleared long enough to reveal a pair of tanks rounding the corner.

"Stay down!" he whispered. But Arno didn't hear. Popping up again, the tank caught the boy in their sights. One of them began to swing his turret.

Arno froze.

"Arno!" Frederick reached for him, stumbling over debris and missing the boy's jacket, he landed face first on the littered floor. He scrambled to get up, barking at Arno to get away from the wall.

Beneath the echoes of machine-gun fire, the cannon boomed. The wall exploded. Arno flew backward, crashing into remnants of wrecked furniture. Frederick pushed himself up to his knees and raced to the boy, who lay beneath shards of wood and glass. A large slice had lodged close to his heart. Others pockmarked his face. Blood oozed over the dirt and filth caking the boy's face.

Frederick cursed, listening for another shot, but the tanks rolled on. Carefully, he lifted the boy and slipped beneath him, settling Arno into his lap.

The boy blinked up at him, his glazed eyes still hinting at a will to go on.

Frederick just shook his head. A few breaths later, he was completely alone.

<hr>

Pounding footsteps abruptly woke him. No time to scramble. Voices approached, speaking English.

There was no way out of this one. Leaving his weapon on the ground, he rose slowly and lifted his hands.

"Achtung!" One of the men yelled to Frederick as he entered the blown-out room. He struggled with a few phrases in German before Frederick finally said in a calm, firm voice with no accent, "I speak English."

The soldier eyed Frederick. "Are you—American?"

"Yes, sir, I am."

The fellow cursed.

Another two soldiers joined him, surveying the debris-scattered room. "There's no one else here, sir. Just bodies."

"Come with us," the sergeant ordered. Frederick followed into the hallway. With a few more expletives, the sergeant asked, "How did you end up here?"

Frederick shook his head. He couldn't help feeling ashamed, even if he was fully convinced he'd done the right thing. "I came in '38."

The obscenities were now laced with pejoratives, yet Frederick sensed a respect emanating from the foul-mouthed man of comparable rank. "Where are you from, young man?"

"New York. Upstate."

"No kidding." The man chuffed. "Only about another month till those apple blossoms, isn't it?"

"You from there too?"

"Born and raised." The sergeant chuckled and let go of yet another expletive. His slight drawl told Frederick he was a country boy a heart—New Yorker or not. He motioned his men to rejoin the rest of the unit, leaned against what was left of a wall, and offered Frederick a cigarette.

"No, thanks."

"Really? Thought all you Krauts smoked." He lit up and continued, "You don't strike me as a Nazi, kid."

"I was a young man looking for adventure." Frederick glanced around. "I hadn't planned on a war."

The sergeant chuckled. "What's your name?"

"Frederick Smith."

He extended a hand. "Pleased to meet you, Frederick Smith. John Parsley."

Frederick shook his hand vigorously.

"So, Frederick Smith. You have a wife and kids here in Germany?"

Not yet. Not a single hour had passed where Frederick hadn't thought about Krystyna and Mischa. In the few days he'd known her, he had memorized every curve of Krystyna's face and could still feel the softness of Mischa's hair between his fingers. To him, they were already family, and it might help his situation if the fellow knew that. "I have a sweetheart waiting for me in Poland," he began. *Just go for it, Freddie.* "A little girl too."

The sergeant dropped his cigarette and looked around. "That country's gonna fall to the Soviets, comrade. You need to get back there and get them. *Pronto.*"

How was that going to happen? Even if he did manage to get back to Poland, what would he find when he got there? Would Krystyna even be allowed to come with him?

He had made a promise. If God allowed him to escape Germany because some eccentric sergeant was willing to stick his neck out, he had to take the chance.

Parsley didn't like his hesitation. The fellow leaned in and growled, "You get that field gray off ASAP, you hear me? I didn't see you, and you didn't see me."

"Your men saw me, sir."

The sergeant lifted his pistol and shot into the air. "You tried to fight me off. I won. Now try to make it out of here without getting caught, you hear?" He leaned in still closer, the stink of his cigarette breath encouraging Frederick to move quickly. "I hear they're taking the sewers."

Frederick nodded and ducked back into the building until he could figure out a plan of escape. Maybe he could reach the sewers from the basement. Could he get out of his uniform first?

His mind raced in a thousand directions as he pressed deeper into the building where a few rooms were still intact. Upstairs, broken doors stood ajar as if they'd been blown open with the impact of exploding shells.

God protect me. Nervously, he forced his way into one of the apartments. A few rats scattered as he peeked into the remnants of a kitchen. *Nothing but debris.* Heading further in, he found an adult's bedroom, pushed his way in, and began rummaging through a wardrobe. What other choice did he have?

Unable to find anything suitable, he headed for the apartment across the hall, a mirror image of the last, and made directly for the master bedroom. A wardrobe had tumbled, its doors broken off their hinges. He dug through and found pants, a shirt, and even a hat.

The man who'd lived there had obviously had more style than he did.

Frederick pulled off his ruined uniform, tossed it on the bed, and slipped on the civilian clothes. He placed his boots together on the floor next to the bed and took a pair of shoes out of the closet. They fit well enough.

He righted a mirror and studied his reflection. *I have no regrets, God. Please continue to protect me as I head back into Poland for my bride and daughter.* Everyone else, he understood, was fleeing west.

He ran his fingers through his hair. It had grown out again but was sufficient for making his way through a war zone. Apparently, he'd probably end up in the sewer. He placed the hat on his head, grabbed a satchel from the closet, and threw a change of clothes into it. With one last look around the room, he dashed out the door.

CHAPTER 52

Poland

May 1945

She barely heard the knock that caused Jan to rise from the table and stride to the door.

"*You?*"

Mischa jumped down from the stool she'd been sitting on and ran to the door. "Papa!"

Krystyna dropped her work and swung through the kitchen door to find Mischa already in Frederick's arms. A wide smile graced his face as the little girl smothered him with kisses.

Krystyna hurried to them, but Jan threw out his arm to hold her back. Mama's voice barked sharply from behind. Jan inhaled deeply, set his shoulders, and invited Frederick in.

Things played out like a drama before her eyes. Her parents were not cold to Frederick, but they took their stance between the two young people. Her father offered Frederick a chair at the table while Mama called her back into the kitchen.

"I am going to make coffee. Please set out some bread and jam."

Her father had formed a high enough opinion of Frederick last summer. All that had changed when he took off, and Krystyna had slowly leaked the story out.

From the kitchen, she heard her father speak to him in broken German. "Krystyna said you went back to the army."

"Ja."

From her peripheral, she saw Frederick reach a hand out to Mischa, who happily ascended his lap. "I'm sorry I left the way I did," he continued. Looking directly at Mischa, he reiterated, "I'm sorry I had to go."

Mischa nodded and looked down at his hands. "Your hands hurt."

"Na, they're fine now. Just scarred."

"Scarred?" She stuck out her lip in sympathy and threw her arms around him again.

He wrapped his arms around her and stroked the back of her head. "Looks like they've been feeding you well."

Krystyna approached and set down some bread and jam, then took a seat beside her father, who asked her to interpret. She nodded.

"Frederick...Krystyna told us you went back to the German Army," he began. "I admit I had my suspicions about you, but my family seemed to accept you, even my boys. You certainly showed yourself to be helpful and beyond reproach, at least in the beginning."

Krystyna bit her lip. Reproach? *Without blame.* She hurried to catch up with her father's words. "We were not pleased when you left Mischa with us without speaking to us first. Krystyna was happy to take her, but Krystyna is little more than a child herself, unmarried, and not ready to make such decisions. God knows we did not need another mouth to feed."

Frederick continued to gaze down at Mischa, clutching her as if she were a guarantee that this awkward conversation would not end in disaster.

"Mischa is a very special little girl, and the family has come to see her as one of our own," her father continued. "Krystyna did as she promised you, taking almost full responsibility for her, though my wife Halina could not help but dote on her. You know how women are."

Frederick looked up long enough to speak his thanks, though his words were tinged with shame.

Her father let out a heavy sigh. "My daughter is in love with you, Frederick. I cannot seem to talk her out of it. Once the truth came out about your involvement with the Germans, we insisted she let go of you, though I would often hear her praying for you late at night." His eyes met Krystyna's, but his words continued to be directed at Frederick. "Six years ago, Jan and Andrzej rescued my daughter from the hands of a German soldier. After that, when Halina and I would try to speak to her of marriage, she would not hear of it. She feared men, hated them. But from the moment she laid eyes on you, she had no hatred, no fear. You completely disarmed her. My daughter is in love, and I cannot deny it."

He turned his gaze back to Frederick. The young man breathed deeply and seemed to force himself to look the older man in the eyes.

"Mischa is quite convinced you are meant to be her father," he went on. "You, yourself, heard her cry *Papa* when you arrived at the door. With these two girls so set on your return, I had to think long and hard over your choices. I must confess that, had I been in your position, I would have done the same thing. You are a man of character, Frederick."

Her father pushed his chair back from the table and fixed a firm, serious gaze on Frederick. "You are also an American, and I believe Krystyna has a chance at a better future with you than she would have here. My condition is this. You will marry Krystyna only if you promise to take her somewhere she will be free. The Soviet grip will only tighten here in Poland. You must marry her immediately and then return to Germany while you are still able. From there, it would be best if you take her on to America."

Frederick nodded. Only Krystyna caught the hesitance that flashed in his eyes. "Understood. We will return to America as soon as the Lord allows."

"There is one more thing," her father added, as if Frederick's words had jogged a memory. "Krystyna was baptized in the Roman Catholic Church. You must be married by our priest, and she must be allowed to continue to practice her religion. Will that be a problem?"

That hadn't even occurred to Frederick, but why would it? By the time he'd met American Sergeant John Parsley, he had fully accepted that he might never see Krystyna again. The mere fact that he was now sitting at her table was nothing short of miraculous. It made his answer clear. "No, sir, it will not."

"Very well." Her father's words were firm, but there was a hint of a twinkle in his eye. "I will give you my blessing. But you must get married immediately."

FREDERICK

The priest came the next day, and Frederick and Krystyna were hurried through simple vows beneath the same tree Mischa had napped under a year earlier. The family shared a special meal, and Frederick and Krystyna escaped to the loft above the barn. His bride had decorated it simply with white sheets, candles, and vases of flowers. It was charming, just enough for a moonlit wedding night before they made their escape the next morning.

Krystyna released her hair and settled down beside him. "Can't you put your worries aside for one hour?"

He pulled her close. "I can't promise we will get to America."

"I know." She nestled into the crook of his arm. "Father only said it would be *best* if we went to America."

"I want to remain with my people."

"Are the Americans not *your people*?"

He shook his head. "When you spend six years fighting side by side with men, sharing in a common suffering, you cannot help but see them as your own."

"And the Americans?"

"What kind of man would I be if I left now?"

Krystyna considered his words. A slight smile appeared on her lips. "I am not angry at the Germans."

"No?"

"No. Not anymore. It is true that I suffered at the hands of a German soldier, but I also grew up seeing the way Germans in our territory suffered at the hands of *my* people. Certainly there were hundreds of women who hated Polish men for the same reasons." She gazed at him through the candlelight. "Hatred, violence, sin—none of these things are the guilt of the Germans alone. We brought much of it on ourselves."

"The German cause was not wholly righteous."

"No, and they have reaped the whirlwind." She sighed heavily, her body relaxing against his. "Sometimes, it seems that life on earth is nothing more than a constant cycle of evil—God, allowing evil men to be punished by other evil men."

Frederick nodded. It sounded like something his father might have said.

"Anyway"—she swept a few tears out of her eyes—"I watched the German columns as they marched through. Enemies or not, they were all so handsome. Little did I know what harm they could do. After I was violated, I wanted to hate them. I tried to pray that they'd be destroyed by hellfire, but I remembered the teaching of the Catechism. It is a sin when one desires great harm toward their neighbor. I did not know how to pray, so for many years, I just *didn't*."

"And then?"

"Then I met you. You were the answer to every prayer I could never speak."

He thought back to those first weeks of war, when Fritz had died in his arms. When he'd witnessed German sins first hand. When he'd wrestled with *not understanding* the way desperation, vengeance, and unanswered calls for peace had culminated in the great German Blitzkrieg. Somehow, even then, their lives had been entwined.

Frederick cradled his wife, relishing the flowery scent of her hair as she drifted off to sleep. Her breath grew soft and rhythmic. Finally, he slipped his arm out from around her and rose to put out the candles. In the morning, he, Krystyna, and Mischa would embark on a new adventure—as a family.

EPILOGUE

HANNAH

Upstate New York

January 1946

Paul arrived home with a fistful of mail.

"Anything interesting?"

He pressed his lips together and flipped through the envelopes. "Bills..." he stopped abruptly.

"What?"

His eyes twinkled. "I think you'd better open this one first."

She received a thick envelope from his hand, and her eyes settled immediately on the word *Germany* scrawled in familiar handwriting. "Frederick!"

She fell hard into a chair and tore the letter open. A metal object fell to the ground. Paul bent to pick it up, observing it curiously as she scanned the words from her son. "Oh, Paul, he's alive!"

"Of course he is, Hannah dear."

Paul set the half-oval down on the table and bent to read over her shoulder as she continued to read, finishing the letter and going over it a second time to be sure she'd not missed anything:

Dear Mom and Paul,

It has been far too long since I wrote you. Please forgive me. I wrote a few times since I received your letter in 1942, but I do not know if my letters got through. Now that there is peace between Germany and the United States, I hope we can begin to rebuild our lives. I am alive, uninjured, and free. I have also married and have a child! My wife Krystyna and I have informally adopted an orphan from Belorussia. Her name is Mischa. She is eight years old and is learning both German and English. She's incredibly smart!

I wish I could tell you all that I have experienced in the last seven years. Thank you for your prayers for me. I felt them every day. Krystyna, too, was praying for me, although I didn't know it at the time.

You will see that I have enclosed an identification tag. It belonged to a German army chaplain named Friedrich Schmidt! One day, I will tell you the fantastic story of how this man truly was the father I never had. He even provided a place for us after the war, at the home of his dear friend and mentor, Duncan Wallace, a Scotsman if there ever was one.

I hope to see you someday soon.

All my love,

Frederick

Hannah finally turned her attention to the metal identification disc that Paul had placed on the table. "A chaplain named Friedrich Schmidt."

"Maybe it's common over there."

"Maybe."

She lifted the tag and examined it. "Frederick said he was the father he never had."

"A wonderful coincidence."

"He has mentioned him before. He seemed to love the man dearly."

Paul nodded.

Hannah set the object down and returned her attention to the letter. "So Frederick's married now."

"And a father."

"Hard to believe."

He rested a meaty hand on her shoulder. Sobs worked their way up from her stomach, and she began to convulse.

"Hannah?"

"I just wish he would come home." She flew from her chair into Paul's arms. "It's been seven years, Paul! Seven."

He ran a hand down her back. "I know, Hannah. I know."

She shook her head. "It doesn't sound like he plans to come home."

"Not immediately."

"The war has been over for months."

"So it has."

"Then why doesn't he come home?"

"Because he didn't go over there to fight a war."

She sucked in deeply and backed away. Paul's words seemed so strange. Dropping back into the chair, she picked up the letter again. "I—I guess I'd forgotten."

Paul settled into the chair next to her. "Either that or you'd assumed that was the reason he needed to be there."

"Yes."

He took the letter from her hand and placed it on the table, enclosing her hands in his. "Frederick is an incredible young man. He has a good head on his shoulders, and he said before that he wants to be in God's service. I can't imagine a better way to serve God than to remain in a devastated nation and help them rebuild."

"He wants to be a pastor."

"We don't *know* what he wants to do, and chances are, he doesn't yet either." Paul shook his head. "The boy just endured six years of war, Hannah. Give him time to figure this out."

She huffed. "I guess I can be glad he's not at a POW camp." *On the other hand, it might've forced him back to the US.*

Paul released her hands and picked up the identification disc once more. "You know I don't believe in signs, Hannah. I wasn't religious for most of my life, and, even now, I'm not one to make a big deal out of things like this, but"—he tucked the identification tag into her palm—"I think you can look at this and remember that God has taken care of your Frederick all along, right down to the details—Friedrich Schmidt, the father your son never had."

A smile blossomed on her lips, and she closed her hand around the disc. Warmth spread in her chest. "I do wish I could hear this story."

"You will."

"I wonder why he didn't just tell me in the letter."

"Because he wants to tell you in person."

She looked away.

"Hannah. It's Frederick's way of giving you a promise. He *will* come home."

GLOSSARY OF FOREIGN WORDS

Absolut nichts: absolutely nothing

Achso: oh I see, oh right

Achtung: attention, respect, or a warning of danger

Also: so (as an interjection)

Alter Hase: a veteran soldier, literally "old hare"

Amis: American soldiers

Armia Krajawa (Polish): Home Army, organized Polish resistance

Bahnhof: train station

Bisschen: a little

Blitzkrieg: lightning warfare

Böhmen und Mähren: Bohemia and Moravia, regions disputed between Czechoslovakia and Germany

Brust raus, Bauch rein: chest out, stomach in

Comment vous-appellez vous? (French): what is your name?

Doch: but (as an interjection, often negative)
Dummokpf: fool, idiot

Einsatzgruppen: an SS formation used during WWII to perform ex-
ecutions on the Eastern Front, literally "task force"

Feldbluse: army tunic, field jacket
Feldgrau: any of a number of shades of gray-green used by the German
army, literally "field gray"
Freut mich: nice to meet you

Gott mit uns: God with us
Guten Morgen: Good morning

Hauptstadt: capital city
Heer: army
Herr: Mister
Hilfe: help
Hitlerjugend: Hitler Youth

In Ordnung: in order
Isba: a Russian peasant's house
Ivan: German army slang for Russian soldiers (often spelled Iwan)

Jawohl: yes sir
Judenhilfe: Jew-helper
Jul: Yule

Jup: yup

Junge: boy

Kein Problem: no problem

Kettenhunde: slang for German military police, literally "chained dogs"

Kriegsmarine: German Navy

Kto to jest? (Polish): who is this?

Kriegspfarrer: military chaplain

Landser: German army slang for a foot soldier

Liebling: Sweetheart

Mutti: Mommy

Na dann: well then

Na ja: well, oh well, I guess

Natürlich: naturally

Nordlich: northern

Oder: or

Ostfront: Eastern Front (the war in Russia)

Pfarrer: pastor

Pommes: French fries

Prost: cheers

Raus: out

Reichswehr: the German Army between 1918 and 1935

Sani/Sanitäter: medic
Schelte: scolding
Schnell: fast
Schön: beautiful
Sicher: safe, secure, certainly
Sitzkrieg: literally, "sitting war"
Sprischt du deutsch: do you speak German?
Stahlhelm: steel helmet
Stollen: German Christmas bread with dried fruit, coated in pow-
dered sugar

Tante: aunt

Und doch: and yet

Vati: Daddy
Verboten: forbidden
Vielen Dank: many thanks
Volksdeutscher: used during the Third Reich, a person of German
ethnicity who did not live in Greater Germany
Volkssturm: the last groups to be called up for military service at the
end of the war, literally "people's storm"

Wie formell: how formal
Wir sehen uns: see you later
Wirklich: really

Wohnzimmer: living room

GERMAN RANKS AND US EQUIVALENTS*

*German military rankings were more delineated and changed over the course of the war.

Feldwebel: Staff Sergeant

Gefreiter: Private

Hauptmann: Captain

Leutnant: Lieutenant

Unteroffizier: Corporal

SS-Hauptsturmführer: Captain

SS-Reichsführer: Special rank for Heinrich Himmler, head of the SS

SS-Schütze: Private

SS-Untersturmführer: Rank equivalent to Second Lieutenant

WHAT TO READ NEXT

CONTINUE THE GOTT MIT UNS SERIES

THE PRODIGAL SONS

What happened between Jakob and Chaplain Schmidt? This book provides the backstory, and introduces readers to other characters who are an integral part of the series.

THE CHRISTMAS WE BOTH NEEDED

Bridging a gap between *The Prodigal Sons* and *The Rubicon*, this Christmas novella provides a snapshot of Christmas 1935 as told by Christian Richter, a side character from *The Prodigal Sons* who takes on a more prominent role in *The Rubicon*.

THE RUBICON (Second Edition Coming in 2027)

This book intersects with *Sani: The German Medic*, and completes the tumultuous love story in *The Prodigal Sons.* Readers will also enjoy a connection to Book 3 of the Separate Ways Series, *Saving Brygida.*

OR, START THE SEPARATE WAYS SERIES

<u>DEAREST GUNTER</u>

Inspired by the experiences of many young men who served in the First World War and postwar German Freikorps (militia), this book is woven with heart-rending romance and sets the stage for future books in the Separate Ways Series, along with its connected novellas.

<u>BORN FOR ADVERSITY</u>

(From the Brave Authors Collection, **Every Life Treasured**)

A story of lost love in post-WWI Germany, this novella is part of a multi-genre collection devoted to the value of life.

<u>BROTHER JOCHEN</u> (Releasing in 2026)

The official sequel to *Dearest Gunter,* answering some of the book's questions while raising others. Set in 1926 to 1935, it spans the latter half of the Weimar period and the rise of the Third Reich.

<u>SCHNEEWITTCHEN</u>

(From the Beyond the Bookery Collection, **A Worthy Love**)

This retelling of the Snow White story invites you into a cozy Bavarian homestead. Beyond Gerda's quiet surroundings, the Second World War rages in its fifth year—but then a threat arrives much closer to home.

<u>SAVING BRYGIDA</u> (Releasing in 2027)

Set primarily in East Prussia, this is the culmination of the Separate Ways Series, and crosses paths with *The Rubicon* as well.